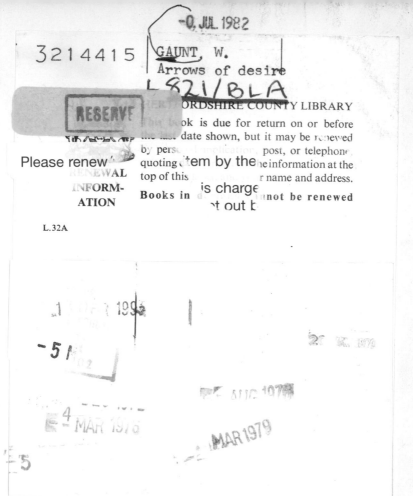

ARROWS OF DESIRE

A Study of William Blake and his Romantic World

By WILLIAM GAUNT

THE PRE-RAPHAELITE TRAGEDY
THE AESTHETIC ADVENTURE
VICTORIAN OLYMPUS

BLAKE'S BIRTHPLACE
Broadwick Street, Soho

ARROWS OF DESIRE
A Study of William Blake and his Romantic World

by

WILLIAM GAUNT

LONDON
MUSEUM PRESS LIMITED

FIRST PUBLISHED IN 1956

B56-15880

MADE AND PRINTED IN GREAT BRITAIN
BY EBENEZER BAYLIS AND SON, LTD., THE
TRINITY PRESS, WORCESTER, AND LONDON

CONTENTS

CONTENTS

ILLUSTRATIONS

I

TOWARDS THE PAST

I

THE SPIRIT OF AN AGE

WHEN William Blake was born in 1757 at the house-cum-shop of a hosier in central London, a change of mood, which he was later to reflect in his own remarkable way, had already begun to show itself in Georgian Britain.

In this change of mood there was—the dawn of wonder, the budding of romance, the beginning of a new emotional life. Such phrases are needed to do justice to its force and indicate its contrast with the prevailing spirit of the time.

The prevailing spirit was exactly opposite. At its lowest level the country was animal and gross, as Hogarth had pictured it in his paintings and prints. (A man of sixty, he was still engraving the brutal humours of election, cockfight and judicial bench.) At a higher level it was urbane, sceptic, polished, rational, judging it, that is, by persons of rank and fashion, philosophers, poets and others who set the style of thought and behaviour.

One would not look for romantic emotion in, let us say, Philip Dormer Stanhope, fourth Earl of Chesterfield, wit and statesman, friend of Voltaire, so typical an aristocrat. Nor would one find, in the famous letters to his son, which had so much to say about good breeding, etiquette, judicious flattery and the conduct of a love affair, any reference to tiresome subjects like morality and religion; though this polite cynic was not devoid of affection and Dr. Johnson was somewhat unfair in saying that he taught the morals of a whore and the manners of a dancing master.

The arts were strictly governed by rules, Augustan or "classic" in the sense of being, it was tacitly agreed, in some

9

way or other derived from the pagan wisdom of ancient Greece
and Rome. Poetry was regular in form, artificial in description
and prosaic in sentiment. Alexander Pope, the great Augustan
poet, had died in 1744, but his orderly couplets, "just" observations and "elegance of diction" were still the model to be
followed. So, at least, the critics held. Samuel Johnson, "last
of the Tories," a middle-aged scholar in 1757, chiefly of note
for his English Dictionary, was soon to become the despot of
literature, defender of Pope and enemy of any departure from
the canons for which he stood. In their various ways, architecture, sculpture and painting submitted to rules of comparable kind. One race of Augustan architects, which included
the illustrious Vanbrugh, Hawksmoor and Gibbs, had completed its work earlier in the century. The grandeurs of Castle
Howard and Blenheim Palace were no longer in favour, but
with the brothers Adam, now at the outset of a brilliant career,
new classic magnificence was to succeed theirs and to illustrate,
both in London and Edinburgh, the value of symmetry and
ordered plan.

Following the well-beaten trail of the Grand Tour, the
noble and wealthy still sought the principles of taste at their
fountainhead in Italy and encouraged their protégés in the
arts to do likewise. After such Italian studies, Joshua Reynolds
was now a successful portrait painter of thirty-four, earning
some £6,000 a year but also destined, until his death in 1792,
to be as powerful an advocate of classic authority as Dr. Johnson himself. A dislike for the past, or that large section of it,
in which civilized standards had perished—or never existed—
was a necessary consequence of their point of view. With its
homage to Greece, Rome and Renaissance Italy the age of
George II combined a great respect for modernity and was
highly satisfied with itself. A poem, or a building, more than
a hundred years old was complacently dismissed as "rude" or
"uncouth". If the genius of Shakespeare was allowed, it was
not without disapproving comment on the flaws and excesses
from which even he, in his relatively barbarous period, was
not immune. Between Apelles and Raphael there was no painting known or worthy of mention. "Gothic", "Gothick" or
"Gothique", as the term was indifferently spelt, denoted
contempt for old buildings that were the product of ignorant

effort and confused minds; and, more generally, contempt for the Dark Ages and all their works. All told, it was an age of completeness, definite in personality and, as we say, well-integrated. Its typical, and very beautiful, creations, were a triumph of Order and Reason. It was the Eighteenth Century, that seems to emerge from the slot machine of history, a neat strip of time, tinted differently from other hundred-year strips, and boldly lettered with its own special motto. Yet, somewhere between the years 1740 and 1760, this eighteenth century began to split in two.

This is less surprising if one considers that change in human affairs goes on all the time, and that the essence of it is to depart from the cherished ideas and established partialities of any given historical moment. The fickle Greeks of the ancient world could get rid of a magistrate on the perverse ground that his verdicts were uniformly just. In the same way certain people in the mid-eighteenth-century found the admirable principles of Order and Reason, the modern-mindedness of their contemporaries, irritating to say the least of it; though there were more emphatic reasons for the feeling of revolt, which appeared in a number of different forms. One form it took was a return to the un-classic past, a movement of sympathy towards and interest in the despised and barbarous "Dark Ages"; in which architecture, poetry, and the sense of history were all involved.

As far as buildings are concerned, it was due, in part, to mere boredom with the classic "orders" and the style adopted from the sixteenth-century Italian architect, Andrea Palladio, which had provided Britain with so many "Palladian" mansions. Like the fickle Greek of old, Horace Walpole, tired of its excellence, turned to the curiosities of mediaeval times, battlements and machicolations, crockets and ogives. "Gothic" was an amusing hobby, proper to the man of fashion, inasmuch as, flouting an existing fashion, it tended to create a new one. This playfully defiant connoisseurship, not without an element of genuine liking (a mixture not unknown in our own century) led him to torture the "little plaything house" he bought near Twickenham in 1747, Strawberry Hill, into the semblance of a "Gothic Castle". He was able in 1766 to persuade so classical an architect as Robert Adam to design for its drawing-room a ceiling like a Gothic rose-window and adapt a chimney piece from Edward the Confessor's tomb.

The little that was known of the vestiges of the past and of those who left them was a serious challenge to the historian (and this was an age of historians). Inquiry, on the largest scale, into the obscurities of barbarism, was to produce that historical masterpiece, Gibbon's *Decline and Fall of the Roman Empire*. It would be impossible to say that Gibbon was stirred by Byzantine or romanesque art. Yet in this typical eighteenth century man of culture, sceptic and rational certainly, classical in style and erudition, a spark of romantic feeling gave the incentive. The sight of "the barefooted friars, singing vespers in the Temple of Jupiter" in 1764, prompted, if not nostalgia, the vast curiosity that, after years of labour, gave the volumes to a fascinated public between 1776 and 1788.

The same curiosity, locally applied, led to what may be called the discovery of Britain, an enterprise in which the antiquary, country gentleman and water colour painter had their share. The nobleman grew interested in the mouldering ruins on his land; the antiquary began to classify them, the artist was called in to illustrate them. Thus during the period of William Blake's childhood, Richard Gough was travelling far and wide in the study of castles, abbeys and sepulchral monuments, a painter like Paul Sandby revealing for the first time the antiquities (and natural beauty) of such unexplored regions as Scotland and Wales.

It was to be a long continued, gradually accelerating process of discovery. Fact-finding came before emotional sympathy, the idea that the relics of rude forefathers were of merit as works of art, or worthy of imitation, came last. Poets were first to feel the sense of wonder that ancient stones could induce, and to discern a quality of art, not only in them, but also in ancient rhymes. In the latter there was relief from that classic correctness which Pope had taken from France and France from the Italian Renaissance arbiters of literary taste; release of the native gift of song, of the primitive epic passion, so far removed from the polite sneer of Augustan satire.

A quiet scholar at Cambridge and an exquisite poet, Thomas Gray, could, in 1757, leave his classical studies for a time, to dream of an old Celtic bard:

"Loose his beard and hoary hair
Streamed like a meteor to the troubled air—
And with a master's hand and prophet's fire
Struck the deep sorrows of his lyre."

The mysteries of a distant time and place were magically
evoked by William Collins, another precursor of the romantic
spirit in poetry in the ode on the Superstitions of the Highlands,
found unfinished among his papers, when he died in despondent
madness, in 1759; in which his muse could

". . . extend her skirting wing
Round the moist marge of each cold Hebrid isle
To that hoar pile, which still its ruin shows,
In whose small vaults a pigmy-folk is found
Whose bones the delver with his spade upthrows
And culls them, wondering, from the hallowed ground !"

The change of mood became sensationally manifest in the
two poets James Macpherson and Thomas Chatterton, in
whom the Celtic and the Gothic past lived once more, and who
were immediate forerunners and, in certain ways, prototypes,
of William Blake.

II

PAST CELTIC

That a Scot should attempt to revive the spirit of an ancient
poetry is understandable: a poetry conceived in wild and
rugged country or retaining its memory and breathing the
patriotism of a still primitive and tribal society. If an unusual
and penetrating note had already, at times, interrupted the
steady and philosophic measure of Augustan verse, it was more
often than not Scottish in origin: and intelligent young men
from Edinburgh University, even when settled in the south in
comfortable sinecures and snug suburban retreats near London, could sound it. In 1727, the son of a farmer in Perthshire,
David Malloch (or Mallet, as he anglicised his name)—"for

there is not one Englishman", he said, "that can pronounce
Malloch") who had come, by way of Edinburgh, to seek
fortune in London—and was later appointed by Lord Bute,
Keeper of the Book of Entries in the Port of London—could
throw himself into the spirit of the old ballad-maker and in his
memorable *William and Margaret* write with a verbal colour
and an affecting simplicity alien to the polite poetic circles in
which he moved.

Mallet's friend (the friend also of Collins), James Thomson,
the son of a minister and born at Ednam near Kelso in Rox-
burgh, is a more famous instance. He too, was educated at
Edinburgh, and enjoyed patronage in London (his appoint-
ments including the nominal post of Surveyor-General of the
Leeward Islands). His *The Four Seasons*, completed in 1730,
which made a deep impression by its descriptions of nature, was
not free, in language or thought, from the conventions of his
time; yet the placidity of Thomson is suddenly disturbed by
such a forceful passage as that in which he tells where

> "The northern ocean in vast whirls
> Boils round the naked, melancholy isles
> Of farthest Thule, and the Atlantic surge
> Pours in among the stormy Hebrides."

In these lines, ostensibly descriptive of nature but in essence
the symbol of emotional freedom and of yearning for the wild,
there is a new, a romantic element, of which James Macpherson was to make sensational use in the dynamic compound
of his "Ossian".

Macpherson was in a way the highly successful victim of
circumstances. He showed in his early days no sign of unusual
ability. Born in 1736, at the village of Ruthven near Kingussie
in Inverness-shire, he had as rough and spartan a boyhood as
any other small Highland farmer's son, was undistinguished
among many poor students of divinity at Aberdeen and
Edinburgh, returned in 1756 to teach in the charity school at
Ruthven. He occupied his spare time in writing verse, of no
great merit, to judge by *The Hunter* and *The Highlander* which
conform to familiar eighteenth-century rules. In 1759 he was
a tall, reserved, young man, tutor in a private family, of whom

no more might have been heard if he had not, in that year, met John Home, Presbyterian minister and of some note for his tragedy, *Douglas*. Home was a patriotic Scot who knew no Gaelic but was curious about the remains of Gaelic poetry. He gathered that Macpherson had interested himself in the poems and fragments of old legends sung and recited in Gaelic by the peasants who still used the old tongue. He pressed him to turn a sample into English. After a show of diffidence and an interval of some days, Macpherson produced for him the fragment entitled *The Death of Oscar*.

It would be interesting to know by what exact process of translation, cooking or invention he arrived at his version: but it foreshadowed the works to come. A prose poem with an insistent irregular beat, it took the reader away into a strange world of storm and stress, of bleak sorrows and fierce lamentations. "How can I relate the sorrowful death of the head of the people? Prince of the warriors, Oscar my son! Shall I see thee no more?

"He fell as the moon in a storm, as the sun from the midst of his course, when clouds rise from the waste of the waves, when the blackness of the storm inwraps the rocks of Ardanmidder. . . ." The excited Home and his friends in the "Select Circle" of Edinburgh took charge. Macpherson was hustled into further "discoveries" by the literary bigwig, Dr. Hugh Blair. The small volume of *Fragments of Ancient Poetry; translated from the Galic or Erse language*, in which the "mighty soul" of Ossian "prince of men" was bared, scored an instant success: though approval was mixed with some incredulity.

What seemed odd to the acute, critical intelligence of Thomas Gray was that Macpherson, with whom he exchanged some letters, in them appeared a person of no talent. The letters were "ill-wrote, ill-reasoned, unsatisfactory, calculated (one would imagine) to deceive, and yet not cunning enough to do it cleverly". This might argue that the poems were counterfeit; and yet on the other hand, if Macpherson could not have written them himself, this was some presumption of their having an original. It was puzzling altogether. "In short," concluded Gray, "the man is the very demon of poetry, or he has lighted on a treasure hid for ages."

The affair had reached a point at which Macpherson was

not to be allowed to stop. In Scotland, northern patriotism
was aroused. England had made many efforts to suppress the
native language and replace it by English, and after the rising
under the Young Pretender in 1745, these efforts were sternly
renewed. It became all the more a Scottish duty to preserve
the precious remnants of a national literature from oblivion.
A subscription was raised in Edinburgh: the young man of
twenty-four was released from his tutorship; despatched to
tour the Highlands; and seek in Perth, Argyle, Inverness,
Skye and the Hebrides for further fragments and traces of the
epic concerning Fingal, the Hero-king, which (he had suggested) was written in the third century by Fingal's son, Ossian.
And sure enough, Macpherson, after three journeys, talks with
local men of learning, and the study of (somewhat mysterious)
manuscripts was able in 1762 to produce the six books of
Fingal, an Ancient Epic Poem to follow them in 1763 with the
eight books of *Temora*, an epic also credited to the son of Fingal:
thus, at the age of twenty-six to twenty-seven, causing that
mighty sensation of which there were echoes throughout his
lifetime and until the end of the century.

The bitter controversy that at once arose involved more
than one issue: patriotism among them. Celt and Saxon had
at one another, and the Irish too were angry, for Fingal seemed
to claim, for Scotland, the person of their own national hero,
Finn McCoull. Fingal was the pretext for attacks on the Scots
by those enemies of Lord Bute's administration, John Wilkes
and the satirist, Charles Churchill. The thistle, observed the
North Briton in November 1762, was choking the rose. Fingal
was "like Hervey's *Thoughts* in drunken prose". The muse,
according to Churchill, was now "disrobed of all her pride" by

"Ossian, sublimest, simplest bard of all
Whom English infidels Macpherson call."

The question whether the epic was genuine also introduced the
question whether a primitive society could produce anything
worthy to be compared with the products of a classically inspired civilization. On any count, it is easy to understand why
"Ossian" should arouse the enmity of Dr. Johnson. It brought
out his prejudice against the Scots and it spurred him to defend

the Augustan culture against an inroad of the barbarous past or alternatively, and less forgiveably, a modern imitation of barbarism.

He concluded (1) that the supposed poems of Ossian were "as gross an imposition as ever the world was troubled with". *Fingal* was in six books: "The Highlanders," he said, "knew nothing of books and nothing of six"—or perhaps, he admitted, "they had got to the length of counting six but certainly no more". Manuscripts were mentioned as evidence, but these, he jeered, were impossible from "a nation that could not write". Dr. Johnson's own expedition to the Hebrides with Boswell confirmed his view that no such material existed. (2) that if the poems had been genuine, they would have been first rate "curiosities" but that (3) whether genuine or not, they had no literary merit, "no end or object, no design or moral". As a modern production, Fingal was nothing. "A man might write such stuff for ever, if he would abandon his mind to it."

It has long been decided, by those who have studied the matter, with more specialized knowledge than either Macpherson's supporters or enemies in the eighteenth century possessed, that he was no Gaelic scholar, that whatever the (elusive) material he drew on, he wishfully gave it an epic form that is not to be found in Gaelic literature.

He did not repeat his youthful success, though he defended himself with great tenacity against Johnson and other critics and came to the point of threatening the Doctor with physical violence, to which Johnson answered in words of courage and weighty abuse. Macpherson's career after 1763 and until his death in 1796 was something of an anti-climax. After a brief adventure in Florida as secretary to the Governor-General of the Western Provinces (which brought him a life pension of £200 a year) he settled down as a political propagandist on the Tory side, became a member of Parliament, speculated shrewdly and made a fortune, and retired to a classical mansion built for him by Robert Adam in his native parish. His only exploit in poetic interpretation, after the Ossian books, was his version of the Iliad in 1773, which contained many of the Ossianic mannerisms and was generally laughed at as "Homer in Kilts"—though from a modern point of view, the aim of getting nearer to the spirit of the Homeric age appears sound

enough, and Macpherson may be considered rather more
Homeric in style than Pope, comparing, for instance, the way
each begins:

Pope. "Achilles' wrath to Greece the direful spring
Of woes unnumbered, heavenly Goddess sing!
That wrath which hurl'd to Pluto's gloomy reign
The souls of mighty chiefs untimely slain;
Those limbs unburied on the naked shore,
Devouring dogs and hungry vultures tore:
Since great Achilles and Atrides strove,
Such was the sovereign doom and such the will
of Jove."

Macpherson. "The wrath of the son of Peleus—O goddess
of song, unfold! The deadly wrath of Achilles;
to Greece the source of many woes! Which
peopled
the regions of death—with shades of heroes
untimely slain: while pale they lay along the
shore: torn by beasts and birds of prey: But
such was the will of Jove! Begin the verse, from
the source of the rage between Achilles and the
sovereign of men."

Yet, during the lengthy period of his not very distinguished
prosperity, Macpherson's fame, which grew tremendous and
extended all over Europe, remains to be accounted for.
Posterity thinks little more of him as a poet than did Dr. Johnson, but by some flash of intuition he had delivered precisely
that message of revolt against the eighteenth century that
subconsciously it had been waiting for. It was destructive; it
broke down the framework of an artificial poetry with a rush
of feeling. It called for a return to the past, not for the sake of
scholarship, but for the emotions the past evoked or had been
able to express. The melancholy and rage of "cold moon" and
"roaring streams" were symbols of elemental and unfettered
being. The importance of "Ossian" at the height of Macpherson's fame, was not that Ossian was authentically a Gaelic
bard, but that, as James Boswell said (before Johnson had

brow-beaten him into silence) "Take my word for it, he will make you feel you have a soul."

The influence of Macpherson was immediate in England. Vague and abstract as were his descriptions of the bleak mountains amid which the old and blind Ossian sadly recalled the battles of his hero-father, they stimulated interest in the actual locality. Reversing the Johnsonian witticism, one might say the "noblest prospect" now before the English writer was the road that led northwards. It was three years after the publication of *Fingal*, when Gray made a journey to Scotland, following it by the discovery of kindred scenes in Wales and among the lakes of Cumberland and Westmorland, which he described with an enthusiasm anticipating that of the Lake school of poetry, and of Sir Walter Scott.

A new feeling for nature was, however, only one of the streams diverging from the mountain torrent of "Ossian" that were to feed the broad river of the Romantic Movement. Whether or no the blind bard of the third century existed, there was now some presumption that the essence of poetry was to be sought deep down in the heart of a people rather than the consciously cultivated attitude of an aristocratic society. The products of any ancient time, not necessarily those of Scotland, became the object of study. Perhaps the Scottish legends were originally Norse: they had an affinity with those of the Scandinavian countries; Gray was incited by them to study the *Eddas* of Iceland and from their lays of Gods and heroes to extract his *Descent of Odin*.

The young rector of a midland parish, Thomas Percy (later Bishop of Dromore), whose research into popular literature had taken the rarified form of Chinese studies (with the help of Portuguese translation) was, likewise, so impressed by Macpherson and the primitive nordic regions that invited exploration as to deorient himself and to produce, in 1763, his *Runic Poetry Translated from the Icelandic*; to collect, greedily, also, the songs and ballads of his own land in which spoke the ancient, popular voice. These, published in 1765 under the title of *Reliques of Ancient English Poetry*, had as deep an effect as Ossian, and were, it may be, an even greater creative stimulus.

Both share credit for the romantic awakening in Germany, the passion for legend and folk song, exemplified in the poems

and poetic studies of Bürger and Herder; though to describe
the full effect on Europe and to say why Ossian in particular
took on a new meaning as the end of the century approached,
would be to go far ahead of the present stage of this narrative.
It is enough to say for the moment that the distant past was
now an air a young poet was encouraged to breathe; that from
it came an intoxicating potion. Macpherson, whose influence
upon his world was far greater in extent than his own abilities,
had shot his bolt and was settling down to lucrative political
propaganda when Ossian was only beginning to excite others,
among them a youth called Thomas Chatterton.

III

PAST GOTHIC

With Thomas Chatterton, music and song came back into
poetry from the past. The famous poems, which he represented as the work of a fifteenth century poet-priest, Thomas
Rowley, which include such immortal lyrics as the minstrel's
song in *Aella*, emerge from shadowy archaism into the clearer
air of beauty. It was a beauty beyond the reach of the interpreter of Ossian; different also in its purely English quality
from that which he sought, though the research accompanying
it and the dissembling it involved, were quite in the spirit of
Macpherson's preceding adventure.

Chatterton, this extraordinary young man, who committed
suicide before he was eighteen, a "romantic" in the fullest
sense of the word, breathed deeply in his short life the atmosphere of the Gothic, as opposed to Gaelic, memory. He grew
to adolescence in the environs of an ancient Church, St. Mary
Redcliff, Bristol, known in Elizabethan times as "the fairest and
most famous parish church in England", a good example of the
Perpendicular style. It bore witness to the mercantile wealth
and the piety of Bristol in the middle ages. The south transept
and south wall of the nave remained of the building erected in
the fourteenth century at the charge of the merchant, William
Canynge; otherwise it had been rebuilt in fresh and graceful
guise, during the fifteenth century by Canynge's grandson and

namesake—also a merchant and five times mayor of the city. St. Mary Redcliff had always been a central fact in the life of the Chattertons. Since the seventeenth century, men of the family had made a living as masons, kept busy by the necessary repairs and care of the fabric. The poet's grandfather was sexton—in the words of his epitaph "Death's Chamberlain here for twenty years". The poet's father, Thomas Chatterton senior, was at the time of his death in 1752 (three months before his son was born) writing master at the Redcliff and St. Thomas Charity School.

In the busy eighteenth century city (second in trade and wealth only to London) the church was a relic treated with the characteristic indifference of the time. Its muniment room, or "Treasury", with its heavily beamed door and massive lock, was open to the comings and goings of such familiars of the place as the Chattertons. From the narrow windows light, in which the dust floated thick, fell on coffers crammed with old deeds and documents, a sight to astonish and delight a modern archivist, though these treasure chests were left carelessly open, their contents treated as lumber, or plunder of the least valuable kind. Thomas Chatterton, senior, was able to make off with loads of parchments. They were useful as dust jackets, protecting the covers of the Bibles his pupils handled.

To a child, the place and its contents could be mysteriously enthralling. In his very early years, the young Chatterton seems to have had an instinctive fondness for every hint and suggestion of the time to which it belonged. He learnt the alphabet from the illuminated capital letters in "an old folio Music book" with which he fell in love (one of the writing master's calligraphic specimens—or part of his equipment as "singing man" in the cathedral). He learnt to read from a black-letter Testament. During the seven years, 1760 to 1767, which he spent at Colston's school, a foundation on the model of the London Christ's Hospital, he haunted the church: a little bluecoat boy in leather breeches, orange stockings and with monkish tonsure; looking up at the empty niches whose crumbling recesses the mind's eye could people with saints and kings; spelling out the crabbed inscriptions on tablet and tomb; pondering over the massive repose of a mailed Knight Templar, tiptoeing among the dusty chests in the silent muniment room or reading, cosily insulated from the bustle of the city, on the roof, invisible behind the cusped tracery of its stone railing.

Bristol was a great place for books and bookshops, and when he was of an age to read for choice, he sought out old texts which could be found, then, even in a local circulating library. At fifteen, after leaving school and becoming articled to an attorney, Chatterton subscribed to Green's Library, there chanced on a copy of the Elizabethan edition of Speght's Chaucer; pored devotedly over it, gaining a threefold pleasure from the poetry, the peculiar savour lent to it by an archaic typography, the copious glossary that glowed with strangely-cut verbal gems. Sometimes he would go to Goodall's bookshop in Tower Lane and sit reading for hours, as custom allowed, a favoured work being a history that dealt, in the speculative fashion of an ignorant age, with Saxon manners and customs, perhaps "Verstegen's" "*A Restitution of Decayed Intelligence, in Antiquities*".

It required, however, an outside and contemporary stimulus to turn this receptive, boyish, love of far-off things into a creative process. Chatterton began to write poetry when he was twelve, and the first poems worthy of note were satires, on the typical eighteenth-century model, deriding "Sly Dick", a schoolfellow accused of theft and *Apostate Will*, a venial Methodist. It was only when the noise of Ossian was in the air, when Percy's "*Reliques*" were being discussed in Bristol as in London, that Chatterton began to devise his own mediaeval source. It is hardly possible to say at what precise moment these influences began to operate, but traces of the style of each are to be found in the Rowley papers, and if the antique form of the ballads in Percy's collection was more congenial to him, the alias of Macpherson also invited imitation.

To return to the past effectively, it was clearly necessary to speak with its voice, to reincarnate, as it were, someone who lived then. The process of reincarnation may have begun before Chatterton left school; it arrived at its outcome when, aged fifteen to sixteen, he was an unwilling junior clerk in the attorney, John Lambert's, office. The brass in St. John's Church to Thomas Rowley, bailiff, when William Canynge was Mayor of Bristol in 1466, gradually called into being the substitute person of a fifteenth century poet. The title deeds and dull commercial documents from Mr. Canynge's "cofre" became, in his imagination, curious verses set down by a priestly hand—in language he derived from a glossary to Speght's "Chaucer" and Kersey's *Dictionarium Anglo-Britannicum*, adding mediaeval-sounding words of his own coinage which he ornamented with fantastic spelling.

All this may suggest the gentle dreamer, destined victim of a harsh world, whom the Pre-Raphaelite Henry Wallis was to depict so affectingly in mid-Victorian days, in his celebrated picture *The Death of Chatterton*; though in several respects this painting is misleading. The attic, with its view of St. Paul's, plausibly represents the attic in which Chatterton died, but Wallis's model for the poet was the young George Meredith, another person in another age. Slender and graceful, his is not the short, thick-set figure of Chatterton (in reported description—no authentic portrait remains). Nor did the artist, in giving so angelic an expression to the features, convey anything of his actual character. It is a more formidable and subtle being that the brief life-history of Thomas Chatterton reveals.

He enjoyed playing a part; which may be assumed not only from the creation of "Rowley" but also the pleasure he took in writing love verses to a Bristol girl, purporting to come from his friend Baker, on whose behalf he wrote them—for Baker had gone to Charleston, South Carolina. In this willingness to deputize in verse, there was a schoolboy love of a hoax, and the deception was innocent enough. "A sad wag of a boy, always on some joke or other", so the sister of his local "patron", George Catcott, described him. Yet there was in him something of that madness, which, as the romantic spirit grew, was so often to take a fatal form. The creation of a "fantasy world" had its dangerous and pathological element. It separated him mentally from others. In doing so, it encouraged an egotistical pride to grow excessive. His sister (whose fanciful spelling unconsciously matched his own) observed, at an early date, his "thirst for pre-heminence". All the more humiliating was his office-boy life in the attorney's household where he slept with the servant lad and took his meals in the kitchen. The sullenness with which he went about his daily duties marked a growing withdrawal into a realm which he dominated, and the growth of a corresponding contempt for those with whom he came into ordinary contact. He was, in his imagination at least, not so much the great lover as the hardened rake, subjecting the girls who paraded on the College green to cynical appraisal. Is there? he wrote

> ". . . . a street within this spacious place
> That boasts the happiness of one fair face
> Where conversation does not turn on you
> Blaming your wild amours, your morals too?"

It was the pose of an adolescent conscious of superior mind to represent himself as a mephistophelean figure in these provincial encounters. His sister did not believe in what she called his "venality"—somewhat mistaking what noun could be derived from "Venus"—though mistaken, perhaps also, as to his behaviour. "Miss W. is now in chase". In such terms the youth of sixteen spoke of his amorous pursuit and with a lordly contempt for his quarry.

This is not "romantic", in a tender sense this word has acquired. As applied to a Don Juan, it is less descriptive of affection than of the egoist for whom such often repeated adventures have a subjective importance : and if Chatterton was a provincial Don Juan of sixteen, this was a role consistent with an egotism that showed itself in several ways. A "genius" fully formed, inhabiting a still immature mind and body, is liable to take on a somewhat demonic cast, to appear to its possessor as beyond the adult conceptions of good or evil. "Enfant terrible" describes Chatterton no less than the French poet, Arthur Rimbaud, whom in some respects he resembles. The imaginative power he showed was accompanied by contempt for a real world in which he played an inferior part, and confidence in his ability to fool it to the top of its bent.

The method by which he concocted his supposedly antique finds was so naïve as to approach caricature. He freely borrowed from all the poets he had read, even so recent as Gray and Collins. He made up words of his own that had a specious flavour of the past. He devised spellings in which there was an almost satirical exaggeration. He produced crude "originals", which it is hard to believe were seriously intended to pass muster as ancient manuscripts.

Yet in the first published piece of 1768, the journalistic hoax, which, topically, when the new Bristol bridge was opened, purported to describe (from an old Manuscript) the opening of the old bridge, there was a touch of magic, a feeling for pageantry that came from a born artist in words. Why, it has often been asked, did not Chatterton admit himself to be the author, in view of the local interest aroused, instead of persisting in the fiction that this, and the splendid poems that he allowed to be seen in the following year, came from among the deeds in the muniment room? A simple answer to this question would probably be wrong in being simple. The genius, the romantic egotist and the schoolboy joker were all involved.

He wished for fame, but may have reasoned that fame was not likely to come to a youth who confessed to an imposture, whatever personal talent he might have shown. The angry cry of forgery would drown the words of praise. Suspect though "Ossian" had become, the fame of Macpherson still seemed to depend on the genuineness of his elusive originals and the genuineness of Rowley, therefore, had to be defended with equal tenacity. Again, it was not too difficult to take in those provincial worthies, the amateur antiquarian, William Barrett, the partners in a pewtering business, George Symes Catcott and Henry Burghum, who had "discovered" him, though in their attitude there was a curious mixture of admiration and credulity, suspicion and cunning, which made them half patrons and half fellow conspirators.

It was naïve, however, to suppose that Dodsley, publisher of Percy's "*Reliques*", and Horace Walpole would be as gullible. It was surely the schoolboy joker, with a poor opinion of his famous elders, who sent to Walpole, author of *Anecdotes of Painting*, what professed to be "The Ryse of Peyncteynge yn Englāde, wroten bie T. Rowleie, 1469 for Mastre Canynge" —beginning with the ancient Britons who "dyd depycte themselves in sondrie wyse . . . wythe the hearbe Wodde" and including an obvious Ossian pastiche, concerning one, Afflem, a glass painter, taken prisoner by "Oscarre the great Dane—," ("Affrighte, chaynede uppe hys Soule, Gastnesse dwelled yn his Breaste"). Almost persuaded at first, though more by the quality of the poems also enclosed than by this strange piece of art history, Walpole could reasonably conclude, on further reflection, that his correspondent was laughing at him.

Yet, in a profound sense, Chatterton had become Rowley; the imaginary poet of the fifteenth century was not a creation he could easily get rid of. To deny him would have been to deny that part of his mind in which a fancied existence had turned into a real one: through which he was alone able to express his immense power and sense of beauty. The past was of value not merely as the past but as a world insulated from his eighteenth century; in which he was free and himself. The coined and barbarous words had a strange magic of sound: musically through the lush growths of archaism ran the clear spring of pure poetry.

> "O! synge untoe mie roundelaie
> O! droppe the brynie teare wythe mee
> Daunce ne moe atte hallie day
> Lycke a reyninge ryver bee;
> Mie love ys dedde
> Gon to hys deathe-bedde
> Al under the wyllowe tree."

The defensive aspect of this split, romantic soul was savage and mocking, morbid also. It was the morbidity of "The Last Will and Testament" which, found on his desk, early in 1770, promptly caused the attorney, Lambert, to cancel his indentures. It expressed his scorn:—"Item. I give and bequeath all my Vigor and Fire of Youth to Mr. George Catcott, being sensible he is most in want of it. . . . To Bristol all my Spirit and Disinterestedness, parcells of goods unknown on her Key since the days of Canynge and Rowley. . . ." It was a death-wish, anticipating by only a few months his suicide in London in August 1770.

The obvious motive for his suicide was his failure in the capital. His trial of strength in the rough and tumble of journalism, his satires, burlettas and political tirades, got him nowhere. It was perhaps reason, or seemed reason enough, that he was penniless, that the baker at last refused him the loaf of bread that would have kept him from starving. To say that these things did not count would be absurd, though others have survived conditions as grim. Yet, to whatever physical plight he was in, must be added a pathological pride. The letters he wrote home show it, together with a disturbing and Hamlet-like irony and self derision. To his sister in July: "I have an universal acquaintance; my company is courted everywhere; and, could I humble myself to go into a compter, could have twenty places before now, but I must be among the great. State matters suit me better than commercial. The ladies are not out of my acquaintance. I have a deal of business now, and must therefore bid you adieu. . . ." His end is no less pathetic because no note of pathos came from him; but it is possible to discern in it scornful impulse rather than passive suffering, the romantic revenge on a world despised.

The untimely death of a poet is apt to correct the indifference with which he has been treated when alive. The first step was publication. The *Bristowe Tragedie or the Deathe of Syr Charles Bawdin* was printed in 1772. Tyrwhitt's edition of "Poems supposed to have been written at Bristol by Thomas Rowley and others in the fifteenth century" appeared in 1777. They were treated at first as part of the detective story that literature now seemed to have become. Were the poems authentic or not? Rowleians and anti-Rowleians took sides. As chief literary sleuth, Dr. Johnson, together with Boswell, went to Bristol to expose Chatterton, as he had gone to the Hebrides to expose Macpherson. They called on Mr. Barrett, the surgeon-antiquary, saw some of the *originals* (Boswell's italics) and "were quite satisfied of the imposture". Johnson puffed and panted up to the muniment room where "honest Catcott" triumphantly showed them the chests from which the manuscripts had supposedly come. They laughed at this "evidence", though Johnson was kinder than he had been about Ossian. "It is wonderful how the whelp has written such things."

Yet "forgery" was the term used by critics typical of eighteenth-century culture to describe the poet's attempts to sing with an ancient voice; the wish of Macpherson and Chatterton to identify themselves with a barbaric time offered, otherwise, no rational explanation. They were not, it is true, the only "forgers". One still has to discriminate with some care between the various "discoveries" that a changing outlook and

changing thought incited. "Say," thus Chatterton indignantly
apostrophized Horace Walpole,

". . . didst thou ne'er indulge in such Deceit?
Who wrote Otranto?"

It was true that Walpole's *The Castle of Otranto* (1764),
wherein his dabbling in mediaeval matters took the form of a
novel of mystery, professed to be "translated by William
Marshal, Gent, from the original Italian of Onuphrio
Muralto", though this was an obviously fictional device. In
a different category were the Shakespearean documents
manufactured by William Henry Ireland later in the century.
An attorney's clerk who took Chatterton as his model, Ireland
could certainly be accused of a fraud on the public in pro-
claiming that he had found the originals of two unknown
Shakespeare plays, *Vortigern* and *Henry II*. The only excuse to
be made for him was that he admired Shakespeare. If the
fraud was so obvious that *Vortigern* was laughed off the stage,
the intention was still to be condemned. But Chatterton had
made no such use of a famous name; he had created Rowley.
If this was an antiquarian fraud, his genius was not, and its
influence on poets who came after him was inspiring. When
the tedious discussion of authenticity was put aside, they could
see what changes he had wrought in the substance of the poetic
art.

In spite of the garbled history, the load of "olde" mannerisms, there was, they observed, much that was fresh and natural.
Coleridge, in 1790, could speak of "young eyed Poesy, All
deftly mask'd as hoar antiquity". Keats, in 1819, asserted that
Chatterton was "the purest writer in the English language".
The adventure into the past showed how worn was the elegance
of the present, into what clichés the special poetic language or
diction had fallen, how void of music its didactic sentiments.
A new world of colour and enchanted strangeness opened in
the *Balade of Charitie*, a wild clarion sounded in the Chorus in
Chatterton's *Goddwyn*

"When Freedom dreste, yn blodde steyned Veste
To everie Knyghte her Warre Songe Sunge."

Chatterton and Macpherson had done much to construct a
new outlook, an alternative existence to that of which the
eighteenth century had been so proud. One who believed in
both of them, took something from each, and was impelled by
circumstances and by nature in the same direction was William
Blake.

IV

THE PAST AND THE POET-CRAFTSMAN

Such a great change as that which people generally agree to
call the "Romantic Movement" cannot be stated in very simple
terms. What, indeed, is a "movement"? It is a force that cannot be seen though we arc as well aware it exists as that an
invisible electric current lights a lamp. It is generated by a
need that some feel intensely, some vaguely, by the march of
political and social events, by economic pressures and develop-
ments. Its progress is marked and brought to notice by assertions of idealism, theories of conduct, controversies, works of
art, and even fashion. The personality of a great artist is no
less great and individual because it is exposed to the force of
this current, to "influences" which take various particular
forms. In considering the remarkable career and works of
William Blake, the curious fact emerges that while, in a way,
no one could be more distinct and unusual as a person, no one
also, could be more typical of the new romantic impulse in
his time, or better express its complex character.

A return to the spirit of the past was only one aspect of it,
but this was as notable in the young Blake as in his forerunners. It was fostered by his apprenticeship at the age of
fourteen to an engraver, James Basire. Of his life to that time,
in the family house which still exists at the corner of Broad
(now Broadwick) Street, Soho, little enough is known. James
and Catherine Blake, his parents, are, for us, names only,
though it may be supposed that they were kindly and not
unprosperous. It showed indulgence that they did not send the
highly-strung child to school. He learned to read and write
at home. Passages read from the Prayer Book and the Bible

would help to account for his childhood visions of God at the window, the Prophet Ezekiel and the angels in the tree at Peckham Rye. The story of these visions, repeated many years after, by his wife, suggests that his mind was unusual in child-hood—though a middle-class home which contained three brothers and a sister was a background normal enough.

His double gift, for writing and drawing, soon showed itself but the desire to draw seems to have come first. It is further evidence of his parents' indulgence and fairly easy circum-stances, that they allowed him to go, when he was ten, to the drawing school in the Strand, of Henry Par (less well known than his brother William Par, one of the travelling water-colourists who depicted classical ruins): and that they con-templated sending him as pupil to one of the successful minor artists of the day, William Wynne Rylands, an engraver who had his own print shop and exhibited portraits at the Royal Academy. The boy objected for two reasons, one of which supposes an early gift of divination and the other, certainly, a sense of fairness towards the rest of the Blake children. He said to his father that Rylands looked "as if he were born to be hanged". Twelve years later Rylands *was* hanged—though a more lenient age would have spared him the extreme penalty for forging bills of exchange.

A further objection was that his premium was too high—the young Blake wished to avoid this cost to his family, and so in 1771 he began his seven years apprenticeship to Basire; through whom he made his first aquaintance with a still legen-dary or only half-historical Britain. James Basire was one of that school of engravers which was growing to meet the demand for illustrations, in antiquarian books, of castles, churches, monastic ruins, and earlier remains. The son of an engraver of maps, he had been appointed engraver to the Society of Antiquarians founded in 1751, a post which became hereditary in the family, passing to his son and grandson (both of whom engraved plates after Turner).

His reproductive craft was advancing towards the perfection it was to attain by the end of the century. There was now an effort to imitate in line that effect of tone which the brush of the water-colourist gave, to impart some look of authenticity to the objects depicted. The craft that William Blake learned was that of digging with a burin, on a copper plate, lines of varying depth which, when printed, represented contour and shading. It was manual work in which there was little scope for an artist's own expression. It did not in any way foreshadow the later modes of engraving, which were to be a personal triumph: yet, technically, it taught two lessons which Blake never forgot; the pride of craftsmanship and the value of definite statement. A firm and decisive outline was essential. One could not be vague when working with a metal point on metal.

In addition, it introduced him to those dim eras on which antiquaries lavished their curious speculations, to their discussions on pre-historic Britain and its mysterious standing stones, mysteries it was then usual to resolve by reference to the Druids. The Druids (who were real enough to have been described by Julius Caesar) conveniently explained a great many things the eighteenth century did not understand. From this amateur archaeology, Blake was to derive the idea of and to personify an ancient British culture, the Cymric "Albion". The impression made by the thought of a "Druidic" Stonehenge persists in the brooding cromlechs that appear in his *Jerusalem* and the illustrations to the *Book of Job*.

Yet the main object of interest to the antiquary was the Gothic past; the love of Gothic churches and sculpture—the religious art of the Middle Ages—was implanted in him by his work for Basire. Some of his fellow apprentices teased him; his master found a way of avoiding friction by sending him, to make drawings for engravings, to Westminster Abbey and other London churches: and the Abbey was as great an experience for him as St. Mary Redcliff had been for Chatterton.

Released from the workshop in Great Queen Street, he would run off along Drury Lane, past the classical splendours of Northumberland House in the Strand, the still brightly-gleaming Portland stone of Kent's Horse Guards in Whitehall; an unnoticed London apprentice in sober worsted among the bewigged gentlemen in their gaily coloured coats and silk knee breeches and stockings, the ladies in their fashionable large hats and be-ribboned gowns; at last to approach the ancient church. The massive door within a door that swung to behind him at once excluded modern London, the rumble of drays and coaches, the street cries, the endless smoking chimney-pots, the up-to-date palaces. As if by magic, eighteenth century reality had disappeared; he had entered another world. The hush, broken from time to time by a chant that welled up from some invisible source like the very voice of the past, the smell of antiquity, the beauty of fretted stone, calmed and entranced him. It was his mission to draw the tombs of Kings and Queens. He had to climb up among and over them to get a satisfactory point of view; would gaze down on the placid bearded countenance of Henry III, the enigmatic features of Eleanor of Castile moulded by a London goldsmith in the thirteenth century; gazing upon them with intense excitement as if they were real persons, and some profound, human secret was contained within the rigid conventions of the Gothic sculptor. Little enough of this passion can be traced in the finished engravings for Gough's *Sepulchral Monuments in Great Britain*, yet here was the source of much that was to be typical of Blake's original work. The Gothic sculptor had defined for him the aspect of an angel. The long, plain folds of dress, carved in stone, opposed themselves in their simplicity and dignity to the trumpery finery of his own time, suggested to him the costume of Heaven. The grandly-bearded head of a mediaeval monarch was a patriarchal type he was to make use of in many a later drawing and engraving.

Thus the idealism of Blake was kindled through the agency of the occupation he had chosen, though his seven years apprenticeship with Basire was a desultory and imperfect training for a painter or draughtsman. We cannot as yet speak of him as either. It might be concluded from his reluctance to become Rylands' pupil, that he had no real desire to be a painter. Westminster Abbey was a contact with an age different from his own, to which he instinctively responded: yet its inspiring product was conceived in a medium different from his; and the prints he liked to collect, the engravings after Raphael and Guercino of which he would see proofs in Basire's shop, were poor, black-and-white travesties of the originals, that gave no genuine communion with their authors, no benefit to the copyist.

Poetry was a different matter. The poet was born, not made. Contact with other minds might call out his powers but the

PORTRAIT OF
JAMES
MACPHERSON
("OSSIAN")

after
Sir Joshua Reynolds

Reproduced by permission of the National Portrait Gallery

PORTRAIT OF
EMMANUEL
SWEDENBORG

JOHN FLAXMAN
by George Romney

WILLIAM HAYLEY
by Henry Howard

FUSELI by John Opie

contact was swift and emotional, the printed word was not that barrier to understanding which engraved lines interposed between the student and the form and colour of Raphael and Michelangelo. If he began to draw before he wrote poetry, he was a poet before he was a draughtsman. In those early poems of Blake, collected and printed under the title of *Poetical Sketches* in 1783 (when he was twenty-six), according to the preface of his first patron—or patronizer, the Rev. H. Mathew "the production of untutored youth, commenced in his twelfth, and occasionally resumed by the author till his twentieth year", two things appear: the occasional flash of a lyrical beauty of expression that was all his own; and the record of an awakening mind in process of freeing itself from the conventions of his time—in this respect showing a marked resemblance, at least of aim, to the efforts of his precursors, Macpherson and Chatterton.

Many years later—in 1826—Wordsworth wrote critically, of Macpherson ". . . much as these pretended treasures of antiquity have been admired, they have been wholly uninfluential upon the literature of the country . . . no author in the least distinguished has ventured formally to imitate them— except the boy Chatterton, on their first appearance". To this remark Blake added one of his pugnacious annotations.

"I believe both Macpherson and Chatterton, that what they say is Ancient, is so.

I own myself an admirer of Ossian, equally with any other Poet whatever, Rowley and Chatterton also."

The belief represented his mature thought. If Ossian and Rowley existed in the imagination of Blake's two predecessors, then they existed as definitely as the Man who built the Pyramids did for him. He expressed a continuing loyalty which the *Poetical Sketches* first reveal.

We must imagine the engraver's apprentice in those adolescent years, a small well-made youth, with large brow and fair hair, full of the mental turmoil that belonged to his period of life and the dual nature of his interests, reading as voraciously as he studied prints after the fifteenth-century Italian painters who were still grotesquely known as "Gothic

3

Primitives". Macpherson was still alive, the Ossian controversy was active and Blake must have read *Fingal* as well as
Spenser, Shakespeare and Percy's *Reliques* and, no doubt, also
Gray, Thomson and Collins. He attempted the Celtic rhythm
in a *Prologue to King John.*

> "Then Patriot rose; full oft did Patriot rise,
> when Tyranny hath stain'd fair Albion's breast with
> her own children's gore. Round her majestic feet
> deep thunders roll; each heart does tremble and
> each knee grows slack. . . ."

Chatterton had been dead some years, Blake was twenty-one,
when the Rowley poems were printed and went through three
editions in the same year. It was then perhaps that Blake
added to his manuscripts the ballad, *Gwin, King of Norway* in
which "Gordred the Giant" recalls Chatterton's *Godred Croven.*
But whatever actual echoes may be detected, he arrived at the
same point as Chatterton in the revolt against eighteenth-
century formality, the release of the lyric impulse in all its
flexible beauty, and surpasses him in the wonderful *Mad Song.*

> "The wild winds weep,
> And the night is a-cold
> Come hither, sleep
> And my griefs unfold. . . .

Even in this first "slim volume" the duality in Blake (apart
from the double character of craftsman and poet) already
shows itself in the contrast between the lyric and epic pieces.
He was as lyrical as Chatterton in the sense that some of the
poems were "song", could, in fact, as opposed to the typical
Augustan verse, *be* sung. The likeness was that of kindred
spirits: the likeness to Macpherson was that of conscious
imitation.

At no period during Blake's lifetime, could the world of
poetry entirely forget Ossian. He projected that intense frame
of mind which became a fever in the later eighteenth and early
nineteenth centuries. When Blake was seventeen, Goethe
appropriated the anguish of the Songs of Selma to describe the

anguish of his disillusioned hero in the *Sorrows of Young Werther*
(1774)—"I sit in my grief! I wait for morning in my tears!
Rear the tomb, ye friends of the dead". Ossian was to be
still more of a power in Europe during the period of Revolution
and war when the French, like Macpherson's Oscar "alone in
the midst of a thousand foes . . . the mark of their arm in a
thousand battles" felt Ossianic exaltation and woe. Tragedy
and opera were based on the Gaelic epic (it would be of curious
interest now to hear the dirge of tenors in Méhul's *Uthal*). In
the Abbé Césarotti's Italian translation it was to be the
favourite reading of Napoleon, who desired the Baron Gros to
paint the entry of his favourite Marshals into the Halls of
Ossian. It is hardly surprising that Blake should feel the powerful contagion, or that its effects should be prolonged, in the
style and rhythm, the thunder and mystery of his later "prophetic books". Essays in the style appear in the *Poetical Sketches*;
also the first mention of that poetic homeland that was always
to haunt his imagination—Albion. Albion was the epic past
of which Macpherson had written, but an ancient Britain, more
comprehensive and even more shadowy than his, in which the
clans of the Highlands were absorbed in the remoter antiquity
(as many ingenious antiquarians then believed) of the lost
tribes of Israel. Land and inhabitants together were represented
in his imagination by a symbolic human giant.

Thus the Gothic church, amateur historical speculation
and the revival of an old poetry all played their part in
encouraging the outlook in which Blake was akin to his predecessors; but the return to the past, so essential a part of the
romantic movement, as it can now be seen in perspective, was
only one phase of the great change of mood taking place in his
time: neither antiquary nor poet had so far been much concerned with religion. The grave beauty of St. Mary Redcliff
had not deterred Chatterton from the defiant, juvenile assertion that he was not a Christian. The thousand bards of
Fingal had little to offer on the subject of faith. Yet religious
revival was parallel with Gothic revival and to understand the
world of William Blake it is necessary to examine it in some
detail.

2

TOWARDS ANOTHER WORLD

I

SCIENCE AND SOUL

A MONG the topics of self-congratulation in an Age of Reason was the brilliance of its scepticism, the calm intelligence which applied itself so acutely to the exposure of "superstition". As a conscious attitude, this scepticism belonged to the upper regions of society. It was the atmosphere of the salons, in which aristocrat and philosopher met on equal intellectual terms, part of the entente that linked the culture and fashion of France with that of Britain. The wit with which Voltaire in his old age attacked Christianity was equally approved by the man of fashion and public affairs like Chesterfield, the historian trained in continental thought like Gibbon. When Blake was writing his youthful poems, the fifteenth and sixteenth chapters of Gibbon's *Decline and Fall* were causing a storm by their manifestly anti-Christian trend: though many approved of them as a sign of progress and enlightenment.

Thought, it might be said, had become civilized and free; once again the eighteenth century showed a marked superiority in its refusal to accept blindly the dictates of more credulous times: but there was another side to the picture if one viewed society in all its dimensions. The brutality, cruelty and hopelessness of a lower class that had neither rational thought nor belief was obvious; nor was "enlightenment" as free as it professed to be from the point of view of those who did not move in its inner circle. For these others it was a ceiling, or prison of the emotions, weighing down the spirit and creating a state of tension that could be unbearable.

The existence of this tension is shown beyond dispute by the remarkable results of John Wesley's missionary journeys through heathen Britain, when as many as thirty thousand people would await the arrival of the preacher on horseback, when rough miners and artisans would burst into tears and welcome Wesley's message with transports of enthusiasm. An eager reception awaited any revelation that gave promise of a spiritual life instead of enslavement to a cynically material system. One such revelation that had its welcome in Britain was that of a distinguished Swede, Emmanuel Swedenborg.

The personal evolution of this remarkable man is an illustration of the contending forces in his century. From science, the purely material explanation of nature, and practical undertakings in which he displayed much efficiency and commonsense, he made the transition to prophecy and the interpretation of Scripture. Born in Stockholm in 1688, he was brought up at Upsala, where his father, Jesper Swedberg, became professor of Theology in the University. His mother died when he was eight, but Jesper married again within a year to a widow, Sara Bergia, of whose seven step-children Emmanuel was the favourite. When his father became Bishop of Skara in 1702, the boy stayed on as undergraduate at Upsala, studying the "exact sciences"—mathematics, physics, astronomy. In 1710 he made his first visit to England, mainly because of its prestige in science. He "read Newton daily", bought all kinds of scientific instruments, stayed with an instrument maker in order to "steal his trade" and competed for a prize offered by the Greenwich Observatory for an improved method of finding the longitude at sea. He went on to Leyden and Paris, studying the work of mathematicians and astronomers and, where possible, cultivating their acquaintance; and returned to Sweden in 1715 with a long list of scientific projects, including like many such lists from the time of Leonardo da Vinci onwards, proposals for a submarine and an aeroplane.

Sweden at this time was engaged, under the heroic leadership of Charles XII, in great wars of trivial or no advantage. The utility of science in making them more destructive was not yet fully appreciated. Nevertheless, the King took sufficient notice of the promising young man to advance him to the unsalaried post of extra "assessor" to the national board that supervised the mining industry. His stepmother, who owned mining property and eventually left him an independent income, allowed him sufficient to labour on his honorary, and somewhat thankless, job for many years before he was granted an Assessor's salary. Yet he was very active, entirely practical, and full of common-sense ideas for the survey and control of imports and the increase of production at home. As a specialized metallurgist and mining engineer, he travelled about the country, assaying the iron ore, going down mine shafts, visiting the forest huts of charcoal burners. This work occupied him until middle age.

Swedenborg (he was ennobled in 1719 and then took this name) was forty-five when he had printed in Leipzig, at the expense of an admiring patron, the Duke of Brunswick, his first important book. It was an investigation of the nature of matter, in which he announced the principle that "Nature operates in the world in a mechanical manner and the phenomena which she presents to our senses are subject to their proper laws and rules". It was the doctrine of a scientific materialism, typical of his age and not completely outmoded since. The book had its practical side—and also contained original ideas. The author's account of metals was well received and we may take the word of scientists that he gave some anticipations of later discovery in molecular structure; but evidently he was not satisfied. There remained to be considered the elusive connection between the finite world and the infinite, and in a further book *Of the Infinite* he found himself compelled to reckon with the existence of the soul. His researches had shown that "matter" was not necessarily solid and tangible. It was conceivable that the soul as the "last and subtlest part of the body" was amenable to "mechanical laws". Faced with the problem of how this might be, Swedenborg in 1736 obtained indefinite leave from his duties as Assessor of Mines, and went abroad to study anatomy under expert guidance, and to establish if possible the nature and workings of the soul by means of "experience, geometry and reason".

The plump, blue-eyed Swedish scientist, a typical eighteenth century figure in his bag wig, travelled to Paris, Rome, Venice, enjoying contact with different types of European society, not averse to music and the theatre, but making it his main business to seek out those who knew most of anatomy. In 1738 he published his *Anatomy of the Animal Kingdom* in which he tried to comprehend soul and body in an ordered structure. The soul or "anima" was the governing factor. It worked through the intellectual mind that thinks, understands and wills. This, in due succession, operated on the "animus" or "seat of emotions" and desires, and so, at last, on the senses and motor organs of the body. It was the turning-point in the process that converted the scientist into a mystic.

To reason that the soul existed was one thing, to enter the spiritual world, claim to talk with spirits, describe their dwellings and occupations was another. It was, in one way, an extension of the ordered system Swedenborg had conceived, to imagine a further series of steps and grades, different levels of "heaven", but this escaped entirely from the region of scientific demonstration into that of personal and emotional experience.

He began, at this period of his life, to consider himself as removed from the material world. He practised a kind of yoga, being able eventually to hold his breath for "a little hour". He noted a tendency towards dreams which became not merely dreams but a waking "ecstasy". At last he converted a scientific study into a matter of faith. "What are truths without an ultimate desire for goodness! Or . . . the intelligence unless to know how to choose the Good." The strange world in which at first he saw no clear and definite image was given shape by Christianity and his reading of the Bible. In Swedenborg himself a new faculty had taken charge. The mystic offered the solution of the problem that had baffled the student of material phenomena. He retired on half pay from his official post. He devoted himself to a description of the new world into which his mind had entered in his *Arcana Coelestia* published in eight volumes between 1749 and 1756. Until his death in London in 1772 his life was exclusively devoted to recording his spiritual experiences and expounding the doctrine to which they gave rise.

There was an element of "revelation" in his account of the "heavenly secrets". He practised "automatic writing", and thus as he reasoned, became the medium of spirits. "Nay, I have written entire pages, and the spirits did not dictate the words, but absolutely guided my hand, so that it is they who were doing the writing." "Sometimes it was also granted me to know by what angel of God Messiah they were thus written."

One passage was supposed to have been "written" by Jacob, who was somewhat indignant at things that had been said about him by others in the spirit world. The possibility that the wrong kind of spirit might gain control was apparent to Swedenborg himself. It seems clear, at the same time, that consciously or unconsciously, he interpreted the Bible in his own way. Historically speaking, it was an allegory—Adam, for instance, stood for the original Church, the Flood marked its disappearance and Noah its reappearance : but the Bible throughout, he concluded, with the exception of certain books which were merely *good* books, was inspired, in the sense of revealing the spiritual world and the spiritual nature of man.

The spiritual world was a structure and Swedenborg's deep-rooted belief in an ordered system came out in his description of it. It consisted essentially in heaven and hell, though heaven and hell were independent of time or space. It was not necessary to suppose that a given number of years must elapse before the Last Judgment took place—indeed Swedenborg affirmed that such a judgment—spiritual re-assessment or shake-up—happened in the year 1757. On the other hand it did not imply ascent in the air or descent to some fiery depth. Heaven was the perfect state of goodness and truth, complete selflessness. Hell was the reverse, complete egotism. There were palaces and beautiful gardens in the one, slums and hideous wastelands in the other, but these were not realities in the earthly sense, they were part of a system of "correspondences" by which the idea of all things good attached to good and of things evil to evil.

There were marriages in Heaven. Swedenborg, though a bachelor, had always been a man with a decided liking for the opposite sex. Of intercourse between the sexes, in the married state or out of it, he had approved so far as it represented love or the union of souls. "Intention being the soul of all action", the desire for self-abandonment or union with another was a virtue, a spiritual intention. It was only lacking this, that he deplored the carnal act (for the body without the soul was dead). He explained in some detail in his book on Conjugal Love that "a similar love exists between married partners in the heavens as in the earths", even "to the utmost delights".

In the spiritual world the entering souls were sorted out according to their nature, and like gravitated to like. To begin with, they might not realize that they were spirits. They existed in a sort of Purgatory for a while : then the true characteristics of each were gradually revealed—the wicked were attracted to their kindred spirits, the good prepared to become angels. It was possible to converse with spirits. Time and space being immaterial, they would come when you did think of them—even if in life they had belonged to a different age, or even a different planet. Swedenborg conversed with the spirits of many he had known in life and many also he had not known. Language was no barrier, thought communicated itself by the telepathic faculty Swedenborg believed to be latent in every living human being.

News of his strange powers and experiences got about by degrees. He made no secret of them, though he did not obtrude them on others and remained in the ordinary affairs of life the practical and level-headed person he had always been. In Sweden, he was a respected "elder statesman", who cogently opposed currency inflation, and put up sound arguments for the nationalizing of the liquor trade. He made no effort to found a sect and the fact that his books were written in Latin showed no anxiety to give them a very wide circulation.

Swedenborg always had a particular attachment to England. Speech there was freer than elsewhere and he valued this freedom as an approach to the complete spiritual frankness of truth. It was in lodgings in a public house kept by a Swede in Wellclose Square, Whitechapel, that he began work on the *Arcana Coelestia*, which "noble repast to a pious mind" as the publisher described it, was issued in London. He returned towards the end of his life, staying in 1769 at the house of a barber and wigmaker in Coldbath Fields. It was there his last days were spent. Partly paralysed in 1771, he was visited by his English disciple, the Reverend Thomas Hartley, and by a Swedish pastor, Arvid Ferelius, who found him "very easy and pleasant". He never spoke about his own views except when he was asked about them though he made Ferelius a little uncomfortable by referring to the spirits who had just been with him or just left him. Early in 1772 he died peacefully at the age of eighty-four.

The small, struggling middle class folk among whom he had

elected to stay composed a human background far different from that of his life on the continent. The well-to-do and greatly esteemed ornament of Swedish society was here a humble, an undistinguished traveller. He had had no part in the "high life" of London, nor had the works he had sent to the dignitaries of the Church and other eminent persons made any perceptible impression. Yet it was that small middle-class, little disposed to the sarcastic intellectualism of a socially higher sphere, with its unsatisfied desire for religious experience, that was by degrees to warm to the Swedenborgian doctrine, to add to the various churches of nonconformity, the "new Church" which he had envisaged as rising, in a purely spiritual sense, on the ashes of the old.

He did not seem insane, any more than those other zealots and other mystics who had dreamed dreams and seen visions. He tested himself for insanity with all the disinterested calm of the scientist. He seemed to others the most normal and well-balanced of men. It was to be left to twentieth-century psychoanalysts to advance subtle explanations that would convict him of mental disease or unbalance. From their point of view, indeed, any kind of mysticism is a sign of defeat in the mind, a falling backwards to the condition of a primitive and infantile humanity. Swedenborg, in this light, was a "mythomaniac". Alternatively, his diversion from the material to the spiritual world has been explained in sexual terms. Thus the early death of his mother, by one theory, set up an unconscious homosexual love for his father, which became symbolized by his love of God. That he had a great affection for his stepmother and she for him is an objection to this theory which the psychoanalyst might regard as simple to the point of frivolity.

On the other hand, while the rationalist might find it a shock to learn that Swedenborg had just had a pleasant chat with the spirit of Sir Isaac Newton or seen the distinguished naturalist, Sir Hans Sloane, in heaven, studying an angelic bird, his thought or belief, stripped of quaintly circumstantial details, had a firm and clear outline. It amounted to this, that the life of the spirit is the only life, without which all created things are meaningless and dead, that it constitutes an ordered system, Good in its perfection; that Good, and Evil (the disorder or perversion of Good) are definite presences in the human mind, which in a sense creates its own heaven and hell and is the stage on which an immense spiritual drama is first performed.

There was no immediate wave of enthusiasm in England for Swedenborg's doctrines as there had been, and still was, for those of Wesley. The circumstances were different. Wesley was a clergyman who had devoted his life to reform, to publicizing and propagating his belief. He spoke—and spoke with singular power—in town, village and hamlet, throughout Britain, in words of which any artisan or farm labourer could feel the force. A foreigner who wrote in Latin, did not set himself out to win converts and merely spent a quiet vacation in London, preparing and supervising the production of his books, would not, obviously, become the centre of like attraction.

Yet, in the curious way in which people will seek out the food they need, though hidden and hard to get at, there were soon followers of Swedenborg. Stripped to its essentials, his message was not unfamiliar but a new and startling affirmation of what, obscurely, many a pious protestant believed. If he had not spoken of the spiritual world in abstract and remote terms, but as one who had penetrated beyond the veil, and "seen for himself", he was entitled to no less respect than such another visionary as John Bunyan. His assumption that a new "Church" would come into being with "the Last Judgment" of 1757 could be taken literally as a call to make such a Church a reality.

The interest he had caused in the humble East End quarters where he stayed widened into circles of discussion. A clergyman understood Latin if the laity did not (Latin was, after all, more universal than Swedish). An enthusiast like the Reverend Thomas Hartley could interpret Swedenborg for the unlearned. Hartley began a series of translations with an English version of *Intercourse of the Soul and Body*; another clergyman, the Reverend John Clowes of Manchester, took up the work. A printer in Clerkenwell, Robert Hindmarsh, organized the following and in 1788, sixteen years after Swedenborg's death, the new Church "signified by the New Jerusalem in the Revelation" came into being.

II

SWEDENBORGIANS

In what precise fashion the influence of the Swedish mystic filtered into the Blake household it is not now possible to say, though that it should is not in itself surprising. Such orderly middle-class family groups with their latent puritanism and their distance from the sceptic and fashionable stratum of society, were receptive to the idea of a spiritual life which removed the oppressive ceiling of the materialist outlook from above their heads. It is assumed that James Blake was a member of the small sect that began to take shape in the London of George III's time, though he died in 1784, before one can strictly speak of a Swedenborgian Church, and his views on the subject of religion are no more discernible than on any other. One cannot tell to what extent he communicated them to his growing sons, though it is conceivable he might remark that the year of Swedenborg's spiritual house-cleaning, the Last Judgment of 1757, was also the year of his son William's birth. There is no reason to suppose that the engraver's apprentice of fourteen ever saw the old Swedish gentleman in his antiquated suit of black velvet with his double hilted sword and gold-headed cane, though the possibility emphasizes their nearness to each other in time. There is no doubt, however, of the influence of Swedenborg on William Blake, nor of the fact that he was, for a time at least, quite specifically a Swedenborgian. And if it were not written plain in the whole of his mature life, the entry in the minute book of the Great Eastcheap Swedenborgian Society of his name and that of his wife (1789) would supply evidence in writing.

Like other influences on Blake, that of Swedenborg was cumulative in effect: his ideas were altered, magnified, exaggerated, destroyed and renewed in the vortex of Blake's mental energy. In his later years he was almost Swedenborg over again—though much else besides. There are few signs, however, of this influence before he was over thirty, though in the decade after he left Basire, a qualified engraver of twenty-one, his character and inclinations begin to appear for us.

Blake, there is every indication, was energetic, opinionated, quick-tempered, determined, impulsive, as capable of hatred as of affection, and capable also of expressing it in terms both forceful and ironic. A brief period spent in the Royal Academy school was a failure, for it is evident he did not want to learn or had already come to opposite conclusions from those of his teachers. No humble student, he contradicted the Keeper of the Academy, Moser, who tried to point out the merits of Le Brun and Rubens. "These things that you call Finish'd are not Even Begun; how can they then be Finish'd? The Man who does not know the Beginning never can know the End of Art."

It is very likely that at this time he submitted drawings for the inspection of the President, Sir Joshua Reynolds. Sir Joshua's reputed advice was in the spirit of those lectures to the students of the Academy which he had been delivering since 1769 (and was to continue until 1790) setting the classics of European painting on their pedestals (the masters of Italy towering above the rest) and recommending equal devotion to the study of them and of nature. He earned Blake's remorseless enmity by his recommendation to work "with less extravagance and more simplicity" and to correct his drawing. Blake in middle age (1808) was still chafing under this criticism when he wrote his fierce annotations to the President's published *Discourses*. It was the sort of criticism which might be given without harm to any normal student; but there must have been some immediate antipathy between the courtly Reynolds and the fiery young man. Possibly Reynolds touched a sore point also, in speaking of correct drawing; and Blake's indignation was partly due to an incompetence in himself he knew and would not admit.

The impatience of Blake with the Academy and its head may be explained on broader ground; aesthetically, by his admiration for the Gothic sculptures in Westminster Abbey, which made Le Brun and Rubens, held up as models by the Academy, seem artificial and insincere. In this respect he was already a kind of Pre-Raphaelite, his remark to Moser that "The man who does not know the Beginning can never know the End of Art" anticipates many such remarks by John Ruskin. Yet there was the Swedenborgian, too, in his attitude; even if he had not argued the matter out consciously. It was not the external but the internal man that was of importance: and this was why he could not bear to draw from the living model, why it "seemed looking more like death or smelling of mortality". Any such copying of appearances, including those rich folds of satin and velvet, those sparkling jewels, those landscape vistas, on which the oil-painter lavished his skill, was to deal with so much dead matter, from which the all-important and active element, the soul of man was absent.

In modern terms, Blake was not a realist. The French word for a painting of still life, *"nature morte"*—"dead nature" would have suggested to him a literal and contemptuous meaning. He would indeed have been astonished at the devotion of a Cézanne to the representation of a plate of apples. It would not have occurred to him that the soul of man was sufficiently present in the result as an element in the painter that transformed and illuminated the "dead nature" before him. He was to remain outside the circle of painters, always disturbed by an activity in so many ways repugnant to him and, it may be, vaguely troubled (and angered) by the inability he refused to confess. He returned to the humbler craft of reproductive engraving which earned him a fair living from his twenty-second to his twenty-ninth year, and through it he came to know other young men who lived by illustration and other forms of designing; notably John Flaxman.

Flaxman, two years older than Blake, born at York in 1755, was the son of a maker of casts and models, who worked for the sculptor, Roubiliac. At the time when he was introduced to Blake, he was a sculptor of promise, trained in the Academy Schools (he won the silver medal for a wax model of Neptune in 1770) and finding employment in what we should now call "industrial design" for the Wedgwood pottery. He was a serious and high-minded young man who had enrolled himself among the followers of Swedenborg and this, no doubt, was one of the reasons why he and Blake became friends. They had, also, a common object of dislike in Sir Joshua Reynolds, a "gentlemanly scholar" in Flaxman's view, who talked nonsense about sculpture. Nor did Sir Joshua endear himself by his remark, when he heard of Flaxman's marriage: "Then your improvement is at an end."

Flaxman plays an important part in Blake's life in having

introduced him (for better or for worse) to more than one patron. Among the customers of Flaxman's father was the Reverend Henry Mathew of Percy Chapel, Charlotte Street. The young sculptor took his friend with him to the "salon", if that is the word, of Mr. and Mrs. Mathew. It was essentially middle-class, far removed from the gay aristocratic gatherings where Horace Walpole and George Selwyn giggled over each other's bon mots. One imagines a solemn company, a meeting of blue worsted stockings rather than the black silks of the card rooms and clubs, including a number of earnest women, sitting very upright in their chairs and talking very profoundly. The learned Mrs. Elizabeth Carter, who knew nine languages, played on the spinet and the German flute, and was noted both for her poetry and puddings, would probably have much to say about her celebrated friend, Dr. Johnson. Mrs. Elizabeth Montagu, the "Mme. du Deffand of London," whose *Essay on the Genius of Shakespeare . . . with some remarks on the misrepresentations of M. de Voltaire* had won great approval, graced this salon as well as her own. Mrs. Hester Chapone, author of *Letters on the Improvement of the Mind*, Mrs. Anna Letitia Barbauld, writer of poems and hymns, and Miss Hannah More, the tireless exponent of duty and religion, seem to have been of the company. Over such an assembly of talented, and, as Dickens would have described them, "middle-aged females", Mr. Mathew (whom the introduction to the *Poetical Sketches* entitles us to think of as somewhat pompous and overbearing), ruled.

It would be unfair to laugh too readily at these blue-stocking meetings, of which there is now only a distant impression. Mrs. Barbauld is certainly not to be despised as a poet and woman of letters, her verses on *Life* are admirable. Hannah More was an able and excellent woman, though Dr. Johnson's stunning pronouncement that she was "the most powerful versificatrix in the English language" goes a little too far. On the other hand, it can be surmised that a good deal of stilted nonsense was talked. Flaxman, earnest in features, with long pointed nose, large upper-lip, and slightly receding chin, may be envisaged as listening with reverence, almost as if he were in church: but what was going on in the mind behind the prominent brow, the blue eyes of his quiet companion, is another matter.

The keen and powerful intelligence of Blake was not to be taken in by claptrap. Nor was he one to suffer patrons gladly. It was pleasant to recite his poems—or sing them—to an attentive audience. They were lyrics that could be sung, and the music was his own though what it was like is now a matter of conjecture. It was kind of the Mathews to subscribe, with Flaxman, to the cost of printing the *Poetical Sketches*. Yet there was much to be endured. Mr. Mathew was all too "conscious of the irregularities and defects" in the poems: his protégé by no means meek in the reception of criticism. There may well have been moments when an embarrassed silence followed some sharp retort, or some bold and devastating paradox. The visits to the salon grew fewer: the eventual outcome was that uproarious little farce *An Island in the Moon* (1787).

In this lunar island, a party of middle-class intellectuals like those he had studied at close quarters, meet and talk in peculiar and erudite fashion. Philosopher, scientist, antiquarian and blue-stocking appeared under such grotesque titles as Sipsop the Pythagorean, Inflammable Gas the Windfinder, his wife Gibble Gabble, Mrs. Gimblet, Mrs. Nannicantipot and Miss Gittipin; though the parody was not so much of individuals as of a general absurdity.

They must have talked a lot in the Mathew salon of the great Johnson; but neither the praise of his women admirers nor *The Lives of the Poets* (appearing between 1779 and 1781) in which the Doctor praised Pope so finely, was indulgent to many a correct nonentity and scathingly hostile to the genius of Gray, was likely to commend itself to the young Blake. Derision grins in the verse:—

> "Lo the bat with leathern wing,
> Winking and Blinking,
> Winking and Blinking,
> Winking and Blinking,
> Like Dr. Johnson."

Buffoonery follows.

> "Oho, said Dr. Johnson
> To Scipio Africanus,
> If you don't own me a philosopher
> I'll kick your Roman Anus."

WILLIAM BLAKE by Thomas Phillips

MRS. BLAKE

Pencil drawing by William Blake

Chatterton, too, was evidently discussed, or at least was much in Blake's mind; but if the latter represented himself as "Quid" in *An Island in the Moon* he distorted his views in harmony with the general silliness of the characters. "I think that Homer is bombast and that Shakespeare is too wild, Milton has no feelings; They might easily be outdone. Chatterton never writ those poems! A parcel of fools, going to Bristol! If I was to go, I'd find out in a minute, but I've found out already." The garbled accounts of Chatterton's end are parodied by "Aradobo". "In the first place I think, I think in the first place that Chatterton was clever at Fissie Follogy, Pistinology, Aridology, Arography, Transmography, Phisography, Hogamy, Hatomy and hall that, but, in the first place, he eat very little, wickly —that is, he slept very little which he brought into a consumsion; & what was that he took? Fissic or somethink—so died!"

Altogether Blake showed himself capable of grotesque fun and rollicking satire, as further in the parody of the Augustan poetical cliché:—

> "Hail matrimony, made of Love
> To thy wide gates how great a drove
> On purpose to be yoked do come!
> Widows and maids and youths also,
> That lightly trip on beauty's toe,
> Or sit on beauty's bum."

Blake could be coarse on occasions; but the power of the born poet animated even the grotesque fragments in this little work.

Meanwhile, his marriage throws additional light on his character. He wooed with a typical impetuosity; as a lover he was romantic—and even Swedenborgian. There came first a disappointment. Realistic, flirtatious and taking her time about her choice, a girl of his own class, Polly Wood, briskly refused idealization; when he objected to other suitors, asked "Are you a fool?" Blake nursed his wounded pride on a holiday in then rural Battersea. Catherine Boucher, the daughter of a market gardener, whom he met there, had, from a worldly viewpoint, little to offer. She had no fortune. She was illiterate: the nearest to a peasant to be found in a country without

a peasantry, far below the intelligent mercantile level of the
Blake family. The lack of worldly goods did not trouble the
young man, no one was less mercenary than he. Education he
was capable of supplying. She was simple, sweet, comely, above
all sympathetic. The gentle eyes misted with tears as he told
of his troubles. "Do you pity me?" "I do." "Then, I love
you." The famous proposal, which might almost be called a
process of reasoning, would certainly have met with Swedenborg's approval. While prudence and intellect were not at all
involved, it was not to be ascribed to a sudden physical infatua-
tion—it was that union of souls which the Swedish mystic had
regarded as the one essential of conjugal love.

Yet until Blake was thirty he showed no obvious signs of
absorption in the spiritual world. He was married at Battersea
Church in 1782, when he was twenty-five and Catherine
twenty-one (she signed the register with a cross). They lodged
for a while at 23 Green Street (now Irving Street, off Leicester
Square); then he went back to work as engraver and printseller
in partnership with another of Basire's pupils, James Parker,
next door to the family house in Broad Street. He was masterful, his wife was adoring, they were both happy. The imprudent
marriage seemed ultimately to have been dictated by excellent
sense. For five years more he patiently pursued his trade and
routine craft: but in 1787 his younger brother, Robert, died
and the event and the year mark, if not a change in Blake, a
new phase in his life and thought. Robert had been his
favourite brother, pupil and assistant in the printselling business and his death from tuberculosis caused William Blake to
think more and more deeply of the mysteries of existence and
the nature of religion. The follower of Swedenborg was not
downcast. He could see Robert's soul depart from the body
"clapping its hands for joy". He was still able to converse
with him "daily and hourly in the spirit, and see him in my
remembrance, in the regions of my imagination". Writing thus
many years later to William Hayley he added the magnificent
phrase "The ruins of Time build mansions in Eternity".

Yet how far was he a follower of Swedenborg? What was
his religion? These were questions to which he sought an
answer. He and his devoted Catherine, who would probably
have subscribed to any religion her husband decreed, were duly

enrolled among the adherents of the New Church though later both (again obviously by his decree) resigned. Blake was too independent and nonconformist a character to accept a creed unreservedly and without giving it his personal interpretation. In his way, like Swedenborg in *his* way, he was a Christian : but each laid his own emphasis on the nature of Christianity. The central fact for Swedenborg was not that Christ had been sacrificed for the salvation of human beings, which indeed he thought a horrible idea. "No good master could so deal with his manservants and maidservants, nor even a wild beast or bird of prey with its young. It is horrible." This was the comment he made in his book *The True Christian Religion*. In Christ, the Invisible had for a space of time become visible. The Crucifixion symbolized the return to, the complete identi- fication that was possible with God. For Blake, the essence of Christianity was forgiveness as he put it in his preface "To The Public" at the beginning of his *Jerusalem*. "The Spirit of Jesus is continual Forgiveness of Sin."

It was always remarkable in Blake that while so vigorous and individual in statement, he took in ideas and stimulus from many different sources. To look on him simply as a follower of Swedenborg would be an error, though the impress always remained in his thought and actions. He studied also the writings of Jacob Boehme, the German shoemaker who died early in the seventeenth century and had caused a sensation, in his own time, by his deep speculations on the nature of God, universal, present in all things. He had acquired attentive readers in England, including Sir Isaac Newton. Interest was renewed by the translations of William Law. Law is known by his own work, the *Serious Call to a Devout and Holy Life* (1729) as a forerunner of the Wesleys, though in later years (he died in 1761), his advocacy of Boehme's views made him anti-Metho- dist. In the days of Blake's youth the complete edition of Law's translations revived controversial notice of the Protestant mystic.

Boehme—"Behmen" as he was usually known in England— was not unlike Swedenborg in ideas. The latter, when questioned on the resemblance, declared he had not read him, though from various books influenced by Boehme he might unconsciously have absorbed his thought. An echo of Boehme, whom he considered a "divinely inspired" person, may be found in the proposition Blake tersely set out in 1788 under the heading *There is no Natural Religion.*

"Man's perceptions are not bound by organs of perception, he perceives more than sense (tho' ever so acute) can discover. . . . He who sees the Infinite in all things, sees God. He who sees the Ratio [Reason] only, sees himself only."

Or, as he put it in the *Auguries of Innocence* with a beauty the German shoemaker never dreamed of:

"To see a World in a Grain of Sand
And a Heaven in a Wild Flower
Hold infinity in the palm of your hand,
And Eternity in an hour."

At the same time Blake must have been strongly impressed by John Wesley. His active and forthright character was not one to lose itself in passive speculation. He was like Wesley, an enthusiast. He admired the preacher who bestirred himself to ride about Britain and give a message of hope; who spoke in language very much like his own. He expressed his admiration in his *Milton* though misspelling Wesley's name.

"He sent us his two servants, Whitefield and Westley.
Were they prophets
Or were they idiots or madmen? Shew us miracles!
Can you have greater miracles than these?"

The famous verses with which the same poem begins are the perfect Methodist hymn:

"I will not cease from Mental Fight
Nor shall my sword sleep in my hand
Till we have built Jerusalem
In England's green and pleasant land."

"England! awake, awake, awake!" The message is again

repeated in Blake's *Jerusalem*. To appreciate its meaning one must think once more of that ignorant and brutal England which Wesley had done his best to change.

Yet Blake was also a romantic and an artist: and these two qualities set him apart from the mystic and the evangelist. As a romantic he could not be bound by the tenets of any sect.

"The bounded is loathed by its possessor. The same dull round, even of a universe, would soon become a mill with complicated wheels."

Gradually he became suspicious of Swedenborg because he had made a system. Into the approving annotations which he wrote, somewhere between 1788 and 1790, to Swedenborg's *Wisdom of Angels* there came a change to sharp criticism. Its author had, in his scientific way, looked with satisfaction on a celestial order in which the good and the evil were neatly sorted out and remained presumably in their respective categories to all eternity. Man "according to his Life here has his *place assigned* to him either in Heaven or in Hell". The words in italics are those underlined by Blake, pounced on, as it were, with displeasure and growing doubt. ". . . he who is in Evil in the World, the same is in Evil after he goes out of *the World wherefore if Evil be not removed* in the *World, it cannot be removed afterwards.*" More italics: and the comment by Blake "Predestination after this Life is more abominable than Calvin's, Swedenborg is Such a Spiritual Predestinarian. . . . Cursed Folly."

He would have found much the same view in Boehme, though how closely he studied Law's translations we are unable to say in the absence of any annotated copy. The kindly Swedenborg seems to have recoiled from the conclusions of his own argument: to have left a way out inasmuch as "there is not wanting to any Man a Knowledge of the Means whereby he may be saved, nor the Power of being saved if he will". Thus "it is a cruel heresy, to suppose that any of the Human Race are predestined to be damned", and here, as Blake pointed out with perfect justice, Swedenborg contradicted the statements he had previously made. Evil, the two European theosophists concurred in regarding as the necessary fissure in the principle of good, the "contrary" that by its opposition contributed to set in motion the forces of the created universe, though Lucifer, (so to personify Evil), was still held in relation and subjection to that infinite unity "he" had disturbed, from which "he" had been turned out—by an effort of will that admittedly remained mysterious.

These efforts to bound the Infinite were the subjects with which Blake's mind grappled, with firmness. In the first place, as he believed in the continual forgiveness of sin, he could not accept the idea that the sinful would languish hereafter in a Sargasso Sea (or Hell) of the spirit, from which it was incapable of moving. His love of freedom, his contempt of all barriers and restrictions, condemned it and rose against it. A methodically ordered, despotically governed, spirit world was just as bad as the materialistic eighteenth century into which he had been born. Understanding, he reasoned, was a good. Understanding was acquired by experience. To gain experience it was inevitable that man should commit errors and even sins. In his ardent desire for freedom to experience, he was led, as were so many romantics, into a position like that of Lucifer himself; or at least to find a paradoxical virtue in the reversal of roles, by which the Devil spoke truth when Jehovah had become false.

The demonic defiance, or essential humanity of Blake was brilliantly expressed some years after he made his notes on Swedenborg's *Wisdom of the Angels concerning Divine Providence* in the *Marriage of Heaven and Hell* of 1793, in which he included the rebellious epigrams of the *Proverbs of Hell*. "The road of excess leads to the palace of wisdom. . . . He who desires but acts not breeds pestilence. . . . Exuberance is beauty." Swedenborg came in for criticism on the score of his one-sidedness. "He conversed with angels who are all religious, and conversed not with devils who all hate religion, for he was incapable thro' his conceited notions." In his romantic defiance he commented acutely that, "Milton wrote in fetters when he wrote of Angels and God, and at liberty when of Devils & Hell, because he was a true Poet and of the Devil's party without knowing it." As much, André Gide has remarked, may be said of Blake himself "but he, at least, was aware of it—and was also able to forget it; whence comes his power".

It seems, at first, not a little curious that Blake who believed

so firmly in the forgiveness and love of Christ, should fling himself so ardently into the tremendous battles of Heaven and Hell
that belong to the Old Testament rather than the New. Yet
he interprets the Bible in his own way and with a consciousness
of his purposes as an artist. He offered an alternative version of
his faith in the exhortation "To the Christians" that forms part,
of *Jerusalem*.

"I know of no other Christianity and of no other Gospel
than the liberty both of body and mind to exercise the Divine
Arts of Imagination. Imagination, the real and eternal World
of which this Vegetable Universe is but a faint shadow, & in
which we shall live in our Eternal and Imaginative Bodies
when these Vegetable Mortal Bodies are no more." The Bible
was not a collection of precepts concerning the moral virtues
but a stupendous series of Imaginations and Visions. The
Prophets were poets in the force of their imaginations—the
word prophet for Blake became the same as poet—a prophetic
book was a "poem". The Heaven and Hell of the prophets were
an allegory of the forces contending in the human mind, where
alone they existed. It was in this way that religious feeling was
transmuted into the terms of art—or imagination—in the
writings of Blake's middle-age and old age and in the great
designs of his maturity.

He ceased, except for a very occasional piece, to be the
exquisite writer of lyrics—who may be compared with
Chatterton and transcends him in the variety of rhythm, the
simplicity and purity of imagery and phrase when he had
composed the *Songs of Innocence* (1789) and the *Songs of Experience*
(1794). Yet in a strange fashion influences on Blake remained
imperishable and as it were suspended in all he did. The
influence of Ossian persisted in the unrhymed "prophetic"
books, with, as he explained, "variety in every line, both of
cadences and number of syllables". (Even the blank verse of
Shakespeare and Milton did not sufficiently escape from "the
modern bondage of Rhyming".) Ossian, too, suggested the
atmosphere of the primæval epic in which vast, uncouthly
named figures struggle in a scene that mixes past and present,
shifts from Camberwell to Golgotha. The example of Wesley
seems to dictate something of that spirit of hopeful enthusiasm
in which he wrote. The Swedenborgian persists in these com-

munications with the spirit world, the report of which puzzled,
alarmed and interested the circle of his later acquaintance. It
was in the series of engravings to the Book of Job that at last
he expressed both the freedom and the subtlety of his interpretation of the Bible. They were not mere illustrations to the
trial of a good man, subject to the whim of a Jehovah resembling an Oriental sultan, who listened to the counsels of a
diabolical vizier. On the contrary, the "power" above and the
"horror" below were contending elements in Job's own mind.
The cruel deity (with cloven hoof) who in one engraving
represents self-righteousness, and the devils who seek to bind
him with physical chains, are, alike, Job himself; what we
witness is indeed the inward battle of the soul.

Into the growing anti-materialism of his time Blake projected
energy, wit, daring. He was not meek, vague, or less intelligible
than the professed men of religion who struggled with the same
deep matters. He took much from them; has a place among the
Protestant thinkers for whom a fresh evaluation of the Bible was
essential; stands in sympathetic relation with the leaders of the
Evangelical movement; but is distinct from them in his ability
to enrich and expand thought both by words and pictures—
that is, as an artist. But no tribute to this man who felt so
violently, reasoned so intensely, could be less appropriate than
that of William Hayley, who in 1800 inscribed his *The Triumphs
of Temper* to

> ". . . My gentle visionary Blake
> Whose thoughts are fanciful and kindly mild".

These uncomprehending lines refer to the fiery romantic who
wrote "Sooner murder an infant in its cradle than nurse
unacted desires"; who pictured in the Book of Job a tense and
terrible, though happily resolved, drama of the human spirit.

3

DREAM AND NIGHTMARE

THE growing sense of "wonder" in the eighteenth century, the conviction that there were more things in heaven and earth than its philosophers dreamed of, showed itself in varied explorations of human emotion. Sombre, melancholy and fantastic thoughts came to involve a certain pleasure: as a relief from a prevailing cheerfulness, frivolity and sophistication. They gave a new meaning to the Augustan dictum that "the proper study of mankind is man". The study changed from that of the social animal, conditioned to its environment and complacent in those "moral virtues" (for which William Blake expressed great abhorrence) to that of the "antic shapes, wild natives of the brain" of which Edward Young wrote in his *Night Thoughts*:

> "Helpless immortal! insect infinite!
> A worm! a god! I tremble at myself
> And in myself am lost!..."

To study man was, in some degree, (contrary to the opinion of Pope) to "scan God", to encounter mysteries, strange depths and prospects, and the poet who had no specifically religious aim, nevertheless brooded on spectres and phantoms, dreams, symbols of death, and ideas of immortality. The feeling that, as Swedenborg put it, "there are marvellous things occurring in the human mind", was ultimately a desire for its freedom like that of the Surrealists in the twentieth century (the Surrealists, it may be noted, have claimed Young among their number). Two poems, appearing in the 1740's, reflect this unaccustomed depth and direction of thought, Young's *Night Thoughts*, and Blair's *Grave*. In many respects, Edward Young was a typical Augustan. Born in 1683 at Upham, in Hampshire, where his father was rector, educated at Winchester and Oxford, he promptly sought out a patron as a young man, and seems to have lived a gay and courtly life, dividing his time between literature and place-seeking.   He became a chaplain to George II, in 1730 rector and lord of the manor of Welwyn in Hertfordshire, in the following year married Lady Betty Lee, widow of a Colonel Lee and daughter of the Earl of Lichfield. In 1741, the lady's daughter by her first marriage, whom Young was very fond of, died; shortly afterwards so did her mother; grief set him to work on the *Night Thoughts* (1742–44) which he addressed to a fictional man of pleasure, Lorenzo. Probably in "Lorenzo" Young rebuked his own son, who was sent down from Balliol. In the nine "Nights" of which the book is composed there is no story, sequence, or action: only a series of concentrated reflections on life, death and future life. The content was more original than the form.   Young's blank verse gives a certain pomp and artificiality to his emotions which does not always assort well with them: but in single and detached images, in a sense of the terrific, he sometimes rivals Blake himself.

The Grave by Robert Blair was published about the same time. The author was a Scottish clergyman, of private means and cultured tastes, born in Edinburgh in 1699, educated at Edinburgh University and in Holland, and appointed in 1731 to the living of Athelstaneford, where he preceded Home, the admirer of Macpherson. *The Grave* (1793) had many points of similarity to Young's main work, so many that it was a nice question whether one had imitated the other—and which it was. There was the same sombre enthusiasm, the same love of immensities:

"The wrecks of nations and the spoils of time
    With all the lumber of six thousand years".

In his description of a church at night there was every in-gredient of budding romanticism, the Gothic past, a strange and dream-like atmosphere, the terrible and the supernatural:

"Doors creak and windows clap, and night's foul bird
    Rocked in the spire, screams loud: the gloomy aisles
    Black-plastered and hung round with shreds of scutcheons
    And tattered coats-of-arms, send back the sound

Laden with heavier airs, from the low vaults,
The mansions of the dead. Roused from their slumbers
In grim array, the grisly spectres rise,
Grin horrible . . ."

Both poets imagined a trance-like state in which the mind
travelled freely through scarcely imaginable distance and could
"dream of things impossible". The dream state, in fact, gave
its own assurance of the independent life of the spirit:

"Active, aërial, towering, unconfin'd . . ."
". . . Ev'n silent night proclaims my soul immortal;
Ev'n silent night proclaims eternal day".

The not unpleasurable meditation among the tombs and
relics of the past made popular by the addition of a love story
and circumstances of material terror became, in due course,
the "Gothic" novel, exemplified in Walpole's *The Castle of
Otranto* (1767) and Mrs. Radcliffe's *Mysteries of Udolpho* (1794).
To this sequence of ideas a visual equivalent may be found in
the work of the painter, Fuseli.

The relation is somewhat intricate, partly because Henry
Fuseli was of foreign birth and partly because he was a painter
and therefore faced, as Blake was, with the problem of translating a romantic depth of emotion into visible terms. Fuseli
was the Italianate version of his name, also used in England.
Born at Zürich in 1741, he was the son of Johann Kaspar
Füssli, a Swiss portrait painter and a man of some learning and
literary ability who wrote a history of the best painters of
Switzerland. Of his eighteen children, three lived to grow up.
The eldest, Rodolph, became an engraver, settled at Vienna
and died there in 1806. Another, Caspar, became an entomolo-
gist. It was the second son, Johann Heinrich Füssli, who was
destined for fame as an artist. As a boy he had a passion for
drawing, but this his father discouraged and the learned
atmosphere of Zürich at that time directed him to literary study.
He became the pupil of Johann Jakob Bodmer, the celebrated
professor of History who had an unusually wide appreciation of
European literature. Through him the young Füssli made his
first acquaintance with Milton and Shakespeare and with the

Nibelungenlied, that ancient epic which was to quicken the romantic spirit in the Germanic lands as Ossian had done in Britain. There is a painting by the artist that retrospectively shows him, a dandiacal youth, receiving instruction from the aged Bodmer—lean and Voltairean in appearance, while a bust of Homer behind has the eerie appearance of taking part in the conference.

Bodmer made Zürich an intellectual capital, was visited by writers and men of learning from many quarters, including such eminent Germans as the poets, Friedrich Gottlieb Klopstock, Kristoph Martin Wieland, and Goethe himself. If Füssli did not personally meet them, he must have shared, through his teacher, in the spirit of their discussions; and certainly acquired that love of Shakespeare which was then so stimulating to a romantically minded Germany. The young student was also a disciple of Jean Jacques Rousseau, whose passionate voice was denouncing the evils of civilization, the crimes of wealth, the wickedness of governments. In imitation of their already notorious compatriot, Füssli and his fellow-student, Johann Kaspar Lavater, attacked these evils, as represented by a local magistrate called Grebel, in an anonymous and libellous pamphlet entitled "The Unjust Judge or A Patriot's Complaint". It would seem that in the inquiry that followed the young men got the better of the magistrate; but the latter was still powerful and his enmity and that of his supporters made life in Zürich difficult for them. Füssli, ordained in 1761 but seeing no hope of advancement in the Church, thought it "prudent to withdraw". In his twenty-second year he started in 1763 on his travels—to Augsburg, Leipzig, Vienna and Berlin.

In a casual yet inevitable fashion, he was drawn towards England: in Berlin came to know a man of letters called Sulzer, who interested himself in the correspondences between English and German literature and had formed a society for the study and furtherance of this relation. For this society, Füssli made a drawing from *Macbeth* and a *King Lear and Cordelia* which attracted the notice of Sir Andrew Mitchell, the British envoy to Frederick the Great. Sir Andrew bought the picture and advised its painter to go to London, supplying him with letters of recommendation. By the time he was twenty-four,

Füssli was lodged in Cranbourn Alley, in the artists' quarter of London, and had contacts with the social, literary and painting worlds. He translated the Prussian art historian, Winckelmann, visited Smollett and made drawings for *Peregrine Pickle*. He showed some of his works to Joshua Reynolds, who highly approved. He became travelling tutor to Viscount Chawton, son of Earl Waldegrave, though a mind nurtured on Rousseau did not long endure this dependent position. "The noble family," he later remarked, "took me for a bear-leader but they found me the bear." He returned from a quarrelsome visit to France with his pupil, his appetite whetted for liberty, to write a pamphlet in defence of Jean Jacques (designing his own frontispiece).

At twenty-six, encouraged by Reynolds, he had determined to become a painter and in 1769 set out for Italy, on the obligatory journey of artistic education. He again started with an English companion—but they soon fell out—over the pronunciation of a word—and like many painters who began the Grand Tour as a tutor or guide in the arts, he settled in Italy on his own and stayed there for eight years.

A Goth, one might call him, a Teuton enamoured of Latin civilization. His literary and romantic mind, by this time half British, half German, fed on Wieland's *Oberon*, Shakespeare's tragedies and the *Nibelungenlied*, was now overwhelmed by the genius of Michelangelo. He lay on his back for days, studying the immense forms that swirled in space on the ceiling of the Sistine Chapel. To attain the great Florentine's knowledge of the human figure, he dissected corpses, and for the rest of his days looked on him as the supreme marvel and instructor. The thought of Rome where he had had his great experience was later to cause "frenzy to take possession" of him. When out walking he would stop, grow silent and with apparent inconsequence utter the word "Michelangelo".

No one could successfully imitate Michelangelo. His influence on Fuseli (as Füssli's name was Italianized during his stay in Rome and as he may, henceforward, be called) was possibly bad in persuading him that he could be a master in the Renaissance fashion. On the other hand there is little direct trace of it in his work except for a certain emphasis on muscle that appears more especially in his drawings. There is much more of the "Mannerists" of the sixteenth century in his style which shows itself in a curious elongation of the figure. An incidental passion for the Roman female busts which he saw in the Capitoline Museum, with their exaggerated and crisply curled coiffure, added another peculiarity of style which seemed eventually to become a strange cult with him, a totem or obsession.

In the art circles of Rome he was hailed as a new Michelangelo which was certainly the term of praise most agreeable to him, though it now appears beside the point rather than over-lavish. Between the visions of Michelangelo and the romantic dreams of mystery, magic and terror which Fuseli began to paint, there was all the difference between the plastic and the literary imagination, the purely visual artist and one in whom the poet and the painter were strangely mingled. A peculiar flavour in his work, which hovered between weirdness and caricature, had none of the atmosphere of Renaissance grandeur, though it made a strong impression on several romantic Britons who were in Rome at the same time as he. It touched with its strangeness the art of a Scotsman, John Brown, who had come to Rome to draw classical ruins, stayed a number of years, and eventually returned to his native Edinburgh where, the magic gone, he settled down prosaically to portrait painting. Yet, for a while, the female figures drawn by Brown were almost as spectral and mysterious as those of Fuseli himself: and the same flavour is to be found in the work of Alexander Runciman (who took subjects from Ossian) and his brother John Runciman in those few years of activity before he died at Naples in 1776.

Fuseli, however, was not satisfied to dominate an expatriate circle—nor was he altogether happy in Italy. The Italians, he remarked, were lively and entertaining but there was the slight drawback of never feeling one's life safe in their presence. He left Rome in 1778 and the following year established himself in London—where he felt safe and free. He exhibited at the Royal Academy, was made R.A. in 1790, Professor of Painting in 1799, Keeper in 1804, an office he retained until his death in 1825; and altogether was so closely associated with the Academy in a tutorial and official role that many people have thought of him merely as a somewhat eccentric and comically foreign teacher in its schools—instead of, as we can now appreciate, a romantic in a romantic age.

Of this Fuseli himself was not consciously aware. He prided himself on his classical learning, which enabled him to correct Cowper's translation of Homer; on the ironic wit so typical of the eighteenth century (he voted for Mrs. Lloyd instead of Benjamin West in the election of the Academy's President, on the ground that "one old woman was as good as another"). He believed himself to be a painter in the classic tradition, yet like other painters in England, he spoke with reverence of great Italians as models to follow—and did something quite different. He was a painter of dreams—his first big picture, completed in London before he went to Italy, was, significantly enough, concerned with Joseph's interpretation of the dreams of the Pharaoh's butler and baker (*Genesis* 40). The later efforts in this vein, when he returned to London, began with a picture that made a popular sensation, the *Night Mare* painted in 1781, when Fuseli was forty.

It depicted a woman asleep, her head thrown back, her arms limply hanging, while on her breast squatted a hideous furry little monster, catlike, dwarfish, demonic. Behind, pushing through a curtain, the head of a white horse stared blankly into the shadowy room. Never before or since, probably, have the forces of the unconscious been so impressively symbolized, the "moment of terror" so well conveyed with all its breathless oppression. One might even say that the wild fancies and workings of the mind, so firmly kept down by eighteenth century reason, had at last got loose; and one sees, in the monstrous imp gloating over its beautiful victim, the original of those demons with which the grotesque draughtsmen of the nineteenth century (Cruickshank, for example) were to fill their illustrations—though (to a different purpose) it became instantly popular with the caricaturists and an election print by Rowlandson parodied the sleeper in the cumbrous and unbeautiful shape of Charles James Fox.

The very large number of Fuseli's subsequent paintings bears witness to the extent of his reading and also to the lasting nature of the enthusiasms he derived from Bodmer. He took his subjects from Hesiod, Homer, Sophocles and Apuleius; Spenser, Shakespeare, Milton, Thomson, Gray (whose *Bard* was inspiring to a number of painters touched by romantic feeling); Wieland's heroic poem *Oberon* suggested many a picture. The Edda of Saemundus accounts for the intrusion into an eighteenth-century Academy of such a "rude" and inelegant theme as *Thor battering the Serpent of Midgard in the boat of Hymer the Giant*. He was capable of inventing his own literary subject. Interested in so romantic a title, Byron asked the aged Fuseli whence he had taken his *Ezzelin Bracchiaferro meditating over the body of Meduna whom he has killed on his return from the Holy Land to punish her for her infidelity*. What writer had conceived Ezzelin, whose name indeed resembles that of a Byronic hero? Fuseli confessed he had made him up.

Shakespeare looms large in his work, not only because of his boyish enthusiasm when at Zürich, but also through the steadily growing Shakespeare worship in the late eighteenth century, which the acting of Garrick helped to propagate. One symptom of this was John Boydell's scheme (1789) for illustrating scenes from the plays, by eminent painters, Fuseli among them. Yet, his choice of Shakespearian subjects was not wide in range: the two plays that most fascinated him were evidently *Macbeth* and *The Midsummer Night's Dream*. The first so full of those "moments of terror" he constantly sought, the atmosphere of oppression and hallucination: the second, conjuring up an elemental world of fairies and elves, of moths and mushrooms taking on a semblance of human form but disquieting as if they maliciously laughed over secrets unknown to humanity, while the ass's head of the metamorphosed weaver adds its fantasy like the horse's head in the *Night Mare*.

There remains one department of Fuseli's work in which he advances further into the realization of a dream. The *Night Mare* is a piece of symbolism. The pictures of Oberon and Titania and their court add to Shakespeare's fancy a grotesqueness of Germanic myth (it was an aphorism of Fuseli's that Germanic mythology was more moving than Greek mythology, because the links that enchained us to its magic were not yet broken). Apart, are those pictures which may be called dreams in a strictly Freudian sense, not illustrations of some famous author or feats of the imagination but products of the subconsciousness. They are to be distinguished from the pictures of our modern Surrealists who have tried, somewhat self-

BLAKE AND VARLEY AT SEANCE
Drawing by John Linnell

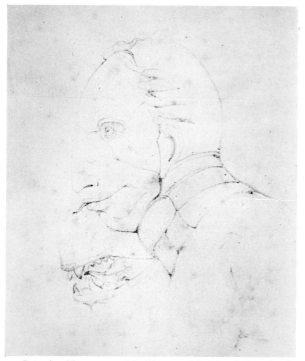

THE
GHOST OF
A FLEA
by
William Blake

JOHN LINNELL,
self portrait

SAMUEL PALMER,
self portrait

consciously, to achieve this result, but tend on the whole to produce a gloss or comment on the irrational processes which the psychologist has analysed. Fuseli, in certain works provided dreams that awaited analysis. The purport of them was something different from what it professed to be. They were unreal, or more than real, charged with hidden meanings. The women in his *The Boudoir* are abnormal and fabulous beings, whose enigmatic faces are such as might be seen in a dream. His well-known painting from *The Merry Wives of Windsor* is, one feels, something other than a representation of Falstaff's concealment in a clothes basket: and for this reason there is discomfort in looking at it. The merry wives are not those Shakespeare imagined but phantoms engaged in some inexplicable ritual: Falstaff is not Shakespeare's fat and genial rogue but, as one looks, seems to turn into an animal-headed monster: the clothes basket must wait for the era of Freud to be interpreted. If the modern psycho-analyst were to give, of the pictures mentioned, the exclusively sexual interpretation that is now common, he would not, probably, be far wrong. From an aesthetic viewpoint, there are many faults to be found with Fuseli, or at least praise must be qualified. It seems in fact somewhat irrelevant to speak of his colour or composition; without the element of fantasy they would make little impression: yet psychologically his pictures are very remarkable. The light of day never shines in them, they come from the shadowy regions of the mind, are, indeed, "night thoughts".

When and where Fuseli met William Blake for the first time is not recorded. He lodged, on his return from Italy in 1779, in Broad Street, before taking a house in St. Martin's Lane; and as Blake was then living in Broad Street, it has seemed to his biographers a reasonable, though it is not a necessary assumption, that they then made contact. Or it could have been at the premises of Joseph Johnson the publisher-bookseller, with whom Fuseli renewed his acquaintance and from whom Blake, the young engraver, solicited work. They would almost certainly meet at the Academy, a few years later, when Blake sent the first of his occasional contributions to the annual exhibition, and thereafter their mutual liking and support, lasting throughout their lives (which ended in the same decade) is recorded by each in his own way.

It is allowable to picture together the anglicized Swiss painter in his forties and the young Londoner in his twenties—both small men—their size may have had a little to do with their large and daring ideas. Fuseli was not much more than five feet two in height. He had keen eyes "of the most transparent blue", a prominent nose, faintly recalling the muzzle of an animal (it caused his pupil, Benjamin Robert Haydon, who has left such a vivid description of him, to use the phrase "lion-headed"). He spoke with a guttural, obviously foreign accent, though he prided himself on his perfect English—he once said he could speak Greek, Latin, French, English, German, Danish, Dutch and Spanish "and so let my folly or fury find vent through eight different avenues". He was excitable, bursting into torrents of words, using epithets of such curious vehemence as "Blastation!", could be sarcastic and biting when he chose, and yet was a kindly person.

In many respects he and Blake were alike—in their energy of mind, their trust in the imagination, their tastes. It was no strain to Fuseli to understand Blake, he was one of the few contemporaries who could appreciate his mind, his poetry, and his designs, and it was precisely the unusual in Fuseli that to Blake made him a kindred soul. The provinces of their imagination were, it is true, not quite the same. The spiritual world of the one is to be distinguished from the dream world of the other. There is a contrast between the Christian Blake, ever occupied with the tremendous conceptions of Heaven and Hell, and Fuseli who, though he had taken holy orders in his youth, was still so much aware of his link with a Teutonic paganism. His fairyland was certainly not a heaven, though neither could one ascribe to it the positive evil of a hell. The Swedenborgian faculty of conversing with the spirits of the departed did not belong to him, though he made some endeavour to put it to the test. He and his friend Lavater agreed that the one who died first should appear to the other. It was Lavater who died first, but "my friend," said Fuseli, "was the most scrupulous man in existence in regard to his word: he is dead and I have not seen him".

By the nature of both his gifts and his beliefs Blake was capable of dreams more tremendous than Fuseli could conceive. "Visions" is the more appropriate word, for there is nothing in the work of Blake, visual or written, that has that oppressive and disquieting atmosphere of secrets untold, that haunts the canvases of his friend. Entirely extrovert, Blake expressed all that was in him, exactly what he felt and thought in a determinate fashion. The light, not the shadows, of the mind gave its value to what he did. One would hesitate to apply to him the apparently apt, modern word "surrealist", which in some degree describes the poetry of those meditative divines, Young and Blair, and the paintings of Fuseli. He rejected pessimism, either in the form of sombre contemplation, abandonment to terror or of that despair which was as much a virulent passion of the Romantic era as of the Surrealists of 1930. He bounded with Wesleyan hope and gladness through those immense tracts in which Young, picking diffident steps, found the pleasures of gloom. It was wonderful that the mind should imagine strange things but the mind was not to be the hapless victim of its creation, lost in its dreams: and this was the message of the *Marriage of Heaven and Hell*.

It includes those wonderful sequences, fantastic enough to be the equivalent of Jerome Bosch's uncanny pictures, wild as the Songs of Maldoror by that hallucinated waif of the nineteenth century, Lautréamont, a romantic challenge to the Book of Revelation.

Here is the likeness to Bosch, pictorially sharp: "So he took me thro' a stable and thro' a church and down into a church vault, at the end of which was a mill: thro' the mill we went, and came to a cave: down the winding cavern we groped our tedious way, till a void boundless as a nether sky appear'd beneath us and we held by the roots of trees and hung over this immensity. . . ." Here is the Book of Revelation ". . . looking east between the cloud and the waves, we saw a cataract of blood mixed with fire and not many stones' throw from us appear'd and sunk again the scaly fold of a monstrous serpent; at last, to the east, distant about three degrees appear'd a fiery crest above the waves; slowly it reared like a ridge of golden rocks, till we discover'd two globes of crimson fire, from which the sea fled away in clouds of smoke; and now we saw it was the head of Leviathan; his forehead was divided into streaks of green and purple like those on a tiger's forehead: soon we saw his mouth and red gills hang just above the raging foam,

tinging the black deep with beams of blood, advancing towards
us with all the fury of a spiritual existence".

The Comte de Lautréamont has scarcely anything to equal
this: ". . . I took him to the altar and open'd the Bible, and lo!
it was a deep pit, into which I descended, driving the Angel
before me; soon we saw seven houses of brick; one we enter'd;
in it were a number of monkeys, baboons, and all of that species,
chain'd by the middle, grinning and snatching at one another
. . . the weak were caught by the strong and with a grinning
aspect, first coupled with and then devour'd, by plucking off
first one limb and then another, till the body was left a helpless
trunk; this, after grinning and kissing it with seeming fondness,
they devour'd too . . ."

Yet these "surrealist" visions are objectively viewed by their
author. "Thy phantasy," says the Angel, "has imposed upon
me and thou oughtest to be ashamed."

"I answered, 'We impose on one another' . . ." In the
wonderful and appalling imagery there can be discerned the
lesson that all things exist in the human mind and the Angel
and the baboons alike give their warning against a one-sided
or a false interpretation of scripture. Lautréamont would have
imagined the baboons to no purpose except to illustrate the
ferocious despair in which he himself existed; for Blake they
were symbols of the type of Biblical commentator, like Bishop
Watson on whose *An Apology for the Bible* he poured forth indignation and scorn.

Blake, in fact, was not a wistful or hallucinated dreamer, but
an optimist battling always on great issues. So ambiguous and
unChristian a realm as fairyland was somewhat beneath the
notice of one pre-occupied with heaven and hell. The question
he asked of a lady, during his stay in Sussex, "Have you ever
seen a fairy's funeral, madam?" seems oddly whimsical and
unlike him, and suggests not so much his own thought as a
passing memory of one of Fuseli's pictures. . . .

". . . I saw the broad leaf of a flower move, and underneath
I saw a procession of creatures of the size and colour of green
and gray grasshoppers, bearing a body laid out on a rose leaf,
which they buried with songs, and then disappeared. It was a
fairy funeral."

A lively imagination could easily endow the insect world

among the flowers with a strange pageantry. Fuseli had
delighted in minute, entomological studies, had found it easy
to turn the moth of nature into the *Moth* of Shakespeare, yet
Blake was not accustomed to look so closely into what he called
"the vegetable universe" for his inspiration. It does not seem
unlikely that the grasshoppers evoked in his mind one of Fuseli's
versions of the *Midsummer Night's Dream* and the insect-like
elves that sported round Titania's throne.

It is on the broad ground that they were not concerned with
the normal and material world that Young, Blair, Fuseli and
Blake come into relation. As a poet Blake is distinct from the
two earlier eighteenth-century men not only in his vastly
superior powers but in his rescue of the dream from darkness
and doubt. "Tell us, ye dead!" said Blair, "Will none of you in
pity
　　To those you left behind disclose the secret?"

The solemn question is very different in spirit from Blake's
rapturous affirmation in his dedicatory lines to the illustrated
Grave:

> "The Door of Death is made of Gold
> That Mortal Eyes cannot behold
> But, when the Mortal Eyes are clos'd
> And cold and pale the Limbs repos'd
> The Soul awakes; and wond'ring sees
> In her mild Hand the golden Keys."

In comparing Blake with Fuseli, we turn from words to visual
design. The links, the exchanges of thought between the two
are a study in themselves. "By gare," said Fuseli to Flaxman,
"all that we do know we have acquired from Mishter Blake";
though there is equally reason to think that Blake with his
capacity for assimilation from all quarters abstracted qualities
from Fuseli and made them his own.

They arrived independently at their enthusiasm for Michelangelo, which was no clear asset to either. If the anatomy of
Blake's figures seems false and even pretentious, displaying,
with emphasis, bunches of muscle without relation to physical
fact, we can only wonder that he should have tried to emulate
the master of physical structure and regret that he should have

adapted these anatomical conventions from engravings that poorly represented the originals. What, perhaps, came—less obviously—from Michelangelo, and through the medium of Fuseli, was the expressiveness of movement by which, alone, it was possible for a painter or draughtsman to make visible the inward stress and force of emotion. The downflung arms of the sleeping woman in the *Night Mare* were as significant of tortured dreams as the apparition on her bosom. The out-stretched arms of the youths in Fuseli's *The Oath on the Rüttli* were a chorus of patriotic determination. Free and violent movement, for the romantic, interpreted the freedom of the spirit, was in itself a language and means of communication.

Blake's biographer, Gilchrist, tentatively noted the resem-blance between the pointing arms of the weird sisters in Fuseli's *The Three Witches* (1785), now in the Kunsthaus, Zürich, and the similar gesture of accusation in Blake's *Job* ("The Just Upright Man is laughed to scorn") of the "satanic trinity" of "Friends". Gilchrist also regretted it as a "mannerism", show-ing himself as blind as most people were in his time to the power and resources of design. There is as little doubt that Blake here copied Fuseli as that both achieved a most impressive pictorial effect; and this is not a single instance. The crouching form of Blake's "Enitharmon" repeats the attitude of the figure in Fuseli's *Silence*. A prostrate figure, lost in an ocean of dreams, with head thrown back and dangling arm, on whom an eagle perches, in Blake's *America* adapts the pose and atmosphere of the *Night Mare*. Blake in Fuseli's words was "damned good to steal from", but so evidently was Fuseli.

Yet the question ultimately was less that of technical borrow-ing, which over a long period of intermittent but always sympathetic association worked both ways, than of a psycho-logical relation between two who were equally opposed to all that was commonplace and worldly in eighteenth-century art. It was this that provoked the dislike of such men as the clever illustrator, Thomas Stothard, an early friend of Blake, and the mediocre and popular portrait painter, John Hoppner. In the conversation recorded (1797) in Farington's Diary, Hoppner based his objection to Blake's designs on the contradictory grounds that "nothing would be more easy than to produce such" and that they looked like the work of a madman.

Stothard "supported his claims to genius, but allowed he had been misled to extravagances in his art, and He knew by whom". The misleader, unnamed by Stothard, can only have been Fuseli.

It was by one of those series of accidents that seem not quite accidents but to have some underlying pattern and intention that the names of Young, Blair, Fuseli and Blake are linked together. There was fitness in the choice of Blake to illustrate those earlier adventures into the realm of "Imagination and Vision", though he rises superior in fervour to the poetry of the *Night Thoughts* and *The Grave* and in such a beautiful design as *The Reunion of Soul and Body* adds to Blair a Swedenborgian rapture and audacious energy of motion which would have astonished the clerical author.

Fuseli's part was to encourage these enterprises. It is, at least, very likely that he would put in a word for Blake with Edwards, the publisher of the *Night Thoughts*. It is certain he wrote the introduction to *The Grave* in which the feeling of goodwill warms a cold and stilted prose very unlike the style of his recorded conversations. It was proper to point out that Blake tried "to connect the visible and the invisible world", though to speak of "those genuine and unaffected attitudes, those simple graces which nature and the heart alone can dictate" seems mere fine and purposeless writing. Nature, in the modern sense, was of no particular interest either to the writer of these remarks or the object of them. "Hang Nature," said Fuseli in another connection (anticipating Whistler), "she puts me out." His arming himself with a raincoat and umbrella to look at one of Constable's landscapes implied a real aversion from the latter's dewy fields and showery skies: Blake's Swedenborgian contempt for the "vegetable universe" was equally a criticism of Nature. If the mind also was "Nature" in the needs and desires that everyone shared, it was not so in those infinite capacities which only the imaginative spirit could give it.

4

REVOLT

I

DANGEROUS THOUGHT

RETURN to the past, escape into a dream world, aspiration to soar above and beyond the narrow range of ideas of an artificial society, materials of which the romantic movement was compounded, required a spark to burst into the fierce flames of the later eighteenth century. It was provided by those wars and revolutions which gave a fresh meaning to freedom, which swept every new current of thought into their devouring and energetic stream. War, of course, in itself was nothing new. The Seven Years War was in its early stages (going, as usual, badly for Britain) when William Blake was born; he was six when, under the direction of William Pitt, all the last battles, in various parts of the globe, had been won; by a series of victories as economical as brilliant, Britain had gained a huge empire. Yet this was a war for property rather than of principle. Satisfactory as the outcome was to national pride it was one more contest in an old-established series, even if the prizes were so unusually large as India and Canada.

Very different was the war going on when Blake was twenty, the war of American Independence. Fought between men of the same blood, it made them feel the more deeply and bitterly; the issue was not one of land or money but whether a group of men and women should be free. Ideas, as the twentieth century has been painfully made aware by its own tremendous struggles, are the most powerful of forces, conducting a war of their own, spreading in the enemy's camp, springing up unexpectedly in different forms. Such was the idea of freedom which not only created an obstinate fighting spirit in Americans on the banks of the Delaware, but travelled thence to arouse discontent, political inquiry and burning ideals among English people in London.

Between the achievement of American independence and the beginning of the French Revolution these feelings simmered among the liberally minded. There was an impressive likeness between the thought of the French philosophers and the fathers of the American republic—an interaction between the two. It was appropriate that the Marquis de Lafayette, after defending Virginia and fighting at Yorktown should, in 1789, produce before the National Assembly in Paris, a declaration of rights modelled on the American Declaration of Independence. In Britain there were many to applaud both, to regard the two revolutions together as steps toward a universal freedom—until, successively, the execution of Louis XVI in 1793, the events of the Terror and the emergence of Napoleon in 1795, changed the views of some and made it imprudent for others to voice them. Freedom, meanwhile, was the operative word, freedom in politics, freedom of thought and action, freedom in love—a romantic exultation fed by the great happenings in the new world and old. To study its effect on the young, the intellectual, the radical and the "advanced", one could not do better than go to the premises of the publisher-bookseller, Joseph Johnson, in St. Paul's Churchyard, and observe the talented and mutinous group that was wont to assemble there.

Johnson was not only the publisher of worthy text-books, medical and mathematical, but one of those people to be found in all periods, who like to be at the centre of a new movement, among the leaders of "new thought". He had an interesting and unusual general list: being the original publisher of William Cowper, Erasmus Darwin, and Maria Edgeworth: but the "new thought" was more concerned with political and social theory and these came to loom sensationally among his publications. In 1787 he started a periodical, the *Analytical Magazine*, which helped to make his offices in St. Paul's Churchyard a meeting place of authors and men of ideas. In this atmosphere of advanced thinking, he sailed dangerously near the wind, was eventually fined and imprisoned for publishing a pamphlet deemed seditious, written by the enemy of Pitt, Gilbert Wakefield. As the times grew more dangerous, the bright watchword of Liberty took on, from a national stand-point, the ugly taint of treason.

And yet about the time of the French Revolution, in their own opinion at least, those who met at No. 72 St. Paul's Churchyard had the purest and most enlightened intentions. The older type of radical was represented by John Horne Tooke, who early in life had discovered that he was not cut out for a clergyman, gave up his clerical dress and office, became the supporter of John Wilkes in his attacks on the government. The money left him by his father had enabled him to devote himself to philology as a hobby and political agitation as a purpose in life. His proposal in 1778 to raise a subscription for the American colonists "barbarously murdered at Lexington by the King's soldiers in 1775" had been punished by a fine and imprisonment; his political views were to cause his trial for high treason in 1794, when the course of events in France had aroused serious governmental alarm against dangerous and subversive thinking; but his dinners gave him a place in society and among the leading intellectuals of the day.

Then there was William Godwin, the son of a dissenting minister, educated at a Presbyterian College, transformed after five years as a Presbyterian minister into a "complete un-believer". He had settled down as an industrious literary man. The philosophy of Rousseau and the advent of the French Revolution encouraged him to write an *Inquiry concerning Political Justice and its Influences on General Virtue and Happiness* (1793), in which, going even further than the author of the *Contrat Social*, he advocated the abolition of every restraint upon the "natural man", of all governments, authorities and laws, including marriage "the worst of all laws". The programme was indeed as subversive as a programme could well be: though the bland calm with which its author proposed the entire destruction of political and social institutions made it seem the most obvious thing imaginable. He believed, however, that it should be accomplished by peaceful means and his expressed dislike of violence as well as the general nature of his theories no doubt prevented the authorities from taking the action against him that the lesser enormities of others provoked.

More militantly alarming was Thomas Paine, whose efforts in the cause of liberty had already aroused the horror of the "right thinking" as well as the anger of the government, a horror the residue of which even now clings to his name. "Distinguished Paine—the rebellious needleman" as Carlyle has called him, thus referring to his early occupation as stay-maker, was a Quaker run amok, a man who candidly told the truth according to his lights, though a truth coloured and warped by his vindictive feelings towards a country in which he felt himself an inferior and where he had been a failure. Like many of the "friends of humanity", he had made no success of personal relationships: after the death of his first wife, had treated his second with indifference bordering on cruelty. He had soon given up staymaking; become a sailor and quickly given that up; been twice an exciseman and twice dismissed for neglecting his unpopular duties; had succeeded only in giving himself the rudiments of an education by becoming a school-master. His chance had come when he had gone out to colonial America in 1774. "It was," he said, "the cause of America that made me an author." His famous pamphlet *Common Sense*, his series of papers called *The Crisis*, had played their part in whipping up resistance to the "Pharaoh of England". He had come back to England in 1787, was to be seen in the group round Johnson in 1791 and 1792 when *The Rights of Man* appeared, in answer to Burke's *Reflections upon the French Revolution*, and had an enormous sale. Described by its author as "one of the most useful and benevolent books ever offered to mankind", its purport was that the people were enslaved, that war was the "art of conquering at home", that aristocracy was a "fungus growing out of the corruption of society", the change to be desired was no less than the "Revolution of the World".

Had not women rights also? Women too could be affected by the inspiration and the virus of Freedom. Notable in the publisher's fiery circle was Mary Wollstonecraft, still quite young, another of those who had not found or could not endure a secure place in the eighteenth-century system. She had learnt by bitter experience how hard was the lot of a girl without home, money or husband. After her father had got rid of his small fortune she had been, successively, a lady's companion, a schoolteacher, a governess in a noble family; had finally discovered a small anchorage in London as a translator and literary help to Joseph Johnson. Full of spirit and intelligence, she threw herself into the discussions of his advanced circle. In 1791, Godwin recorded in his *Memoirs*: "Dine at Johnson's with Paine, Shovel and Wollstonecraft: talk of monarchy, Tooke, Johnson, Voltaire, pursuits, religion": though on this occasion they were "mutually displeased with each other". Godwin wanted to listen to Paine, who apart from some occasional "shrewd and striking remarks" had little to say—and apparently could say little, for Mary monopolized the conversation. She, too, fell upon Burke tooth and nail, to rebut his *Reflections*; like Paine she viewed Burke's attempt to rouse sympathy for the fate of Marie Antoinette as the plea of a sentimentalist who shirked the real issues. Her *Answer* to Burke: "Your tears are reserved, very naturally, considering your character, for the declarations of the theatre or for the downfall of Queens whose rank throws a graceful veil over vices which degrade humanity" matches Paine's remark on him who "admired the plumage and forgot the dying bird". Her most famous work, the *Vindication of the Rights of Women*, was a complement to Paine's *Rights of Man*, and a plea that women should first and foremost be regarded not as a privileged sex but intelligent human beings.

It was a hotbed of dangerous thought, a revolutionary "cell", in which Fuseli in his fifties and Blake in his thirties found themselves—strange creatures thrown into prominence by the convulsions of the century. One sees the men in the plain, dark clothes which now distinguished the average citizen from those who frequented court and society, but worn with some of the carelessness borrowed from Goethe's hero Werther, and showing a suitable contempt for convention. They were not, in person, very attractive. The smile of Godwin, indicating universal benevolence, was perhaps a little sly though he was not as yet that bulbous-nosed individual whose portrait by John Opie in the National Portrait Gallery suggests a combination of Micawber and Pecksniff. The ferocious sneer with which Tom Paine regarded what he called "the No-ability" seemed to be imprinted on his face rather than his kindliness towards humanity in general. Mary Wollstonecraft, in contrast, had a fine, forthright handsomeness though she had been at some pains to show her contempt for feminine coquetry and was got up as a "philosophical sloven", wearing black worsted stockings, a milkmaid's dress, a mannish beaver hat, while her hair was combed out into lank tresses; (even so the effect may not have been without its charm).

Yet this circle had its importance in the lives of both Fuseli and Blake. Fuseli did not come into it as a revolutionary thinker —in spite of his early attachment to Rousseau, his denunciation of the local unjust magistrate, he was content with such freedom as the imperfect government of George III afforded, and was as English as any in his condemnation of the violence that accompanied the upheaval in France. When in 1802, at the time of the truce of Amiens, he crossed the Channel, like many other artists long confined to the island by war, and met that grim painter and fanatic, Jacques Louis David, he "could never divest his mind of the atrocities of the French Revolution nor separate them from the part which he (David) then acted, for they were stamped on his countenance". Fuseli knew the friends of the publisher Johnson. He was an old friend of Johnson and his adviser on foreign works suitable for translation or illustrators when illustration was called for, frequently in demand to turn out the right sort of laudatory preface and was intimate with all his circle. It was Fuseli who in 1788 translated a work by the companion of his student days, Johann Kaspar Lavater, the *Aphorisms on Man*—providing for it a frontispiece which Blake engraved : and no doubt it was on his advice that Johnson some years later embarked on a translation of Lavater's celebrated work on Physiognomy, that art of judging character from the features, which so much influenced Balzac and caused him to refer to Lavater as a leader in science. It was on this work that Mary Wollstonecraft was engaged as Johnson's editorial assistant, and this was one of the factors that brought them into close relation.

The same kind of significant accident links the names of Fuseli, Mary Wollstonecraft, Lavater and Blake, as those of Fuseli, Blake, Blair and Young. Mary was, in a sense, their ideal woman, though Blake would not think of her individually in that light and Fuseli, with a trace of eighteenth-century cynicism and cautious propriety, rejected her efforts to impose this ideal on him. She was in completeness the Romantic Woman, a type that was frequently to be encountered in the agitated

transition of the eighteenth to the nineteenth century. A
creature compact of passion and energy, reckless courage and
ultra-sensitive emotions, intellect and daring, defiance and
scorn. She was the "woman of feeling" who corresponded to
the characteristic invention of the time, the "man of feeling".
To her, the idea of the timid helpless female, needlessly pro-
tected and coddled, the passive centre of male admiration, was
an affront. It was an indignity that some strutting and complacent fellow should rise to pick up her handkerchief or
hasten to open the door she was perfectly capable of opening
herself. In the history of woman's emancipation she follows
shortly after those earnest "bluestockings" whom Blake had
met at the house of Mr. and Mrs. Mathew, yet, by comparison,
how undomestic, untamed and capable of grandeurs and
miseries beyond their ken.

That this handsome and wild young woman should have
fallen in love with the little Swiss painter, aged about fifty, is
somewhat surprising; though he had, it would seem, never
been unattractive to women and had been regarded with
affection by the women painters Mary Moser and Angelica
Kauffmann. His talk certainly delighted her. "I always catch
something from the torrent of his conversation": and though
he was no Godwin or Paine he was able to discuss no less
acutely the ideas of the formidable Jean Jacques Rousseau. She
placed their relations on the highest level. "Designed to
rise superior to her early habitation," as she avowed, she had
"always thought with some degree of horror of falling a victim
to a passion which may have a mixture of dross in it". To
discuss and analyse an emotion at length was a necessity and
even a pleasure (no less acute because it might approach
anguish) of the romantic mind. "Immodesty in my eyes is
ugliness; my soul turns with disgust from pleasures tricked out
in charms which shun the light of day." Examining her soul
and her desires, she wrote in terms of Platonic idealism, that
her wish was to "unite herself to his mind". To this superior
union, practical objections were trivialities to be swept aside.
One such objection was that Fuseli was married; but this did
not deter her. There is pathos in the fact that she instinctively
used, to win his affection, the conventional means that her
principles might have condemned. The milkmaid's dress, the

black stockings, the beaver hat, were exchanged for fashionable clothes; the home-making sense led her to furnish nicely a presentable apartment in Store Street, Tottenham Court Road.

Fuseli, it must be admitted, did not behave in this affair with that romantic ardour he showed in the appreciation of painting and books. He was, after all, married, and the former Miss Sophia Rawlins of Bath, now Mrs. Fuseli, was an old-fashioned woman not instructed in the higher thought or responsive to the gospel of liberty. It may seem astonishing that Mary should direct an appeal to her that they should all live together—"I find that I cannot live without the satisfaction of seeing and conversing with him daily"—though such triangular arrangements were not uncommon among those who despised institutions, including marriage, and extended a disinterested affection to all their fellow-men—and women. Mrs. Fuseli, however, was quite clear that it would not do: and Fuseli himself was not of a different opinion. He "reasoned" with Mary Wollstonecraft, a cruel answer to emotion. He grew bored: the letters she wrote stayed unopened in his pocket. Disappointed, yet determined at all costs to extract the utmost sensation from life, to plunge into the fiercest of maelstroms, she snapped "the chain of this association"; in the winter of 1792, alone, set out for a France dominated by the Terror.

The letter she wrote to Fuseli when she was back in London in 1795, asking for the return of her previous letters, summed up, with rapid and fluent emotional analysis, a feverish three years. Her devouring and unsatisfied passion had seized upon the American timber merchant, Captain Gilbert Imlay. She had had a daughter by him, born at Le Havre in 1794, had been to Norway as his agent, had been deserted, had, in romantic despair, tried to commit suicide by throwing herself over Putney Bridge. And now "I have long ceased to expect kindness or affection from any human creature and would fain tear from my heart its treacherous sympathies". She spoke of injustice, of hopes "blasted in the bud", of "thoughts adrift in an ocean of painful conjectures". "I have been treated brutally, but I daily remember that I still have the duty of a mother to fulfil."

Her subsequent association with William Godwin was at once a triumph and a defeat for the revolutionary philosophy.

Here, from his point of view, was the means of putting his principles into practice. "We did not marry . . . certainly nothing can be so ridiculous upon the face of it as to require the overflowing of the soul to wait upon a ceremony . . ." The soul overflowed into two separate establishments, which asserted the independence of two people between whom there was affection, independence not only of the bonds of institutions but of each other. "Absence," wrote Godwin, "bestows a refined and aerial delicacy upon affection. It seems to resemble the communion of spirits without the medium or impediment of this earthly frame."

Yet the defeat followed; when Mary in 1797 was again to have a child they agreed that for its sake they must make the surrender to conformity that they both deplored. Ironically, when he heard of the marriage, Fuseli remarked that the "assertrix of female rights has given her hand to the balancier of political justice".

It is necessary, here, to pause with the death of poor Mary in 1797—she was then only thirty-eight. It is not a concern of this narrative to examine the tangled relationships of Godwin's family after he married again, though these, involving Shelley and Byron, traced afresh the strange patterns of liberty. It may be thought that too much space has already been given to recalling events that are not unknown; yet without them, without laying stress on the reckless and defiant spirit that grew up in the revolutionary era, with which Blake came in contact through Johnson's circle, the defiance of his own work and life would be underrated.

The great revolutions made as deep an impression on him as on any. They confirmed and increased his natural love of a freedom without bounds. He had the sort of pride that did not accept authority: action on behalf of great ideals appealed to his impulsive and energetic temper: and he had the courage of his convictions which he showed by wearing the revolutionary red cap in the streets. It was another aspect of that brave and even bluff honesty, that refusal to truckle to any man, that appears in his annotations (1788) to Lavater's *Aphorisms*, the first of a long series of comments (which Lavater himself had suggested it was useful for a reader to make)

"A sneer is often the sign of heartless malignity."

SAMUEL PALMER, by George Richmond

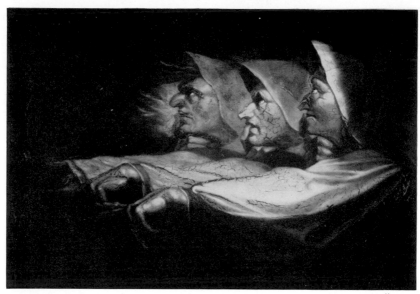

THE WITCHES, by Fuseli

THE JUST UPRIGHT MAN, from Blake's *Job*

Damn sneerers! comments Blake like a true John Bull.

"I know not which of these two I should wish to avoid most; the scoffer at virtue and religion . . . *or the pietist who crawls, groans, blubbers and secretly says to gold thou art my hope* . . . I hate crawlers" (Blake).

"He who is master of the fittest moment to crush his enemy and magnanimously neglects it, is born to be a conqueror." Blake's occasional flash of ironic humour comes out in his remark, "This was old George II."

Predisposed to liberty in thought and action, he was stimulated by the more specific arguments of Johnson's circle—once again showed himself the most receptive of men to the thought by which a generation was formed. The signs of it are in the growing intensification of mood in his writings: and the poems in which he sought in his own fashion to convey the epic grandeur of the revolutionary struggle.

Thus one might contrast the *Songs of Innocence* and *The French Revolution*, the first work appearing in 1789 and the other, it is likely, written in the immediate excitement that followed the taking of the Bastille in July of that year. The *Songs of Innocence*, there can be no doubt, was intended as a children's book:

"And I made a rural pen
And I stain'd the water clear,
And I wrote my happy songs
Every child may joy to hear."

It is distinct from other children's books of the time only in the exquisite beauty of its simple lyrics, and of the designs in which they were set: it has a similar charm though raised to a higher power. Blake's famous process of etching in relief, here for the first time used to reproduce both text and drawing, was, in result, sufficiently like, technically, the woodcuts tinted by hand that were generally popular. It had the advantage of being less laborious: and allowing more fluency and freedom of style. It would indeed have been very difficult to cut out from a wood block the verses, which were not set up in type but lettered so delightfully by Blake's own hand: though the marginal design of *The Lamb* for instance might, as far as effect is concerned, just as well be from a woodcut as an etched copper plate.

6

Apart from the pleasant suggestion of an old illuminated manuscript, there is a period charm, an innocence of draughtsman-
ship as well as poetry, in which Blake shows some indebtedness
to the light and facile touch of the friend of his youth, Thomas
Stothard.

To turn to *The French Revolution* is to see the limpid spring of
lyricism replaced by a roaring torrent. The force of Blake's
ideas could no longer be contained or adequately expressed by
the lyric form, master of it as he was. The memory of Ossian
came to the fore, of a poetry that exulted in its own verbal freedom. Strange names, resembling those of Ossianic characters,
became the signs and symbols of conflict. An age was dis-
integrating before his eyes and everything that he wrote about
this time had some bearing on the theme. The aged "Tiriel"
in the poem of that title (written about 1789) might be taken to
represent the decay of eighteenth-century beliefs bound to
materialism. The virgin in the beautiful *Book of Thel* stands,
fearful and questioning, on the threshold of experience. The
Bastille in *The French Revolution* was the emblem of all tyrannies
over the mind: the "den", in "the tower nam'd Order"

. . . was short
And narrow as a grave dug for a child, with spiders' webs
wove, and with slime".

Announced as "a poem in seven books", *The French Revolution*
never got beyond the first, and though set up in type in 1791,
does not seem to have been issued to the public: whether
Johnson thought it too incendiary or whether Blake realized
the difficulty of writing an epic about events still in progress, is
uncertain. The *America* of 1793 (first of the books produced
when Blake and his wife were living at Hercules Buildings in
Lambeth) had the advantage of retrospect and was "a Prophecy" only in the poetic meaning he attached to the word: but
celebrated in joyous terms the triumph of revolt, naming in its
thunderous lines, "Washington, Paine and Warren with their
foreheads rear'd toward the east."

Whether one tries meticulously to explain and give an exact
meaning to the symbolism in this and other "prophetic books",
or whether one is content to look on them as Wagnerian

opera, to surrender oneself to the surge of emotion, the crash
and tumult of words, is a matter of taste. There is every reason
to be grateful to the scholars who have elucidated Blake's
"giant forms". Without realizing that a "Urizen" is a false
Jehovah, a universal spoilsport, constantly hindering and at
war with the true spirit of inspiration, Los; that Orc is the
necessary demon, the revolutionary principle; one would miss
the point of action that is sometimes obscure. Yet the magnificent reverberant sound has its own meaning and in addition
there is the thread of personal experience. Blake named not
symbolically but by their actual names those he admired and
it is clear that he admired Paine, as the necessary demon of
whom it could well be said "that stony law I stamp to dust".

He was responsible for Paine's escape to France in 1792,
after the latter had delivered a provocative address to the
"Friends of Liberty" that at last decided the authorities to take
action against him. "You must not go home or you are a dead
man." In these words the little poet warned Paine, showing
not so much uncanny foresight as a common-sense estimate of
the situation. Paine had gone out of his way to advertise his
sedition, had insulted the King in a letter to the Home Secretary, referring to George III as "His Madjesty". *The Rights of
Man* had an unhealthily wide circulation, though its author in
many places was burnt in effigy. The speech to the "Friends of
Liberty" made his arrest a practical certainty. Blake's advice
persuaded Paine to slip off to Dover, to set sail on the Channel
packet, not more than twenty minutes before the warrant for
his arrest pursued him.

It may seem strange that Blake, Christian as he was, should
have continued to defend Paine when, from the prison he did
not escape in France, he launched his further bolt against the
"adulterous connection of Church and State", and against
organized religion in *The Age of Reason*. It is not necessary to
suppose that Blake agreed on all points with its author, but he
certainly disagreed on practically everything with Richard
Watson, Bishop of Llandaff, who took Paine to task in *An
Apology for the Bible*.

Watson was the typical worldling of the eighteenth century,
just the person to arouse Blake's ire. Some might account it in
his favour that he was interested in chemistry and farming,

though an indifference to spiritual matters accompanied these pursuits. He had an income from several livings and was always ready to speak up for the system that produced it. He had written an "Apology" in answer to Gibbon (1776); his answer to Paine was published in 1796. Two years later Blake wrote his own indignant notes in a copy of the book: and they illustrate his revolutionary state of mind and that quickness to anger that was natural to him.

"I hope," says the Bishop (to Paine) "there is no want of charity in saying that it would have been fortunate for the Christian world *had your life been terminated before you had fulfilled your intention.*" "Presumptuous murderer," is Blake's remark. His blood boiled at the misrepresentations of this "state trickster"—"O Fool! Slight hippocrite and villain!" "It appears to me," said Blake, in conclusion, with all his bias towards an honest intention rather than a pretended righteousness, "that Tom Paine is a better Christian than the Bishop."

The revolutionary spirit long continued to ferment in Blake. He was not interested in politics and yet, if he was anything, he was a republican. He had as obvious a contempt for the Hanoverian government and its forces as William Hogarth whom, in many traits of personal character, he resembles. Both were true Englishmen, pugnacious and obstinate, free of speech, full of insular pride which still resented a German king and the German-trained redcoats of his army. Hogarth had shown it in his painting of the Guards at Finchley mustering for their northward march against the rebels of the '45: the scene of disorder that incensed George II against its burlesque of his soldiers. Blake showed it, or so one might think, in his sudden violence against the "disgraced sergeant", John Scholfield, in that curious episode which in 1803 brought him before a court at Chichester on the charge of sedition.

It was eleven years after he had advised Paine to make his escape: he was forty-six and living in Sussex in that quiet retreat at Felpham near Bognor that suited him so little. With all the vividness of one of Hogarth's military types, the soldier appears in Blake's garden, cursing, malevolent, perhaps drunk and refusing to go. It is amazing to think of the "gentle mystic" pouncing on the obstreperous dragoon, who threatened to "knock out his eyes", frog-marching him to the gate, and pushing him violently down the road. There is something Pickwickian in the good man's outburst of anger: but Blake's temper was certainly fiery—one recalls the early story of his having hurled to the ground the Westminster schoolboy who had climbed on a tomb to jeer at him when drawing in Westminster Abbey. And perhaps the red coat brought out a surge of remembered hatred against the enemies and hinderers of freedom. "As to sedition," said Blake, "not one Word relating to the King or Government was spoken by him or me." He was always truthful and the little group of Sussex villagers who gathered round, the landlord of the *Fox* (who owned Blake's cottage), his wife and daughter, the hostler and the wife of the miller who lived next door, bore him out. There is little doubt that Scholfield and a comrade who stood by, trumped up a case and falsely accused Blake of saying that the People of England were like a Parcel of Children, that if Bonaparte should come he would be Master of Europe in an hour's time, etc., or that he "damned the King of England his country and his subjects, that his soldiers were all bound for Slaves, and all the Poor People in general". It was preposterous that poor Mrs. Blake should be credited with saying that she would fight for Bonaparte "as long as she had a drop of blood in her". In the record of the trial, which ended in triumphant acquittal, the flashing fire of Blake's eyes, the vigour with which he cried "False" when the accusations were made, stand out.

That a trial should take place at all on such grounds is surprising unless it is recalled that real danger was in the air, that the atmosphere when Napoleon threatened to invade was as tense as when Hitler threatened in 1940, that speech in 1803 was no longer as free as it had been in 1789. Even the opinion of a "miniature painter", as Blake was inappropriately described, required to be carefully examined. It is no less absurd to suppose that Blake welcomed invasion than that the Government, "knowing him to have been of the Paine set," should have sent the soldier to entrap him. Yet some hearty damns may have been uttered in the heat of the moment and in the explosion of Blake's anger there was, it may be, a residue of the feeling of his circle that saw in soldiers a symbol of universal oppression that hindered the "Revolution of the World".

II

THE ROAD OF EXCESS

To say that Mary Wollstonecraft was, in a sense, Blake's Ideal Woman needs some explanation. So that there should be no misunderstanding, let it be added at once there was no question of love between the two, as there was between Mary and Fuseli; or even of a distant worship. Their relations were strictly in the line of business. Mary, the ex-governess, with literary ability, was encouraged by the publisher Johnson to write for him some of those children's stories which were becoming a popular department of letters. Blake was commissioned to provide six engravings for her *Tales for Children* in 1791. They were routine work, in strong contrast with the beautiful designs in his own *Songs of Innocence* of 1789 or the complementary *Songs of Experience* of 1794. There is in the frontispiece, the lady with the mob-cap, the two little girls, all in the simple dress with a long straight line that we now call "Empire". the type that he drew also in the Songs; though how different was the dull line-engraving with its meaningless cross-hatching, its imperfect attempt to render light and shade, from the abounding vitality, the springing and simplified outline in, for example, the illustration of a similar family at play that accompanies the exquisite poem *The Fly* in the *Songs of Experience*. As Mary's illustrator he was Blake, the journeyman engraver, turning out an acceptable commercial commodity; as his own illustrator an individual genius.

Nor does he make any direct reference to her, unless, as it has been surmised, in the poem *Mary*, the subject of which is a beautiful outcast: but whether it is Mary Wollstonecraft he portrays in the lines:

> "And thine is a Face of sweet Love in despair
> And thine is a Face of mild sorrow and care
> And thine is a Face of wild terror and fear
> That shall never be quiet till laid on its bier"

is not a matter that allows of proof.

It may further be objected even with indignation that Blake had his Ideal Woman in the person of Catherine Blake. Was there not here the perfect marriage, the best example perhaps that history affords of the harmony of two human beings. Anode and cathode, learning and innocence, vigour and compliance, fantasy and common sense: their qualities balance completely and arrive at an entire equilibrium. Their love and trust in each other were without alloy. She identified herself with his interests, learning, under his instruction, to take off impressions of his plates and tint them herself; became able to write a letter, quite admirable in choice of words and reflecting some of his fervour, gave to their modest quarters an atmosphere of gentle sanity, the happiness of a true home.

It might be added that a Mary Wollstonecraft would, in comparison, have been not nearly so good for Blake. It is likely that the domestic economy that Catherine carefully administered would, with Mary, have gone quite to pieces. The fire of two fiery spirits together might have caused some awful and unexpected combustion. She could have introduced into his life the element that in fact it never contained even when things were at their worst—the element of tragedy.

Yet in a theoretic way and without reference to his own happy state, Mary Wollstonecraft was the type of woman towards whom his ideas pointed, despising Prudence (the "rich ugly old maid courted by Incapacity"), free, passionate, romantic, embracing experience. That liberty of the sexes that was so much a part of all the desired liberties of the revolutionary epoch was ingrained in his mind.

> "That pale religious letchery, seeking Virginity,
>   May find it in a harlot and in coarse-clad honesty
>   The undefil'd, tho' ravish'd in her cradle night and morn;
>   For everything that lives is holy, life delights in life,
>   Because the soul of sweet delight can never be defil'd."

He was well aware of social evils in his time; his awakening to them can be traced in the *Songs of Experience* which are as certainly for adults, as the earlier collection of lyrics was for children. Walking "thro' each charter'd street, near where the charter'd Thames does flow" he noted as keenly as that earlier social critic, Hogarth, the signs of misfortune and corruption :

> "But most thro' midnight streets I hear
> How the youthful Harlot's curse
> Blasts the newborn Infant's tear
> And blights with plague the Marriage hearse."

Hogarth had had the same thought, though in his pictorial cautionary tale *A Harlot's Progress* he had said no more than that, if you were unwise enough to go wrong, you would certainly pay the penalty in misery and physical ruin. He did not probe more deeply into the nature and causes of this social problem and perhaps it never occurred to him there was any need to do so. It was enough to set up his puppets and make them enact a simple morality play. Hogarth was revolutionary only in that he determined to tell the truth, as he saw it, about a serious matter, to employ his art realistically instead of on the false elegance and meaningless pomp which, especially in the work of foreigners, he so greatly despised. He told a vivid story. The most commonplace thing about it was its moral. In taking another view, Blake, who in words though not in pictures, gives us, for a moment, as desperate a glimpse of eighteenth-century London by night, obviously did not wish to say anything in favour of prostitution. This indeed was the material slavery, in which the soul had no part, which Swedenborg had called hell. He did believe however that it was the result of repression : and if evil thus resulted it followed that repression should be attacked. This was the burden of his *The Garden of Love* :

> "I went to the Garden of Love,
> And saw what I never had seen
> A Chapel was built in the midst
> Where I used to play on the green
>
> And the gates of this Chapel were shut
> And "Thou Shalt Not" writ over the door;
> So I turn'd to the Garden of Love
> That so many sweet flowers bore;

And I saw it was filled with graves,
And tombstones where flowers should be;
And Priests in black gowns were walking their rounds
And binding with briars my joys and desires."

It was the burden also of his *Visions of the Daughters of Albion* (1793) which lamented the woes of pure instinct (Oothoon) maltreated by restraints religious and moral (Bromion), attached in misery to thwarted desire (Theotormon). In its surges of magnificent poetry there is a sustained onslaught on the blind laws that in creating a system of morality crush virtue and encourage vice. "Arise and drink your bliss, for everything that lives is holy" wails Oothoon, while Theotormon broods "conversing with shadows dire". To enjoy love to the full, to drink deep of experience was the true health of the spirit and in this sense the road of excess led to the "palace of wisdom".

Whether Mary Wollstonecraft arrived at the palace of wisdom is a question in which there is a little sad irony, yet her struggle against sex prejudice was that to which he gave the grandeur of his poetic support. "The regulating of the passions," said Mary in her *Vindication of the Rights of Woman*, "is not always wise. On the contrary, it should seem that one reason why men have superior judgment and more fortitude than women is undoubtedly this, that they give a freer scope to the grand passions and by more frequently going astray, enlarge their minds," which may be compared with Blake's lines

"Abstinence sows sand all over
The ruddy limbs and flaming hair
But Desire Gratified
Plants fruits of life and beauty there."

It was, at any rate, clear to both that to marry prudently and correctly for money was a miserable idea. "She must not," said Mary Wollstonecraft, "be dependent on her husband's bounty for her subsistence during his life or support after his death," or, as Blake put it, "she who burns with youth and knows no fixed lot" should not be "bound, In spells of law to one she loathes". It was clear also that the two extremes of a withered and futile chastity on the one hand and a sordid physical commerce on the other were equally repellent. There was it is true a difficulty, as always, when the romantic defiance was confronted with prosaic, or domestic, actuality, when it came to a question of what Mary Wollstonecraft described as "the absurd unit of a man and his wife". The simplicity of theory was then disturbed by a number of complications, as Mary discovered in her relations with Fuseli and Godwin, and as Blake seems to have found on a single occasion. There is something very amiable in the thought of this good and fiery man, shouting, as one might say, with the joyful shout that Walt Whitman was later to echo, the generous freedom of passion, while living quietly the most regular of married existences. It seems that, just once, the intoxication of advanced thought led him to propose the introduction into 13 Hercules Buildings of some other woman, but Mrs. Blake was no more favourable to such a fashionable triangle than Mrs. Fuseli. She wept and her tears were the most effective of tyrannies: so distressing him that never again did he think of converting the poetic "girls of mild silver and of furious gold" into reality. Yet the spirit of rebellion, in a pure and intense form, caused him ever to imagine the shaking off of all the restrictions which to him were vice, to praise the ardour of love as beyond law and prudence, as the Swedenborgian union of souls and the most important thing in life.

III

RUSTIC INTERLUDE

In tracing the growth of the romantic spirit, there is to be noticed a hopeful feeling in all its discontents and proclamations, which only began to wane as a new century approached. It was a feeling that a wonderful dawn promised for humanity, the first rosy streaks of it were to be seen in the sky: the "rights of man" were about to be universally recognized. This feeling became a political fever in the early days of the French Revolution, it reached its crisis in the last decade of the eighteenth century—and then, the situation once more resolved into an

uncertain struggle, which sometimes took a desperate and even
morbid turn, or was lost to view in other struggles that seemed
of more immediate importance.

Regicide and the massacre of an aristocracy in France, the
outbreak of war with that country, the threatening rise of
Napoleon Bonaparte, made many people think twice about an
idealism that was now squarely confronted with patriotic
opposition. Tom Paine had never had quite the stature or the
status of a hero but he did have a multitude of readers and
potential disciples who turned against him when the issue was
suddenly made plain. War transformed the friend of humanity
into a traitor, an object of detestation, burnt in effigy like Guy
Fawkes, in every part of the country. The gross caricatures in
which the popular draughtsmen had lampooned the physical
defects and moral failings of their rulers were diverted to attacks
on the enemy. The brilliant Gillray now devoted himself to
picturing the "cannibalism" of Frenchmen instead of the
peccadilloes of the Prince of Wales. In 1797, the *Anti-Jacobin*,
conducted by George Canning, applied its indignant parody
to the products and propagators of subversive thought and spoke
out for the conservative British way of life. The *Anti-Jacobin's
Progress of Man* was a satire on Payne Knight's *Progress of Civil
Society*. It antedated Blake's *Visions of the Daughters of Albion* but
the satire is directed against the same trend of ideas. When
Canning describes sarcastically the idyllic state of Otaheite,
visited by Captain Cook, where

> "Each shepherd clasp'd, with undisguised delight
> His yielding fair one—in the Captain's sight
> Each yielding fair, as chance or fancy led,
> Preferr'd new lovers to her sylvan bed"

he might almost be making a genteel parody of Blake's "heaven
of generous love"

> "I'll lie beside thee on a bank and view their wanton play
> In lovely copulation, bliss on bliss . . ."

Blake was too little known to be the object of attack, but the
members of the circle he had known, including Paine and

Godwin, were stigmatized as "creeping creatures, venomous
and low", the freedom so dear to his heart as "folly, madness,
guilt", while a younger generation did not avoid the lash: the
young wild Oxford and Cambridge republicans, still excited
by Jean Jacques Rousseau——

"C – dge and S – th – y, L – d, and L – be and Co" – the
line marks the appearance on the scene of Samuel Taylor
Coleridge and Robert Southey (together with their friends,
Charles Lloyd and Charles Lamb). In their twenties, Coleridge
and Southey projected the vision of a changed, an ideal society
that had haunted the minds of their elders, into the form of a
self-governing community to be founded in America on the
banks of the Susquehanna. The "Pantisocrats" as they styled
themselves were evidently Jacobins and in *The Friend of
Humanity and the Needy Knifegrinder* Canning made merciless
play with the young Southey's poems lamenting the mis-
fortunes and mistreatment of the poor.

By degrees, though not necessarily because of such on-
slaughts as the *Anti-Jacobin* made, poetry lost the fervour of
political hope: and individuals went through their own
revolution of feeling. It was a revolution that made those
who were romantically inclined, not less romantic, and even,
as we nowadays define the word, more so: but it certainly
guided them along an altered path. The path led away from
the attempt to meddle with contemporary affairs and human
destiny towards a comparative isolation. The first jubilance in
the rising of a people changed into the desire to be far from the
madding crowd. The rights of man became an object of less
interest than the beauties of nature. After the period of
hazardous adventure and opposition to laws and governments,
there was a retreat.

The dispersal of artists in various parts of the country in
Britain was partly due to this altered attitude or reaction,
though it must be admitted that unless they went to the wars,
or remained part of the London society that so many of them
disliked, it was the obvious recourse. A Britain continuously
at war with France, from 1793 to 1815, save for a brief interlude between 1802 and 1803, was an island fortress cut
off from its most direct access to the Continent. The artist
(using the word in its broadest sense) was driven to find within

its boundaries, or in those dreams that knew no boundary, all his inspiration. It was not necessarily a hardship. The travelling water-colourist, simple and happy soul, not always romantic in spirit, but a symptom of the romantic mood, found the interest intensified in his explorations of Britain, continued his voyages of discovery, in Wales, Scotland and Yorkshire, to general admiration. Such explorations held out to young men, born in the 1770's, like Joseph Mallord William Turner and Thomas Girtin, the promise of a pleasurable and profitable career. If the course of the Romantic Movement brings us again, as in the days of Macpherson, to Scotland, and focuses attention also on the lakes and crags of Westmorland and Cumberland, all this must be taken into account. The young poets held up to scorn by the *Anti-Jacobin* (though Canning might have omitted Lloyd and Charles Lamb, who scarcely come into the question) illustrate a change both of heart and locality. In Robert Southey, for instance, there was all the difference between the rebellious undergraduate of Balliol College, Oxford, in 1794, and the man of thirty who came to rest at Greta Hall, Keswick, Tory in views and in 1807 the recipient of a Government pension of £200 a year. In the meantime the dream of an ideal community, the "Pantisocracy" so ardently wished for by his friend, Coleridge, had been proved impossible to realize. Southey, married in 1795, had wandered for some years, and contrived to visit an uncle in Lisbon, had held an official appointment in Ireland for a short time, had been in and out of London, but in 1803, cured of any desire to reform the world and yet averse to settling in the capital, had begun his industrious career as author, in the Lake District.

The curious and intricate early adventures of Samuel Taylor Coleridge are parallel and connected with those of his friend. He was also an unruly undergraduate—at Jesus College, Cambridge, though his brief enlistment in a regiment of Dragoons was due rather to despair over his university debts than any coherent intention. But again the pattern is repeated. "Pantisocracy", a word, and idea, for which he was mainly responsible, having been discarded, he took his wife and child (he had married in 1793) to a cottage at Nether Stowey in the region of the Quantocks, where, in 1797, at the age of twenty-five, he proposed to become a market-gardener. After this, a few years of wandering brought him, in 1800, to Keswick. But neither Coleridge nor Southey expressed, as clearly as William Wordsworth, the hope that the French Revolution inspired in this younger romantic generation:

> "Bliss was it in that dawn to be alive
> But to be young was very heaven! O times
> In which the meagre, stale, forbidding ways
> Of custom, law and statute took at once
> The attraction of a country in romance."

Wordsworth was in his third year at St. John's College, Cambridge, in 1790, on a vacation tour through France with his friend Jones, when he saw the first excitements—"songs, garlands, mirth, banners and happy faces" of the Revolution. Nor did anyone else express so deeply the conflict after war broke out with France between ideas that he did not give up *as* ideas but was compelled to set aside by the demands of patriotism: and by the unpleasant fact he could not hide from himself that they did not seem to have helped a country where

> "Tyrants strong before
> In wicked pleas were strong as demons now."

Cure for the mental stress thus set up by divided loyalties and a feeling of disillusion was only to be found in the simple life. The process of mental healing took Wordsworth and his sister to Crewkerne in Dorset, thence to a house in the Quantocks near Coleridge at Nether Stowey (1798). Germany was still open to the traveller and Wordsworth visited Germany, Coleridge being his companion part of the way, but the true solace was only to be found in his own country and in nature. He was twenty-nine when (in 1799) he settled at Grasmere. Lakeland, it seemed, was a necessary answer to the French Revolution.

It may be significant that Blake went to live in the country at about the same time as this dispersal and resettlement of younger poets took place—in the year 1800. He was then

forty-three—a time of life when many men take stock of themselves and sometimes conclude their work is over, sometimes
that it has just begun. He had arrived at a state of depression
unusual to one of his hopeful and active mind. "I begin," he
wrote to his friend, George Cumberland—that "respectable
literary person at Bristol", who had interested himself in
Chatterton and had a taste for art—"to Emerge from a deep pit
of Melancholy, Melancholy without any real reason for it, a
Disease which God keep you from and all good men". Always
an extrovert, he did not dwell on and analyse his melancholy.
It is possible that there was in it that fading of hope in the
rebirth of human society that Wordsworth so keenly felt:
though the core of religious optimism in Blake was not,
probably, affected by events in the world, even when they took
a disappointing turn. Yet any stimulating personal contact he
had so far had, was with those whom events in the world had
made suspect. He had known no writers save the propagandists
for a cause, and the fate that had overtaken it and them could
scarcely escape his notice and fail to impress him.

The great amount of work he had done in a period of some
ten years may have brought with it the reaction of a weariness
that bordered depression. He had toiled at his craft as an
engraver, delighting to think that though it produced no glory,
it was honest labour that kept him free and independent. He
had written his immortal lyrics, and set them in a splendid
framework of design, engraved by his own process and coloured,
with the assistance of his wife, by hand. He had created his own
mythology in a long series of "prophetic" books, which however
obscure in detail were consistent and well defined in their
championship of freedom against repression, instinct against
calculation. He had made many paintings in water-colour and
latterly in a sort of tempera which he called "fresco".

Some part of this work had been enough to keep him and his
wife in moderate comfort in the quite large house at Lambeth
yet he was not, materially, on a very firm footing. As a commercial engraver he was at the mercy of the market. He did
not, with the help of his own process of engraving, specialize,
as he might have done with success, in children's books (though
he had begun with one). His epic poetry was a form of self-
expression that sometimes, like the long poem *Vala, or the Four*

Zoas, did not get beyond the manuscript stage. In 1799 things looked black. "For as to Engraving, in which art I cannot reproach myself with any neglect, yet I am laid by in a corner as if I did not Exist, since my Young's Night Thoughts have been published. Even Johnson and Fuseli have discarded my Graver." He was made aware, perhaps for the first time, of the gulf that existed between his and the average mind, by the failure of his negotiations with the Rev. John Trusler to whom Cumberland recommended him as illustrator. Trusler, author of *Hogarth Moralized*, required moral pictures but such as would be acceptable to popular taste. The letter in which Blake argued the point is of note as showing his lucidity and good-humour when he chose to explain himself, though even his common-sense was enough to baffle the worldly divine. He had proposed as a design for "Malevolence", a "Father, taking leave of his Wife and Child, watch'd by Two Fiends incarnate, with intention that when his back is turned they will murder the mother and her infant". Dr. Trusler objected that no motive for the intended murder was given. "Is not," Blake answered, "Merit in one a cause of Envy in another, and Serenity and Happiness and Beauty a cause of Malevolence?" which was a question both searching and uncomfortable.

It seems that Trusler sought for such a picture of ordinary life, flavoured with humour, as Rowlandson gave. Thomas Rowlandson had now succeeded Hogarth as the interpreter of modes and manners, though his style was disburdened of Hogarth's moral purpose. He was the exact contemporary of Blake but his life was spent far differently, in the pleasure gardens and taverns, at the race meetings and boxing matches, among the soldiers and sailors. His was the spirit of the old eighteenth century continuing gaily and unchanged. The emotional release of Methodism touched no religious sympathy in him, was merely subject for laughter, for a drawing of grotesque beings shuffling out of a chapel in the Tottenham Court Road with hypocritical sighs and groans. That two such men as he and Blake, exactly of an age, should live in the same country—and in two different worlds—is a dramatic indication, not only of the contrast between two personalities, but of the gulf now existing between the romantic and the realist. No compromise was possible. Blake could not appreciate a line as

firm and colour as delicate as his own but directed by what was
to him trivial mockery. "I perceive," he admonished Dr.
Trusler, "that your eye is perverted by Caricature Prints, which
ought not to abound as much as they do." He could not stand
the "eternal guffaw" (as Douglas Jerrold was later to call it) of
the professional humorist. "Fun I love, but too much fun is of
all things the most loathsome. Mirth is better than Fun, and
Happiness is better than Mirth." The clergyman's criticisms
rankled. "I am sorry," he wrote to Cumberland, "that a man
should be so enamoured of Rowlandson's caricatures as to call
them copies from life and manners, or fit things for a Clergyman to write upon."

He told Trusler, with naïvely deliberate attempt to impress,
that orders for his designs and paintings, "I have the pleasure
to tell you, are Increasing Every Day" : and it was true that one
of those rare people who were interested in unusual gifts because
they were unusual, Thomas Butts, a man in a comfortable
official post (of somewhat famous descent, for his ancestor,
physician to Henry VIII, had been painted by Holbein) who
lived with his family in Fitzroy Square, had given him an
order for "Fifty small pictures at one Guinea each". Yet these
occasional guineas did not go very far : nor did giving lessons
in painting and drawing provide the answer to Blake's material
difficulties. The kind of teaching that was in demand was in the
topographical style of water-colour landscape that was now
popular. A Paul Sandby by this means could enjoy the favour
of court and aristocracy : but Blake's "small pictures from the
Bible" scarcely recommended him as drawing-master to
members of the Royal Family and the story of George III,
confronted by such works, saying "Take them away! Take
them away!" seems likely enough. The conclusion was that in
this period of war, disillusionment and patriotic bustle,
Blake was less than ever "socially integrated". "I live by
Miracle." It was in this state of affairs that Flaxman, that
friend so full of wise and sensible advice (which never turned
out quite as intended) came to the rescue.

Flaxman, in 1800, had "arrived". In that year, aged forty-
five, he became a full member of the Royal Academy. He had
spent seven years in Italy, from 1787 to 1794. His outline
illustrations to Homer, in which there is some of the Sweden-

7

borgian feeling for a spirit world, had appeared in Rome and created a sensation (Blake re-engraved them for the English edition in 1795). As a sculptor he was in great demand for memorial tablets and monuments. A capable, well-meaning man, with a clerical solemnity. "Farewell friends, farewell wine, farewell wit!" said Fuseli when the time came for Flaxman to lecture on sculpture, "I must leave you all and hear sermon the first, preached by the Reverend John Flaxman." Wishing to help his friend, Flaxman thought of his own early patron, to whose son he had given lessons in modelling, William Hayley. It is possible that he persuaded this distinguished person to visit and take tea at Hercules Buildings and as with the introduction he had given Blake to the Mathews, the results were important.

Hayley was that type of being with which the middle-class Blake had had small contact—a "gentleman". He had been to Eton and Trinity Hall, Cambridge. He had a fortune and like many other eighteenth-century gentlemen had settled on a country estate, in Sussex, where he entertained distinguished guests and devoted himself to various cultural pursuits. He wrote poetry in which there was the correct Augustan elegance of expression. He had written an *Essay on History* addressed to his friend, Gibbon, and in 1800 was addressing to Flaxman his *Essays on Sculpture*. He was, like many other gentlemen, an amateur artist, and also a patron of the old school, one who could pull strings in high quarters. It was he who spoke to Pitt on behalf of William Cowper in his last clouded period and secured for the unfortunate poet the pension of £300 a year (which he lived to receive for only two years). A benevolent and wealthy man of fifty-five of no small influence, and a decided taste for the arts, he seemed exactly suited to be useful to Blake in his difficulties and to help him on his way.

In 1800, moreover, there was a gap in his life which one like Blake could fill. His son, Thomas Alonso, died. His more intimate connections with the world of the arts had come to an end. His friend Gibbon had died in 1794, Cowper in April, 1800. That strange artist, who was also his friend, George Romney, was lost to him. Torn between conventional eighteenth-century portrait painting and a thwarted desire to excel in imaginative art, Romney had reached the stage of collapse, had returned in 1798, shattered in mind, to Kendal and the wife he had deserted thirty-six years earlier.

That Blake should live in a small cottage near Hayley, that the latter should give him work to do and introduce him to others for whom he could work seemed an ideal arrangement. To go into the country was an escape from an oppressive world, as it was also for Wordsworth, Coleridge and Southey; and a promise of better things. Save for those fields where the houses of London ended, Blake had never known the country. He had never been (and never was to go) abroad—except on those immense journeys which the imagination could take. Sussex was a land of golden hopes, his enthusiasm rose to fever pitch. With all the extravagance of Swedenborgian language (which his co-religionist, Flaxman, would understand) he thanked the sculptor as "Sublime Archangel, My friend and Companion from Eternity". He and his wife went in July to see the cottage at Felpham near Bognor, viewed with delight its "thatched roof of rusted gold". Near by was Mr. Hayley's "marine turret" (he had all the liking of his time for an architectural folly)— designed for him by Samuel Bunce, whom he whimsically called "my little Palladio". The cottage (now part of a seaside suburb) was rented for £20 a year from Mr. Grinder of the Fox Inn.

The great adventure for the Blakes began in September, 1800. Boxes and portfolios were shifted from one post-chaise to another during a tiring journey: but the arrival was blissful. The cottage was as good as a palace. There was a fine view of the sea. Mrs. Blake, and her sister who came to help, in the morning "courted Neptune for an Embrace" from which it may be gathered they paddled, if they did not swim. Optimism cast its glow on everything. The villagers of Felpham were not "mere Rustics"—or Rowlandson caricatures—they were "polite and modest". Meat was cheaper than in London, the air sweeter. An unaccustomed sense of physical surroundings and atmosphere pervaded the lines Blake wrote to Butts

"To my Friend Butts I write
My first Vision of Light
On the yellow sands sitting
The Sun was Emitting
His Glorious beams

> From Heaven's high Streams
> Over Sea, over Land
> My Eyes did Expand
> Into regions of air
> Away from all Care."

And yet there was, perhaps, a certain amount of self-deception in the wild delight with which he made the change. If he had listened to his "spirits" (that is, the voice of instinct) he might have thought twice. He had in fact been entrapped into a position which did not in the least suit his independent character. For the time being, the outcome of revolt was captivity and submission.

Hayley has been treated unkindly by many critics. Poets have been, and with reason, harsh. Southey remarked that "everything about that man is good except his poetry". His goodness might be said to consist in his benevolence, his temperate living, his addiction to hard work, his love of the arts: but there was in it some element of irritating obtuseness and self-assertion. Women had not been able to endure it— if one may judge by the fact that one girl jilted him, and that his wife left him. Swinburne has described him as "the master bantam cock of the henroost who fluttered and cackled round this bird of foreign feather (Blake) with assiduous if perplexed patronage" though whether his patronage can rightly be called "perplexed" is a question. He had at least established in his own mind the nature of their relationship. Blake was "a most worthy, enthusiastic, affectionate" engraver, who had "so much attached himself to me that he has taken a cottage in this little marine village . . . to pursue art under my auspices". With their suggestion of humble abilities and dog-like devotedness, these words subtly distorted the truth: but they give the key to Hayley's programme. Blake was to be a tame engraver, illustrator and decorator. He was also to be brought on, and to provide a little diversion for the county circle, as a painter of miniature portraits. He had the job of decorating Hayley's library— with the heads of poets, Milton, Homer, Camoens, Ariosto, Spenser; of engraving the illustrations for Hayley's life of Cowper and other works by his industrious patron: in addition to giving drawing lessons to Lord and Lady Bathurst. . . . The

only thing Hayley did not allow for was what Blake himself
might want to do.

With an unusual meekness in one of his temper, probably
feeling that he must subdue his touchy pride as a defect in
himself, he set himself to carry out his patron's requirements.
He worked hard and long—Time seemed to go faster than it
had in London, yet by degrees his view of the whole situation
changed.   Admiration and gratitude faded into criticism,
criticism became anger. The process took three years. After
one had gone by, Blake had not quite finished the heads of
poets; was, he thought, improving in miniature portraits; was
principally occupied on the plates for Cowper's Life, on
"which Mr. Hayley is now labouring with all his matchless
industry". His letters, however, had lost their tone of ecstatic
enthusiasm, had become plain and serious and in 1802 the rift
began to appear.

It was not to be expected that the miniature painting would
go well. The portrait was of all forms of craftsmanship the
least congenial to Blake: though the specimens now in the
British Museum preserve that firmness of outline by which he
set so much store. Yet they had no flattering grace and Hayley's
circle was critical of them and of his other productions. Lady
Hesketh, with a special interest in Cowper, remarked that
people of taste "found many defects in your friend's engravings". "The faces of his babies are not young": and Hayley,
in making excuses, was able to be pleasantly superior.

"I endeavour to be as kind as I can to two creatures so very
interesting and meritorious." Creatures! It is easy to imagine
the effect of that little smile of superior and pitying affection,
of the amiable commands that dictated another day of useless
labour. Well might Blake say "those who act with benevolence
and virtue they murder time on time". He was made to feel
incompetent, a failure, a quaint and gentle idiot, and though
he struggled for a long time to be dutiful and grateful, dissatisfaction broke through. He found "on all hands great objections
to my doing anything but the mere drudgery of business".
Moreover Felpham was not the earthly paradise it had first
seemed. The cottage was damp. Mrs. Blake, ageing visibly,
constantly suffered from rheumatism.

It is a relief to find him speaking out with all his old forth-

rightness in the letter to his brother James, written in January,
1803. He had at last assessed the position. Behind Hayley's
condescension, he discerned jealousy. "The truth is, As a Poet
he is frightened at me and as a Painter his views and mine are
opposite; he thinks to turn me into a Portrait Painter as he did
poor Romney but this he nor all the devils in hell will never
do." This clearly explains Blake's idea of a real Enemy
—"a Man (who) is the Enemy of my Spiritual Life while he
pretends to be the Friend of my Corporeal". He was "deter-
mind to be no longer pestered" with Hayley's—"Genteel
Ignorance and Polite Disapprobation". Though one would
not say that Blake was jealous or envious, it can hardly
have made him feel more kindly towards Hayley that in this
year the Life of Cowper appeared and scored an immense
success. The success, it was true, was due to the interest of
Cowper's letters, which formed a large part of it, to the affecting
circumstances of the poet's life: and yet the patron, with irritating ease, had now assumed the role of literary lion and best-
seller. It was in August, 1803, that occurred the encounter with
the soldier, Scholfield, that resulted in Blake's trial at Chichester for sedition. In his vigorous action there was not only
a surge of the old revolutionary feeling, but with it the vent of
a long series of indignities and humiliations, repressed but
at last exploding in violence and anger. Hayley provided him
with an advocate at the trial which followed (though, having
fallen off his horse a little while before, he did not appear at
Chichester in person) but Blake, while expressing gratitude,
did not change his mind about leaving Sussex forever.

IV

REVOLT AESTHETIC

At the age of forty-eight, he was himself again. The return
to London, though only to limited accommodation in lodgings
at 17 South Molton Street, was pleasant. Catherine Blake,
benefiting by "Mr. Birch's Electrical Magic", got over the
worst of her rheumatism. Yet, in what he called his "three years
slumber on the banks of the Ocean", he had certainly missed

the tide that leads on to fortune. It is from now onwards that he seems less a part of the great romantic flood, one of a group in which like ideas and feeling are interchanged and developed: and becomes really isolated, and marked out by his contemporaries as an odd, an incomprehensible or even an insane person.

To be with Hayley and to move in county society was isolation in itself. Throughout his life Blake suffered from the absence of the comfort and inspiration that those of comparable intellect and gifts can impart to one another. It was in such communion that Coleridge and Wordsworth, neighbours at Nether Stowey, rambling together in the Quantocks, had exchanged thoughts, made plans, and conceived the *Lyrical Ballads* of 1798. Whatever the differences between the "Lake poets" each took heart from the presence of others. At Malta, in 1805, Coleridge found the climate suited him and he himself showed an aptitude for the secretaryship he held there for a while; yet he pined in its spiritual isolation and returned with relief to the affectionate company of the Wordsworths at Grasmere. In imagination, on the Sussex shore, Blake had the company of Milton like a vast and friendly phantom, but this was not the same as the lively intellectual intercourse between living beings.

Nor did it help that he was an engraver and designer, a poet and a painter. This complexity of expression made it hard for his contemporaries to focus attention on any one of its forms. Explicable in one context, he became a mystery in another. Stothard, who could understand him as an illustrator sufficiently to deplore the departure from his own mildly agreeable standards, was obviously not capable of appreciating Blake's poems. Whether from jealousy or obtuseness Hayley chose to see only the engraver. Flaxman, who had admired him as a poet, considered him unqualified to paint large pictures, "either by habit or study". Nor to a world accustomed to the authenticity of print did the books etched with Blake's own calligraphy and ornamented with his designs present the poet very effectively: literary folk were put off by the intrusion of another medium. Never knowing him, or reading his work in the books distributed by publishers in the ordinary fashion, the poets and critics of the new romantic age came to hear of and appreciate him only by slow and indirect means and through a veil of misunderstanding created by garbled reports of his eccentricity.

All that generous revolt in which he had shared against eighteenth-century conventions, tyrannies and injustices now became a more solitary and personal defiance, embittered by poverty and by the series of unsatisfactory dealings in which he was the sufferer—poverty causing every disappointment to stand out starkly and take on the aspect of malignity and fraud. "I must say," wrote Blake, in 1804, "that in London every calumny and falsehood utter'd against another of the same trade is thought fair play. Engravers, Painters, Statuaries, Poets, we are not in a field of battle, but in a City of Assassinations."

It is not altogether easy to understand his relations with Hayley after the return to London. The irritations of Felpham seemed to have been smoothed over. Blake showed even an over-anxiety to please and collaborate with the man of "Genteel Ignorance". He did research work on the Life of Romney, with which Hayley was to follow the success of the *Cowper*, expressed great enthusiasm for the engravings he was to do for the new work. Though Blake cannot be accused of fawning or hypocrisy, the eagerness to please, so marked in the letters to his patron, was evidently the result of his dire want of money. There came a moment when the falsity of this correspondence was apparent, producing his epigram on "On H. the Pick-Thank"

"I write the Rascal Thanks till he & I
    With Thanks & Compliments are quite drawn dry."

When all the work had been done and the accounts drawn up, it was clear that he had been edged out of Hayley's undertakings. The engraved portrait of Romney by him was not used, only one of his plates appeared (*The Shipwreck*), the remainder being given to other engravers—Caroline Watson, Raimbach, Haines. Caroline Watson supplanted Blake in engraving the head of Cowper for the new edition of the *Life*. Hayley's *Ballads* which Blake had illustrated, proved unsuccessful in a fresh edition with extra plates. The ridicule heaped on the poet fell also on the artist and cannot have made him feel any the better about their collaboration.

The caustic epigrams in which Blake relieved his feelings, with their variations on the theme of enmity and friendship (anticipating the paradoxical wit of the 1890's) are the signs of final disillusion and disgust. Unfortunately his next employer, the engraver turned art-dealer, Robert Hartley Cromek, proved even worse. Blake neglected the business precaution of getting a written contract, but there seems no doubt that Cromek cheated him over the illustrations to Blair's *Grave*. Blake was to make a set of forty drawings. Cromek accepted only twelve, but promised that the artist should engrave them himself and receive extra payment. The promise was repudiated; the Italian-born engraver with a fashionable reputation, Luigi Schiavonetti, was employed instead to make the engravings. Cromek refused to pay anything for the vignette to accompany Blake's dedicatory verses to the Queen, though he gave Schiavonetti ten guineas for engraving it. He could he said do without it . . . . had paid more than he could afford . . . had imposed on himself the labour "and a herculean task it has been to create and establish a reputation for you"—in which there is a note of injured guilt.

The famous affair of the *Canterbury Pilgrims* is somewhat less definite in outline. Stothard seems to have accepted the suggestion of Cromek, his neighbour in Newman Street, that he should paint a picture of Chaucer's Pilgrims, without being aware that Blake had made a drawing of the subject, which Cromek had seen. Blake was under the impression that Cromek intended him to complete the work and had once more tricked him, by betraying the idea and his general conception of it to Stothard.

There was, of course, no copyright in an idea; that a subject should be valuable in itself is nowadays looked on as a laughable misconception of the past and more especially of the Victorian era when the subject in painting made all the difference between success and failure. Yet the subject had its importance before the Victorian era began—even in 1807. An illustration of Chaucer had the attraction of novelty: it was also a logical addition to those other illustrations of the great English poets that had become popular since Boydell's Shakespearean venture: and it fitted in with the growing attention now being paid to the Middle Ages. That Stothard's

picture was completed and exhibited first was half the battle:
it was in fact an immense success. The picture was admired by
other artists—Stothard had introduced twenty horses, which
were approved by the expert in equine anatomy, George
Stubbs, R.A. The public took to it. It was exhibited all over
England, multitudes paying a shilling to see it. It was sold for
300 guineas by Cromek to Mr. Hart Davis of Bath: and there
was a large return to come from the proof-engravings at 6
guineas each, the ordinary prints at 3 guineas. Cromek cheated
Stothard a little on financial details, but the painter could
afford to be indulgent and on the whole seems to have been
sympathetic to the "petty sneaking knave" of Blake's furious
epigram.

It is easy to imagine his annoyance: though he was ill-
advised (in 1808) to follow Stothard's success with a painting,
showing how it ought to have been done, accompanied by
remarks running down his rival. There was a peevishness in
this that Blake's poverty and many previous disappointments
must excuse. His criticism that "the scene of Mr. S——'s
Picture is by Dulwich Hills, which was not the way to Canterbury" is, for him, trivial, and shows a regard for topographical
exactitude which is quite at variance with his usual contempt
for nature or fact. Indeed, in many ways it is a picture that
comes oddly from Blake. It entailed the pictorial description
of modes and manners, of the average worldly type, which was
far from being congenial to him. He was no longer conveying
great emotions of his own, but was compelled by the objective
and humorous genius of Chaucer to adjust himself to the task of
characterization. What a problem, for instance, the Wife of
Bath set him! With painful effort he arrived at a figure somewhat between a Devil (in the Swedenborgian sense) and a
caricature by the Rowlandson he despised. The costume, he
asserted, was "correct according to authentic monuments",
though this correctness is not apparent to the modern eye. His
horses, dignified creatures as they are, were clearly not, as
Stothard said of his own horses, the result of "everyday
observation", would not bear as well the scrutiny of a Stubbs.
Though the painter anxiously strives to give them life, they
are certainly inferior to the spectral steeds in the more congeni-
ally supernatural surroundings of his *Elijah in the Fiery Chariot*.

Neither Stothard nor Blake had produced a masterpiece; but certainly a cause of contention. Both were angry; old friends turned into enemies. Cromek, with his sharp little schemes (which did him no good—he died a few years after in straitened circumstances) became, in Blake's eyes, a monster. The epigrams multiplied: and if some of them were very amusing, there was a hint also of persecution-mania. Even the "archangel" Flaxman, as the friend of Hayley, and one inclined to take the part of his fellow-academician Stothard, one also who was put out by the failure of his efforts to help and tended to ascribe it to the eccentricity of his friend, was now numbered among the "spiritual enemies". The only friend remaining to Blake apart from Fuseli was Thomas Butts, that ideal patron, who made no demands, never irritatingly obtruded his own egotism, was so unlike Hayley, who, as Blake observed

> "When (he) finds out what you cannot do
> That is the very thing he'll set you to."

If in these dark years, save for the final "prophetic" poems, the *Milton* and *Jerusalem*, on which he worked without haste, Blake devoted himself mainly to painting pictures it was because of Butts' encouragement and financial aid. In his painting and his views on painting (tinged as these were by the rancour of his personal struggles) there was an aesthetic revolt of greater coherence than his contemporaries realized, and consistent with the whole of his earlier development.

It was Blake's aim to revive an art that had been lost; and here his early attachment to the Gothic past was, if unconsciously, again in his mind. He had not formulated opposition to the Renaissance in such definite terms as the Pre-Raphaelites were later to do. Raphael, as well as Michelangelo, was his idol (though it is to be assumed that he knew them both only through the medium of engravings). On the other hand he had the greatest dislike for the related schools of Venice and Parma, as represented by Titian and Correggio; for what we now call Baroque art, as represented by Rubens; for Dutch realism as represented by Rembrandt; all of which comprised a dislike of oil painting itself. Though Raphael and Michelangelo used the oil medium, their greatest works were in tempera or fresco. In this respect they were the last of a long succession of painters who had used a well-defined outline and clear colour. They were to be distinguished from those who had cultivated, in the oil medium, a distinct technique and purpose. The technique destroyed outline in order to represent solid form by means of light and shade. The purpose was to attain a richer and fuller sense of material substance. Both, in Blake's view, were destructive of imaginative art. He pointed out that oil yellows and darkens, he poured fierce criticisms on "that infernal machine called Chiaro Oscuro" which produced, to him, unpleasantly dark and dirty effects and resulted in "blots and blurs".

He had been revolving all this in his mind during the servitude of Felpham, and set it out afresh, in the indignation of his penury and neglect, first privately in his annotations to the published collection of Reynolds's *Discourses* and a little later in the *Descriptive Catalogue* that accompanied his unsuccessful exhibition in 1809, held in the old family house that had become his brother's, No. 28, Broad Street, Golden Square.

No one would now take Blake's opinions with great seriousness as a valid system of criticism. The statement that "Till we get rid of Titian and Correggio, Rubens and Rembrandt, We never shall equal Rafael and Albert Durer, Michelangelo and Julio Romano" is fantastic in its arrogance. He overlooked or impatiently dismissed all the qualities that make painting distinct from drawing. "His lights," he says of Rubens, "are all the colours of the Rainbow, laid on indiscriminately & broken one into another" : which a modern critic might well understand as a term of praise though to Blake this was "Contrary to The Colouring of Real Art & Science".

"The great and golden rule of art, as well as of life," said Blake, "is this: That the more distinct, sharp and wiry the bounding line, the more perfect the work of art, and the less keen and sharp, the greater is the evidence of weak imitation, plagiarism and bungling". To apply this dogma to such a painter as Velazquez or Blake's own contemporary Goya, whose effort was directed to getting rid of outline, so that form might take on life and dimension, is to realize its inadequacy. To ask what was the point of painting the yellow face of an ugly, old woman, as Rembrandt did, was to reveal a blindness

to the profound insight and sense of mystery of one of the
greatest of masters. It is interesting that the "mystic" could not
bear mystery, nor the poet comprehend the material and
earthy substance in which the beauty of European painting has
taken shape.

His was an insular and romantic revolt against that organized
arrangement of artists who were forever to be regarded as
classics, the standards of indisputable authority, which
Reynolds had, in his *Discourses*, so carefully put together. In
picking out those passages where Reynolds recommends the
careful study of the masters, Blake certainly distorted sensible
advice to pursue the traditional path of an ancient craft into
the idea that "Genius may be Taught & that all Pretence to
Inspiration is a Lie & a *Deceit*". It is hard not to conclude that
his early encounter with the President still rankled, that speaking of "Inspiration" in general, he had in mind his own
inspiration (which Reynolds had deprecated), that personal
dislike dictated his strictures on the *Discourses* as "the Simula-
tions of the Hypocrite who smiles particularly where he means
to Betray. His praise of Rafael is like the Hysteric Smile of
Revenge. His Softness & Candour, the hidden trap & the
poisoned feast. . . . Such Artists as Reynolds are at all times
Hired by the Satans for the Depression of Art—A Pretence of
Art, to destroy Art".

Yet Hogarth before him had been goaded into intemperate
speech by the connoisseurs' preference for the dark canvases of
old masters and in criticizing the attempts to imitate these
smoky effects both had some reason. Reynolds himself was
misguided in his attempts to gain richness of shadow by the use
of bitumen, the destructive result of which had begun to show
in his lifetime. Blake combined wild derision of the Academic
technique and of royal patronage in the words

> "The Queen dropped a tear, Into the King's Ear
>   And all his pictures faded."

It is not however because he gave a well-balanced view of the
art of painting but because of the unappreciated truth that
was embedded in much perverse and ignorant defiance, the
personal attitude that was not merely personal but revealed
stretches of aesthetically unknown country, that Blake's

remarks had importance. In them, there was the beginning of
that new perspective in which the nineteenth and twentieth
centuries were to regard the so-called "primitives" of painting.
It is possible for a moment to forget that period of three hundred
years in which the easel picture had developed to serve the
requirements of the secular patron; to see Blake as one on the
farther side of the great division in the arts that in Britain had
come with the Tudor regime. Instinct, in the absence of correct
historical information and the absence of actual examples,
directed him towards the Florentine School, in which Michelangelo had a claim on his affections, not only in respect of
"determinate outline", but as a poet and a man with a vision
of the universe; but the sympathies of Blake would, if he had
seen them, certainly have been equally, and perhaps more,
with the works of Giotto. He spoke as a man of the Middle
Ages: though he did not say so in so many words, he was
ultimately advocating a return to the spirit, the method, the
religious feeling of that bygone era.

Thus, with a verbal flourish, he announced his recovery of
the art of "Fresco"—or tempera, water-colour with a binding
of glue size on a specially prepared plaster ground, suitable
either for a small "cabinet picture" or a large mural space, the
medium, he said, in which "all the little old Pictures" were
executed. As compared with oils, he asserted, it had the merit
of permanence, though, in fact, several of Blake's still-existing
tempera paintings have deteriorated and darkened consider-
ably, requiring in recent times careful expert treatment to
restore them in some degree. When coats of varnish were
removed, those painted in his later years, like the *Count Ugolino
and his Sons and Grandsons in Prison* (in the collection of Mr.
Geoffrey Keynes and exhibited in the Arts Council's exhibition
of Blake's Tempera Paintings, 1951) proved in good condition.
Gold, said Blake (in the spirit of a Fra Angelico) could be used
with tempera but not with oil, and these paintings still retain
their traces of gold. He had at the back of his mind the
ecclesiastical function of the mediaeval painter. Four water-
colours in Blake's Catalogue "the Artist wishes were in Fresco
on an enlarged scale to ornament the altars of churches, and to
make England, like Italy, respected by respectable men of other
countries on account of Art".

In this one can see the life-long bias of the boy who had come so profoundly under the spell of the sculptures in Westminster Abbey, who had described his early engraving of a Michelangelesque figure as "one of the Gothic Artists who Built the Cathedrals in what we call the Dark Ages, Wandering about in sheepskins & goat skins, of whom the World was not Worthy", the designer whose illustrated books with their beautiful writing and borders seemed to arrive by an independent way of their own at a similarity with the illuminated manuscript. In the subjects of the exhibition of 1809 there was the same harking back to the past—not only in the *Canterbury Pilgrims* but in that lost work *The Ancient Britons*, in which he sought to recall the last epic splendours of Arthurian legend.

Looking towards the Middle Ages, anxious to revive an exalted spirit in painting, the purity of the fresco painters' outline (as opposed to the oil painters' "brushwork"), Blake may be compared—in intention though not in result—with those first "Pre-Raphaelites", the German Nazarenes, who had formed a group warring on materialism in art at about the time he gave his Exhibition. It is strange to think that the same trend of romantic thought and feeling in Europe that set the Germans, Cornelius and Overbeck, to work in monastic seclusion and devotion in Rome, impelled this solitary Londoner along the path of a forgotten idealism.

When as much as this has been said, the nature of Blake's revolt in the visual arts has still not been fully examined. In attempting to shatter that Pantheon of aesthetic heroes that Reynolds had laboriously built, he disturbed, without consciously intending to do so, the fabric of European exclusiveness; his art threw out its gesture of welcome and sympathy to that of other lands where the spiritual life was valued: not only to the Gothic centuries but to the timeless East. This can be seen in the two pictures "*The Spiritual Form of Pitt guiding Behemoth*" and "*The Spiritual Form of Nelson guiding Leviathan*". In depicting the national heroes of the Napoleonic struggle (Nelson died in 1805, Pitt in 1806) together with the monsters respectively of land and sea, Blake had, it may be supposed, no less a patriotic intention than Turner who contemporaneously painted the Battle of Trafalgar; and yet the conception of these works of Blake has ceased to be European. "We might almost

think," says Sir Charles Holmes, who as Director of the National
Gallery, put aside literary speculation and advised taking
Blake's painting "as we find it"—"that the artist had actual
Oriental paintings in mind, for the glittering golden halo round
the head of the central figure recalls Indian or Buddhist
imagery." Did Blake perhaps see some of the artistic souvenirs
brought back from India by servants of "John Company"? He
was not, at least, unaware of the existence of India. Number
X in the *Descriptive Catalogue* is *The Bramins—a Drawing*. "The
subject," Blake observes, "is Mr. Wilkin translating the Geeta;
an ideal design, suggested by the first publication of that part
of the Hindoo Scriptures translated by Mr. Wilkin. I understand that my Costume is incorrect, but in this I plead the
authority of the ancients . . ." There is again a strongly oriental
character in the attitudes of the figures (for instance that of
"Wantonness") in the tempera painting of 1811, *The Spiritual
Condition of Man*, now in the Fitzwilliam Museum, Cambridge.
If he had no actual Indian painting or work of sculpture to
prompt him, it might well be concluded that a likeness of
spiritual outlook between people otherwise so far apart,
produced a likeness of symbolism and gesture in their art. The
spiritually-disposed artist, East and West, has, in any case,
always had resort to the "determinate outline" on which Blake
insisted: paintings by him would harmonize perfectly with
those in a collection of masterpieces of the Far East: only in the
context of European realism did they appear abnormal: though
in a London still governed by the principles of Sir Joshua's
Discourses the abnormality was marked indeed. The unusual in
painting, even more than the unusual in literature, commonly
gives rise to the aspersion of insanity. The report of Blake's
madness gained currency not so much because of his Swedenborgian thought, or of poetry that was little understood, as
because of his one-man art exhibition and in particular through
the savage attack of Robert Hunt in *The Examiner*. It is true
that Hunt was the type of vigorous journalist who saw madness and folly everywhere: in the "stupid and mad-brained"
projects of politicians, even more than in art. "The present
worthy Keeper of the Royal Academy" (Fuseli) was not,
perhaps, actually "touched", "though no one can deny that
his Muse has been on the verge of insanity, since it has brought

forth, with more legitimate offspring, the furious and d'
beings of an extravagant imagination". Moderately r.
of the authority represented by Fuseli's official position, Hun
felt entitled to give no mercy to the entirely unofficial and
defenceless Blake, describing him as "an unfortunate lunatic,
whose personal inoffensiveness secures him from confinement".
It is small wonder that Blake spoke in the *Public Address* written
in the following year, of "the manner in which my Character
has been blasted, both as an artist & a man". He retorted with
as much pugnacity as Hogarth to his critics; was goaded to
intemperate comment on the art world in general. To this
period belong those epigrams in which he refers defiantly to the
accusation:

" 'Madman' I have been call'd: 'Fool' they call thee
     I wonder which they envy, Thee or Me?"

Flaxman had joined (or Blake thought he had) the number of
his detractors:

"I mock thee not, tho' I by thee am Mocked
     Thou call'st me Madman, but I call thee Blockhead".

Thus it was that in the period when the romantic feeling in art
was in other respects gaining ground, when enthusiasm for the
Middle Ages had already produced attempts to imitate its
architecture, an artist genuinely Gothic in spirit seemed entirely
apart from his fellows, and his work a solitary freak.

5

ROMANTIC CROSSROADS

I

NATURE AND THE SUPERNATURAL

TRACING the course of the Romantic movement, one
arrives sooner or later at a point where there is a choice
of ways. One leads to close communion with nature, the
other into the human mind and through it into the realm of the
supernatural. Coleridge, in explaining his collaboration with
Wordsworth, showed his exact awareness of this divergence in
the *Lyrical Ballads* of 1798. "It was agreed that my efforts
should be directed to persons and characters supernatural, or at
least romantic, yet so as to transfer from our inward nature a
human interest and a semblance of truth sufficient to procure for
these shadows of imagination that willing suspension of dis-
belief for the moment which constitutes poetic faith. Mr.
Wordsworth, on the other hand, was to propose to himself as
his object to give the charm of novelty to things of every day,
and to excite a feeling analogous to the supernatural, by
awakening the mind's attention from the lethargy of custom and
directing it to the loveliness and the wonders of the world before
us; an inexhaustible treasure, but for which, in consequence of
the film of familiarity and selfish solicitude, we have eyes yet
see not, ears that hear not, and hearts that neither feel nor
understand."

Each contributed to the *Lyrical Ballads* a masterpiece within
the limits of these definitions: Coleridge, his *The Ancient
Mariner*, and Wordsworth his *Lines, composed a few miles above
Tintern Abbey*: the strange sorcery of the one being beautifully
complemented by the descriptive beauty of the other. Yet if
both poets were romantic, their temperaments were opposite.
It was in 1810 that Coleridge left the Lakes, "flying" as De

Quincey put it, "from the beauty of external nature". He was in that way nearer to Blake than to Wordsworth, who stead-fastly remained "A worshipper of nature . . . unwearied in that service". As De Quincey further remarked in his *Lake Reminiscences*—"Coleridge himself most beautifully insists upon and illustrates the truth that all which we find in nature must be created by ourselves: and that alike whether nature is so gorgeous in her beauty as to seem apparelled in her wedding-garment or so powerless and extinct as to seem palled in her shroud:

> "O Lady, we receive but what we give
> And in *our* life alone does nature live . . .
> I may not hope from *outward* forms to win
> The passion and the life whose fountains are *within*."

These lines would certainly have won Blake's hearty approval for he never lost the contempt instilled by Swedenborg for the "vegetable universe". It is necessary to contrast them both with the Wordsworth who explained that

> ". . . The sounding cataract
> Haunted me like a passion; the tall rock,
> The mountain, and the deep and gloomy wood
> Their colours and their forms, were then to me
> An appetite; a feeling and a love,
> That had no need of a remoter charm,
> By thought supplied, nor any interest
> Unborrowed from the eye."

In this contrast, no doubt, there is some part of the reason why Wordsworth and Blake seem to view each other from an immense distance or across a gulf, even in admiration. It is hard to understand why Wordsworth should have thought the author of the *Songs of Innocence and of Experience* mad, on the evidence they supplied, although he did add that "there is something in the madness of this man which interests me more than the sanity of Lord Byron and Walter Scott!" It is easier to appreciate why Blake disapproved of Wordsworth's nature-worship, although his delight in Wordsworth's poetry, as the diarist, Crabb Robinson, recorded, was intense. Blake resolved the question by looking on Wordsworth as two people: "the

Natural Man rising up against the Spiritual Man Continually, & then he is No Poet but a Heathen Philosopher at Enmity against all true Poetry or Inspiration". When Wordsworth spoke of the "Influence of natural Objects, In calling forth and strengthening the Imagination in Boyhood and early Youth", Blake commented severely, "Natural Objects always did & now do weaken, deaden & obliterate Imagination in Me. Wordsworth must know that what he writes Valuable is Not to be found in Nature". A passage in *The Excursion*, wherein Wordsworth expressed his disregard for a religion only to be conveyed through the attributes of humanity

> "All strength—all terror, single or in bands,
> That ever was put forth in personal form
> Jehovah—with his thunder and the choir
> Of shouting Angels, and the empyreal thrones,
> I pass them unalarmed . . ."

impressed Blake by its grandeur of sound and shocked him as the statement of belief in an impersonal universe.

One must refer once more to the power of the sceptic, the rationalist and the materialist to be reassured as to the equally romantic character of the love of nature and the interest in the supernatural. They both stemmed from dislike of an artificial and essentially urban culture, of its disciplines and limitations. They both represented the desire for strange and adventurous experience. By "nature", it is to be understood, the romantic meant *wild* nature, untamed and therefore corresponding to the craving for freedom in the human mind. The typical eighteenth-century man had hated the undiscipline of the wild, had found the world beyond the formal gardens, the classic mansions, the well-groomed cornfields, the "sweet security of streets", full of ugliness (that is, disorder) and menace. Among the Alpine mountains Edward Gibbon had drawn down the blinds of his coach, with a shiver of distaste, to shut out the unpleasant spectacle of nature outside human control. A Wordsworth, on the contrary, rejoiced in the height of mountains, the unbridled force of waterfalls, the depth of woods, precisely because they defied subjugation and thus aroused, as Coleridge put it, "a feeling analogous to the supernatural".

The pattern is repeated in painting. Turner was romantic in the same way as Wordsworth: in his delight in the Alpine heights, the magnificent confusion of storm, the endless recession of distance. Fuseli belongs in the other category of romance, seeking the thrill of adventure in the idea of a more than natural agency at work. Even so, there were painters who attempted to show that it was only a step from the immense to the impossible—or rather from the strangeness of nature to the strangeness of imaginative vision. Freely compared with Turner in his own time was that other younger contemporary of Blake, John Martin, who also painted "immeasurable spaces" and "prodigies of landscape" but made them the setting for the apocalyptic destruction of cities.

This balance between nature and the supernatural helps to explain why Milton was the favoured poet of the romantic movement. *Paradise Lost* was, although the fact is sometimes overlooked, a wonderful repository of landscape. Time and again it inspired Turner. In 1798 the young man's Royal Academy picture of "Morning among the Coniston Fells" was accompanied by the eminently pictorial quotation:

> "Ye mists and exhalations that now rise
> From hill or streaming lake, dusky or gray
> Till the sun paints your fleecy skirts with gold
> In honour to the world's Great Author rise."

In 1813 his *The Deluge* had its lines from *Paradise Lost*:

> "Meanwhile, the south wind rose and, with black wings
> Wide hovering, all the clouds together drove
> From under heaven . . .
>   . . . The thicken'd sky
> Like a dark ceiling stood, down rush'd the rain
> Impetuous, and continued till the earth
> No more was seen."

It was the same year in which Martin sent to the Royal Academy a painting suggested either by the Old Testament or by Milton of *Adam's First Sight of Eve*.

But on other grounds Milton's epic had a peculiar significance for the romantic generation. It dealt boldly with the supernatural in the most exalted terms: and in addition it described a situation which, derived as it was from the Bible, appeared in quite a new light. *Paradise Lost* came from a Puritan century, in which the fall of man and the demand for unquestioning obedience to the will of God were fully and literally accepted. Yet in the demand for unquestioning obedience there was, if one chose to look at it in that light, an element of tyranny, that in merely human government would have been unbearable. Sympathy might well be directed to Satan who did rebel against the All-Powerful: though at the same time there was an unresolved problem or contradiction in the fact that an all-powerful Being should find it necessary to make war on His creatures and to allow the tide of battle to sway, the issue to hang in the balance. In describing the uncertainty, the almost equality of the contest, Milton himself seemed to oppose what he ostensibly wished to establish, and to make "the adversary" into a hero. His Satan, it is hardly too much to say, was the hero of the Romantic Movement.

A noble and very human being—this is what Milton had made of Satan; a being of intellect, capable of conducting subtle and powerful argument, with a pride that spurned submission, noble even as the leader of a party that could not win but would not be beaten. It was this great figure that made a special appeal to the romantics at the end of one century and the seemingly hopeless dawn of another. Perhaps unconsciously they associated him with the revolutionary struggle against the organized governments of Europe and as values became confused Satan was less a symbol of horror than of such hope as a hopeless defiance could contain. Good and bad were confused. The lofty and benevolent ideas with which the French Revolution began had in the eyes of other countries turned into blood-thirsty malignance, and the revolutionary himself in the age of Napoleon was confronted with the armed camp of absolutism planted on the foundations of liberty, equality and fraternity. Changing form, the thwarting tyranny that Blake represented by his "Urizen" was stronger than ever; the spirit of freedom, cut off from political and social aspirations, retained only the valour of opposition.

Something of this may have been in Wordsworth's mind, when, in 1802, the same year that Blake thought so often of Milton by the sea at Bognor, he wrote the famous sonnet that begins "Milton! thou should'st be living at this hour". Which Milton was it of whom "England hath need"?—the Puritan of rigid faith or the creator of an immortal rebel? Milton, Wordsworth said, could "give us freedom" yet there was indecision and anticlimax in his conclusion that Milton was a great example because he travelled "on life's way in cheerful godliness", that his heart "the lowliest duties on herself did lay". The sequence of thought in Wordsworth's sonnets of this time, often hesitant in direction, seemed confusedly to applaud the freedom which half of Milton's epic had asserted and the other half condemned.

"We must be free or die." So Wordsworth wrote, but still there remained the question whether this was the plain necessity of repelling a foreign invasion from the standpoint of one country proud of its independence and institutions, or whether in another sense it applauded a possibly quite unpopular freedom of mind and spirit, such as was to be found in his younger contemporary, Byron. The vast and disdainful liberty—"Eternal spirit of the chainless Mind"—claimed by Byron, could place him at war with all the virtues (so easily represented as hypocrisies) of the country to which he belonged, cause him to idolize that universal enemy, Napoleon, as well as fight for the independence of Greece. This outcast, self-made, might have modelled his own personality on that of Milton's "grand foe", and in the heroes of his poems—Manfred, Childe Harold or Don Juan—there was always some trace of the satanic defiance.

In painting, too, Satan was no longer deformed and animal-like, with horns and hoof, but a human, desperate figure; for a time, indeed, a popular subject. Fuseli's "Milton Gallery" of 1799 appropriately followed Alderman Boydell's collection of Shakespeare illustrations, and Blake thought his *Satan building the Bridge over Chaos* should be "ranked with the grandest efforts of imaginative art". Sir Thomas Lawrence, so successful as a portrait painter but not without a trace of romantic feeling, contributed to this venture and painted an athletic figure in his *Satan calling His Legions*—though of this picture Fuseli remarked it was "A damned thing, but not the Devil". It was again the humanized Satan that John Martin depicted in 1824 in his *Satan presiding at the Infernal Council*, vigorous and darkly handsome, with arm raised as he sits on a stupendous dome in a vast amphitheatre.

To sum up the situation of romantic art in these later days of George III, the Regency (1810–1820) and George IV is to observe a growing disaffection for the world of commonplace reality—a division of interest becoming more strongly marked between escape into the past, escape into the wild, and adventure into a world beyond nature; though in each there was a delight in immensities, of time or space or emotion, an exercise of the imagination. It was in this period when the names of Byron, Wordsworth, Turner, Walter Scott were on everyone's tongue, when in so many ways a general definition of romanticism might seem to comprise much that is typical of Blake, he nevertheless was most alone, more now than in the first part of his life, isolated, and like an astral visitant to an uncongenial planet.

For the worship of nature, wild or otherwise, he had little regard. The lesson he had learnt from Swedenborg, that nature was so much dead matter and that only the human spirit was a living reality, stayed in his mind. Turner, contemplating the most mysterious and remote of distances, intoxicated by the magic of light, was still the slave of physical laws, a blind devotee of the sun. The "expressionist" Turner, whose canvases dissolved in glorious confusion of colour, would have seemed to Blake a man sinking without the determinate value of belief into the degradation of "blots and blurs". The painter of Biblical subjects, John Martin, had, superficially, more in common with him. He extended the far distances of Turner into the world beyond and daringly constructed the landscape of Heaven, yet inferior to Turner as a painter, in spirit he was as far from Blake. How different the impressions they had taken from the Bible. Read in the home of the Martins, it had been a devastating force, impregnating the mind of John with images of wrath, gloom and catastrophe, and helping to drive his weak-minded brothers into lunacy. The Bible had been no less of a power in the early life of Blake; had he not seen, when a child, God "put his head to the window" of the house at the corner of Broad Street? yet he was never overwhelmed by it in the same way. The tremendous conflict was not, for him, a war waged by some outraged and implacable Being on the human race, but a spiritual conflict in humanity. It was physical destruction that Martin and his imitator, Francis Danby, depicted, the wrath of heaven descending in electric storm and flood, overturning cities from which the inhabitants ran in pitiable terror. It was a physical landscape adapted from the scenery of the South Tyne, that made his Paradise. Martin's "Plains of Heaven" were still the "vegetative world" that Blake despised and the apocalyptic anger that occupied Martin was entirely opposed to Blake's belief in an infinity of forgiveness.

In fact these "religious" pictures were not so, viewed intellectually or emotionally, but were part of that supernatural machinery which was a vulgar aspect of romanticism, producing at all costs a thrill of fear or amazement. It relied on effect though it was under no obligation to reveal an actual cause—and the mystery (which was very different from Blake's mysticism) was essential to it.

Biblical subjects apart, the mystery was that of witchcraft, magic and superstitious legend, frowned upon by the sturdy common-sense of the rationalist Dr. Johnson (who had gone to as much trouble to expose the "Cock Lane Ghost" as to discredit Ossian) but gaining impetus from the revolt against rationalism of this kind and reinforced by the wave of myth and marvel that swept in from Germany. Even Sir Walter Scott, romantic in his delight in the trappings of the Middle Ages, and in the wildness of mountain scenery, though by temperament disposed to take a naturalistic view of life, could not resist an effort—in which there was, however, no real conviction—to meddle with the supernatural. The *Ivanhoe* of 1819 was a straightforward tale of adventure but followed by *The Monastery* (1820) in which Scott made use of the "machinery" of spiritland and half-heartedly introduced a Germanic sprite, the "White Lady of Avenel", the most implausible of his creations. This kind of thing was better left to the "Gothic" novelists, who made a popular commodity out of the impossible and played upon the love of horror and fantasy like the present-day writers of "thrillers" and "science-fiction": Matthew Gregory Lewis, whose *Ambrosio, or The Monk* (1795) was full of phantom presences, of a furious mixture of licentiousness and diablerie; and Charles Robert Maturin whose *Melmoth the Wanderer* (1820) described the career of one who had sold his soul and "gleams with a demon light" for a century and a half of weird and revolting incident. Yet, merely as a narrative, in which the belief of neither author nor reader was involved, romantic genius could make a masterpiece out of the supernatural, as full of wild humour as Robert Burns' *Tam O'Shanter*, as vivid as the account of hell in Wandering Willie's tale in Scott's *Redgauntlet*.

This is the background against which the life and work of William Blake in his later days can be viewed. In the leaning of the full-fledged romantic movement towards the wonderful, the more-than-human, the background is not inappropriate, but all the differences between Blake and his contemporaries clearly appear. Personal belief, with him, was involved in a peculiar fashion. He could not tell light-hearted legends as legends, nor would he have anything but contempt for the "machinery" of the commercial novelists, the more or less physical participation of phantoms in human affairs. This visionary who so freely and familiarly conversed with spirits in the mind only once encountered anything so material as a "ghost", visible to "the gross bodily eye". This was at Lambeth when he saw coming downstairs towards him a grim figure "scaly, speckled, very awful". It was also the only occasion on which he was at all disturbed. "More frightened than ever before or after, he took to his heels and ran out of the house."

Yet, as he said, "A Spirit and a Vision are not, as the modern philosophy supposes, a cloudy vapour or a nothing: they are organized and minutely articulated beyond all that the mortal and perishing nature can produce". It was natural to Blake to form clear-cut pictures in his mind of anything wonderful he had read or been told of, so distinct as to seem reality, like those visions of God, the prophet Ezekiel and the angels in the tree at Peckham Rye, which (if his later memory was accurate) he had seen when only a small child. The visionary was born, not made; but the "mysticism", the thought that gave to such visions some deep meaning, was a mature development to which Swedenborg and Swedenborgianism added a great deal. The hopefulness of this special form of Christianity, so closely relating the human and the divine, so firm in the belief that an eternity of ecstatic experience awaited the soul, always remained a distinction between his work and that of the romantics around him, who could indulge (as he never did) in despair and take refuge in the "nature" that to him was mere lifeless matter. It was this hopefulness that had enabled him to see the soul of his brother, Robert, rise from his deathbed through the ceiling at the house in Broad Street, "clapping its hands for joy".

Though, on certain points, he quarrelled with Swedenborg's argument, there are many respects in which they are alike. Both had the curious gift of intuition or divination. It enabled Swedenborg to state, at a dinner table, that a devastating fire had at that very moment broken out in a distant city. There was no way in which he could have known of it, yet it had in fact broken out then. It may be compared with the occasion when Blake in old age, among a group of young disciples, on his visit to Shoreham in Kent, suddenly remarked, "Palmer is coming." Samuel Palmer, it was pointed out, could not be coming as he had gone to London by coach; yet he arrived not long after, the coach having broken down.

They claimed equally the ability to converse with spirits of those who in life had belonged to any race or time, and gave a similar explanation when questioned as to how the spirits became comprehensible and what language they spoke in. Blake, for instance, having talked with the shade of Voltaire, was asked if he spoke in French, and gave what to Crabb Robinson seemed an "ingenious answer", though it was, from a Swedenborgian point of view a simple and obvious one, as showing the perfection of spiritual understanding: "To my sensations it was English. It was like the touch of a musical key. He touched it probably French, but to my ear it became English". Did Blake imitate Swedenborg? If so it was not in any conscious or artificial way but in the fulness of his belief (as expressed in his *Vision of the Last Judgment*) that the "world of Imagination is the world of Eternity: it is the divine bosom into which we shall all go after the death of the Vegetated body".

But, again like Swedenborg, he did not obtrude his visions upon others and it would be difficult to make a connected history of his faculty for communicating with the spirit world: for there are many years in which we do not hear of it and sometimes no date is given: and sometimes he seems to have enjoyed his little joke with those who were sceptical. Thus, when, at some unspecified time, he showed Fuseli a drawing and Fuseli observed, apparently in a critical way, "Now some-one has told you this is very fine", Blake's answer seems deliberately calculated to provoke the infidel friend (described in his celebrated epigram as "both Turk and Jew"):

"Yes, the Virgin Mary appeared to me and told me it was very fine. What do you say to that?", which called for one of Fuseli's flashes of sarcasm. "Why nothing—only that her lady-ship has not immaculate taste."

In the rural quiet of Felpham, the "voices of Celestial inhabitants" were "more distinctly heard and their forms more distinctly seen". This was suitable language to use to the Swedenborgian Flaxman. Blake put it in another form when writing to Butts: "my Abstract folly hurries me often away while I am at work carrying me over Mountains & Valleys, which are not Real, in a Land of Abstraction where Spectres of the Dead wander": though "folly" was used only in the deprecating sense of what others thought to be folly and Blake's real criticism was directed not against himself but "the world of Duty & Reality" that chained him to his maddening labours for William Hayley. The great grey forms that appeared to him as he walked by the sea, seeming to take shape and voice from the clouds, the wind and the murmur of the waves were those of the great writers whose works he had been reading, whose meaning he pondered. Milton, Dante . . . why indeed should they not seem real presences, for if not with Blake's intensity of vision it is a common enough human experience to see in the mind's eye those with whom we communicate through books, combining perhaps with residual memory of a portrait once seen to recreate a living impression.

Yet it is possible to speak of a "visionary year" when Blake "saw" visions far more various than the consoling literary giants. This was between 1819 and 1820 when he became acquainted with the water-colour painter, John Varley. They were introduced by John Linnell, that strange man who in his younger days claims our liking for his sympathy for and help-fulness to Blake, who later hardens into one of the typical domestic tyrants of the Victorian age. Linnell had met Blake in 1818. He was twenty-six, recently married, a capable painter already making a profitable living by portraits. Apparently the son of Blake's friend at Bristol, Cumberland, had suggested that Blake could help Linnell with the engraving of a portrait. Friendship followed and in due course Linnell brought Blake to the house of his own master in the art of painting, Varley. Varley was a "character", a large and genial man who, it was said, "began the world with tattered clothes and shoes tied with string", and by his likeable personality and remarkable industry had made himself one of the most popular of drawing-masters and a successful painter of landscape. He rose at daybreak and regularly worked fourteen hours a day. He once produced forty-two drawings in six weeks, and, as this suggests, tended to rely on the conventional formulas of picture-making, though Ruskin was to praise him as the only man who could draw mountains except Turner.

Where he was unconventional was in his athletic prowess and his devotion to astrology. He once fought a cabman in Oxford Street for an hour (watched by two thousand people) and encouraged the pupils who boarded with him (Linnell had been among them) to put on the gloves for a sparring bout. Every morning he worked out his horoscope for the day, planning "directions and transits", and many stories were told of his astrological mania. He ascribed to the conjunction of certain stars the fact that he was several times attacked by bulls while sketching. The discovery of a new planet, Uranus, made him wonder what effect it had in store for him: he predicted some effect on his person or property at a certain hour and was positively delighted when the hour came to find that his house was on fire, a clear indication of Uranus's influence. Such was the eccentric and credulous person for whom Blake drew the famous "visionary heads" . . . Wat Tyler striking the tax-gatherer on the head, Richard Coeur de Lion, the Man who built the Pyramids, William Wallace, King Edward the First, King Saul and, most curious and famous of all, the "Ghost of a Flea", though the mood in which these were carried out is still a matter for speculation.

Blake and Varley were very unlike; it was, indeed, Blake's lot always to consort with an unimaginative type of middle-class person, or with those whose leanings and eccentricities were very different from his. Of no one could it be further from the truth to say that "birds of a feather flock together". Superficially, it might be thought that mystic and astrologer were well-matched, but any apparent similarity between them, derived from their interest in matters beyond ordinary ken, disappears when closely examined. For one thing, Varley believed that he was pursuing an exact science, and the idea of an exact science governing human affairs by some inescapable cosmic process was of all ideas the least acceptable to Blake. It was another form of that predestination for which he had taken Swedenborg to task. It clearly offended against his belief that in the human spirit was the controlling force of its destiny. As "nature" was so much dead matter in his view, the substance of another planet was no more than this, however far distant it might be, even a million miles away, and also assuming, which he did not necessarily allow, that the spatial heavens were more than a figment of man's constructive mind.

Thus the tables, for once, are turned, and he appears in the unaccustomed role of sceptic, who regarded Varley's carefully plotted horoscopes as a puerile superstition, and was not to be convinced that the movements of the planet Uranus could set fire to a house in London. Varley, on the other hand, professedly a disbeliever in religion, fell an easy victim to any alternative, and, as the shrewd Linnell noted, was more credulous than Blake and "believed nearly all he heard and read"— at least where his hobby was concerned.

All this gives an element of comedy, or something other than their ostensible frenzy, to those evenings when, watched by the gaping and burly watercolourist, Blake burst out into wild descriptions of the spirits before him, whom Varley strained his eyes to see—"William Wallace!—I see him now, there, there; how noble he looks—reach me my things . . ." Was there, perhaps, an impish desire to astound Varley by a series of imaginative tours-de-force? There are several points in the narrative of Alan Cunningham, which he had either from Linnell or Varley, or both, which suggest either an embroidery of the writer or else that Blake was not in his most intensely serious mood. First, the idea that Blake copied the aspect of his spiritual sitters in much the same way as one of the professional portrait painters, whom he so greatly despised, copied the appearance of an ordinary sitter in his studio, being put out when the sitter moved. "I cannot finish him," Blake is represented as saying of the Scottish hero, Wallace—"Edward I has

stepped in between him and me." Or again, "Lais the courtesan
—with the impudence which is part of her profession"—
stepped in between him and the lovely Corinna—"he was
obliged to paint her to get her away". He had even to wait
while the "Ghost of a Flea" closed its mouth before he could
proceed with his picture of it. The conclusion may well be that
the artist, who was so little dependent on drawing from life,
by showing an uncharacteristic regard for accurate imitation
steadily pursued in drawing with the mind's eye, was obliging
(or baffling) Varley by thus suggesting a physical presence.
The wonderful Flea, "his eager tongue whisking out of his
mouth, a cup in his hand to hold blood and covered with a
scaly skin of gold and green", was a triumphant effort of the
imaginative faculty, a vivid symbol of the bloodthirsty man;
yet it is hard to accept that Blake really believed the souls of
bloodthirsty men were condemned to take on insect form—as
Varley understood him to have thought, and related in his
Treatise on Zodiacal Physiognomy. This would imply a transmi-
gration, a change of the human into another form, which Blake
in serious exposition would certainly have refused to contem-
plate. Nor can he have taken seriously the thesis of the *Zodiacal
Physiognomy*, that the zodiac produced different types of human
face which an engraving of the Flea was used to support. "It
agrees," said Varley, "in countenance with a certain class of
persons under Gemini, which sign is the significator of the
Flea, whose brown colour is appropriate to the colour of the
eyes of some full-toned Gemini persons." This rigmarole is a
comment on the hazy processes of Varley's thinking rather
than Blake's drawing.

II

THE NATURE OF MADNESS

It is not tenable to suppose that there came a mental parting
of the ways in Blake's development when, in the crude and
unsatisfactory phrase, he "went mad", because of his belief in
the spiritual life. Signs of strain, of a mind sorely assailed,
appear from time to time in his defiant manifestos, his lampoons.
His hardships and disappointments led him to exaggerate the
enmity of others; he seems more than once to show signs of

persecution mania but this is not the kind of "madness" in question and in any case he rallied from it. The peasant simplicity and sanity of his wife was no doubt a source of strength as well as comfort: but the spiritual life, far from unhinging him, was also a mental safeguard, recalling him to a sense of proportion when he was enraged by the trivial wiles of Cromek, childishly put out by the innocently offending Stothard, darkly suspicious of Flaxman's good intentions. The spiritual life made him proof against every material blow. Unbeaten by adversity, confident in his powers and convictions, he was one whom the tragedy that lurked in wait for the romantic soul could not harm.

Only those who did not know him thought him mad. Wordsworth, in his growing conventionality, found madness in his poetry, yet used the word admiringly, was still a great poet recognizing the greatness of another, when he declared that the madness appealed to him more than the "sanity of Byron or Sir Walter Scott". Southey, it is true, went to see Blake in 1811 and considered him "evidently insane", but Southey by this time hugged normality with a timorous caution that made any unusual expression of feeling not only beyond his understanding but something he did not wish to understand. "You could not have delighted in him—his madness was too evident, too fearful. It gave his eyes an expression such as you would expect to see in one who was possessed." Thus he referred to that light in Blake's glance, in which those who were more intimate found both kindliness and inspiration. It did not deter or disagreeably affect Coleridge, who was reported by Crabb Robinson to have visited Blake and talked "finely about him". It was one of the few occasions when Blake had the opportunity of conversing with a kindred spirit and an intellectual equal and it is to be regretted that the details of this great romantic encounter are lacking.

There is nothing so effective as an unusual painting in giving rise to the accusation of madness and neither Blake's poetry nor his personal behaviour probably affected general opinion as much as the unfavourable publicity that greeted the Exhibition of 1809. As has been mentioned, Robert Hunt in *The Examiner* wrote in a vein typical of the Philistine in other and later days but with the particularly offensive license of his own day.

SATAN ON THE BURNING LAKE, by Martin

COMBAT OF THE DEMONS, by Blake

THE NIGHT MARE
by Fuseli

"WITH DREAMS UPON MY BED," from Blake's *Job*

To the lesser men around him, who were admitted to his intimacy, Blake's was in no sense the "distempered brain" whose "wild effusions" Robert Hunt condemned. The cool, practical Linnell could not "for a moment feel there was the least justice in calling him insane. Blake could always explain his paradoxes satisfactorily, when he pleased, but to many he spoke so that 'hearing they might *not* hear!'" The circle of adoring young artists that eventually formed itself, found in him a saintly calm. If they deplored anything it was no palpable unbalance of mind but an audacious freedom in his written opinions (which he courteously did not obtrude in conversation), shocking in contrast with the precepts on which they had been brought up. Even a man like Henry Crabb Robinson, who began by regarding Blake as a mental case and an object of psychopathological study, one of those who "compel our admiration by their great mental powers, yet on the other move our pity by their claims to supernatural gifts", reluctantly, or to his own surprise, was compelled to modify his views on personal acquaintance.

Crabb Robinson was another of those middle-class dissenters and liberals with whom it had been Blake's fortune so often to be thrown in contact. He was a great talker and reader and one with considerable experience of the world. Born in 1775 (at Bury St. Edmunds) he had been in youth one of William Godwin's supporters, had studied, later, at Jena and Weimar, where he knew Goethe and other great figures of the German literary renaissance, was war-correspondent for *The Times* (perhaps the first of war-correspondents) during the Peninsular War. When he was thirty-eight he became a barrister, and had a successful and lucrative career from which he retired in 1828, thereafter devoting himself to a social round and living on well into the Victorian age (he died in 1867 at the age of ninety-one). It was his ambition to be a Boswell and, while disclaiming Boswell's literary gifts, he sought to outdo him in the number and importance of the people he described—— ". . . the names recorded in *his* great work are not so important as Goethe, Schiller, Herder, Wieland, the Duchesses Amalia and Louisa of Weimar, Tieck; as Madame de Staël, La Fayette, Abbé Gregoire, Benjamin Constant; as Wordsworth, Southey, Coleridge, Lamb, Rogers, Hazlitt, &c., &c., &c., for I could

add a great number of minor stars." Blake, whom he met at
the house of some friends of Linnell in 1825, was evidently an
"&c.," one of the "minor stars". They were not long in
contact; yet in his reports of their conversation (Blake was then
sixty-eight and Crabb Robinson fifty) the latter is the nearest
Blake had to a Boswell—and he was not in the long run so
unsympathetic to his subject as he had been before they met.
His cross-examination was parried in an intelligent and
graceful manner. Robinson believed no more in Blake's visions
at the end of their talks than at the beginning, yet he was bound
to admit that his observations in general were "sensible and
acute". They could almost agree in nearly identifying the
"Genius" that inspired Socrates and the "Spirits" Blake spoke
of, though Robinson could not swallow the idea of an actual
conversation with Voltaire or Shakespeare ("he is exactly like
the *old* Engraving" said Blake of Shakespeare, "which is said to
be a bad one—I think it is very good"). For the reader, the
remarks quoted somewhat at random by Robinson fit into the
consistent pattern of Blake's ideas. They seem to have really
upset the barrister only when they were subversive rather than
insane and the fire of the rebel suddenly glowed in the aura of
gentle mysticism. "He was led," we read, in June, 1826, "to
make assertions more palpably mischievous if capable of influ-
encing other minds and immoral, supposing them to express the
will of a responsible agent, than anything he had said before."
The witness under cross-examination had evidently scored a
hit; he stands down from the box of the *Reminiscences* unharmed
by the ordeal.

A growing complexity in Blake's work during the long years
of poverty and struggle in South Molton Street and finally in
Fountain Court, Strand, was not the result of failing power but
of the attempt to realize more difficult aims, to pour so much
more of personal experience into his epic imaginings that they
became in a sense autobiographical. The receptiveness of his
mind has been noted often before. The primeval and Gothic
past, the revival of religion, the poetry of Ossian, the ideas of
Swedenborg and other mystics, the fantasy of Fuseli, the
doctrines of political and social revolution, not only made a
deep impression on him but remained essential substance of his

imagination. He was receptive even to the "Nature" of which
he had so many hard words to say. The time spent at Felpham
made him, either as mystic or cockney, more aware than otherwise he would have been of field and hedgerow, of birds, flowers
and insect life. They became incorporated in the large design
of his *Milton*, as such details are incorporated in the illuminated
pages of a mediaeval missal. There is the extraordinary ballet
of "The gorgeous clothed Flies that dance & sport in summer,
Upon the sunny brooks & meadows"; of the weeds and small
creatures that dance round the Wine-presses of Luvah——

> ". . . the Centipede is there,
> The ground Spider with many eyes, the Mole clothed
>   in velvet
> The ambitious Spider in his sullen web, the lucky golden
>   Spinner
> The Earwig arrid, the tender Maggot, emblem of
>   immortality . . ."

He sees the lark

> ". . . Mounting upon the wings of light into the Great
>   Expanse,
> Re-echoing against the lovely blue & shining heavenly
>   shell
> His little throat labours with inspiration; every feather
> On throat & breast & wings vibrates with the effluence
>   Divine."

Joy "opens in the flowery bosoms . . ."

> "Joy even to tears which the sun rising dries; first the wild
>   Thyme
> And Meadow-sweet, downy & soft waving among the
>   reeds . . .
> . . . the Rose still sleeps,
> None dare to wake her; soon she bursts her crimson
>   curtain'd bed
> And comes forth in the majesty of beauty . . ."

Yet beautiful as these and many other passages are, they are
incidental to the immensely complex fabric that was built on

the simplicity of Blake's logic. These delightful aspects of nature were but the "shadow of eternity". The universe was not to be viewed objectively, the Earth was not "that false appearance which appears to the reason, As of a Globe rolling thro' Void-ness" ". . . every Space that a Man views around his dwelling place (his mental and spiritual point of vantage) such space is his Universe." In a sense Blake told the story of his tribula-tions at Felpham and the comfort he derived from the thought of Milton, in spite of those errors which had divided Milton against himself. His conviction that, as he said to Crabb Robin-son, "we are all co-existent with God, Members of the Divine Body", made it possible for him to identify himself with Milton, (and both of them ultimately with Jesus), to follow in spirit the stages by which casting off "selfhood" and false reasoning the spirit attains redemption. A manifold "hero" passing by no obvious transition from the land of allegory to "Felpham's Vale", South Molton Street and Stratford Place. A detailed explanation of the intricacies of its symbolism can never probably be perfect in that it requires an identification with the way in which Blake's mind worked and also an exact knowledge of what he had read and extracted from his reading, but without this, as a quarry in which the seams of pure poetic gold are easily traceable, the *Milton* is full of wonders and no one could fail to understand its reiterated onslaught on materialism.

> "I come in Self-annihilation & the grandeur of Inspiration
>   To cast off Rational Demonstration by Faith in the
>   Saviour
>   To cast off the rotten rags of Memory by Inspiration
>   To cast off Bacon, Locke & Newton from Albion's cover-
>   ing
>   To take off his filthy garments & clothe him with
>   Imagination
>   To cast aside from Poetry all that is not Inspiration."

Still more complex was the *Jerusalem* on which, after his return from Sussex, Blake worked for some sixteen years, both on the composition of the poem and the designs which make the coloured copy one of the most beautiful and remarkable of the world's illustrated books.

What is it, this enigmatic poem, that has claimed and continues to incite the speculative study of scholars, and learned commentaries longer than the poem itself? It is the whole mind and experience of Blake, expressed without reserve or restraint. It tells us once more what an unworldly man he was, with how little thought of success and fame. He wrote it without any idea of publication, other at least than in those few copies, personally printed, which only a few would see; and as "commanded by the spirits", which clearly made it impossible for him to shape and alter it in such a way as would make it comprehensible to "the public". It was largely "automatic writing", such as that which Swedenborg had found himself practising, which the modern surrealists have practised in their attempt to elicit and allow free egress to the true inward man— caring as little as Blake whether this was acceptable and intelligible to the ordinary understanding and with a similar enmity towards the artifice and conscious process of reasoning—in André Breton's definition, "Thought's dictation, in the absence of all control exercised by the reason and outside all aesthetic or moral preoccupations".

Yet this "inspiration" does not, in Blake, imply any confusion or contradiction of ideas. He was a tenacious and consistent man and *Jerusalem* is the most elaborate statement of beliefs from which it was impossible for him to depart in any degree. It restates his own Christianity, his belief in infinite forgiveness ("The Glory of Christianity is to Conquer by Forgiveness.") It renews his unending attack on materialism in every form:

> "I turn my eyes to the Schools & Universities of Europe
> And there behold the Loom of Locke, where Woof rages
>   dire
> Wash'd by the Water-wheels of Newton; black the cloth
> In heavy wreathes folds over every Nation . . ."

It was the duty of every Christian to "build up" Jerusalem, though "Jerusalem" is not to be understood as anything material but as the divine essence (or "emanation") of the human being—the Imagination with which, after many sufferings, due to their separation, Albion (the "eternal man") is to be conjoined. The whole poem could be said to describe the search for spiritual completeness: with a happy (and still Swedenborgian) ending.   By "self-annihilation"—that is, through infinite love and understanding—the human soul at last becomes identified with God and immortal and the concluding illustration to *Jerusalem* symbolically represents the great moment—"End yet Beginning".

The apparent simplicity of a brief synopsis or summary of essential purpose leaves untouched or unexplained magnificent obscurities, a host of minor puzzles, of mysterious "characters", an intricate confusion of time and space. *Jerusalem* shows the strange fashion in which all that Blake had read, learnt, or personally experienced remained immanent and without perspective in his mind.   Intensified now is that clamour of roars and howls, that atmosphere of storm and conflict that he had borrowed from Ossian; yet with signal effect he returns more than once to the lyric measure, and though this recalls the exquisite and individual mastery he had shown long before, it would not be unreasonable to suppose that he had thought of, or re-read, Chatterton.   Comparison might be made of a passage from Chatterton's *Elegy, written at Stanton Drew* (1769):

> "Ye dreary altars by whose side
> The druid priest in crimson dyed
> The solemn dirges sung
> And drove the golden knife
> Into the palpitating seat of life"

with a verse from the poem interpolated between the first and second chapters of Blake's *Jerusalem*:

> "Where Albion slept beneath the fatal Tree
> And the Druid's golden knife
> Rioted in human gore
> In offerings of human life."

In the same way there remained in his imagination the thought of those cromlechs, which the antiquarians for whose books in his youth he had made engravings, ascribed to the "Druids".   The eighteenth century's gropings in early history pointed out to him huge and fabulous vistas in the past—long and (allegorically speaking) endless eras of cruelty and sacrifice, succeeding some primal and happy state. Caesar's account of the Druids gave him the haunting image of the "wicker-man", the human victim bound in a wicker basket and sacrificially burnt. His myth of "Albion", at once place and person, had its background of poetic legend. Spenser's description of Albion in the *Faerie Queene*, Bacon's account of the *New Atlantis*, have, with probability, been included among Blake's sources.

This strange mind reached out and absorbed its material from sources of many different kinds. There are words and passages which seem to refer to an esoteric tradition of thought. Perhaps we shall never know for certain whether, or how far, Blake delved into the Jewish cabbalistic writings, though it is certain he studied Hebrew (as well as Greek) during his stay at Felpham, and no doubt his Hebraic studies led to his addressing an interlude of *Jerusalem* to the Jews. In this he refers to "your tradition" ("tradition", it may be significant, is the meaning of the Jewish "Cabbala"). In the cabbalistic doctrine of "the world of emanation" proceeding from the "first or ideal man", essential spiritual qualities, dividing into male and female, enumerated in threes, or Trinities, Christian thinkers have found points of contact with Judaism. Blake may well have discovered a likeness to his own thought, and his phrase, "Take up the Cross, O Israel, & follow Jesus" suggests it: while in that use of mystic numbers, so marked in *Jerusalem*, and perplexing to the average reader, the "Seven eyes of God", the "fourfold man", he seems to adopt the magic of numbers that plays a mysterious part in the cabbalistic works.

Except possibly to the special student of theology and metaphysics, this adds, rather than otherwise, to the obscurity of *Jerusalem*. It is of interest as showing what Blake's mental experience was, and the recondite matter on which he drew. That his own time, immediate surroundings, and an event such as his trial at Chichester are interwoven with the "world of emanations", shows still further his delight in complexity, his belief in the unreality of the real and the reality of the unreal.

How did he view the Industrial Revolution which had been steadily gaining impetus during his lifetime, this new and formidable manifestation of materialism? In the years when he was working on *Jerusalem*, the cotton and woollen mills using steam as a motive power were growing in the industrial towns, the Luddites were breaking machinery in a desperate effort to turn back the tide of "progress", conditions in Manchester had led to the "Peterloo" massacre. The famous line from the prefatory poem to his *Milton*, "Among these dark Satanic Mills" evokes unintentionally the grim atmosphere; Blake was thinking no doubt of the machinations of the enemies of the poetic imagination. He never visited an industrial town or went anywhere outside London except to Sussex: nor does he anywhere comment on the growth of industry and population in a specific fashion. He had observed the wretchedness of child labour in the *Songs of Experience*, the "notes of woe" of the chimney-sweep—"a little black thing among the snow", but not the greater wretchedness of children in the new factories. It was only the smoke of domestic chimneys that caused him to write in his *London*, "Every black'ning Church appalls". Yet the fact remains that *Jerusalem* seems full, as none of his previous poems had been, of the whir and pounding of machines. Wheels whiz round, furnaces belch forth flame, hammers clang on metal——

> "cruel Works
> Of many Wheels I view, wheel without wheel, with cogs
>   tyrannic
> Moving by compulsion each other . . ."

The counties of England

> "Labour within the Furnaces, walking among the Fires
>   With Ladles huge & Iron Pokers over the Island White."
> "Scotland pours out his Sons to labour at the Furnaces
>   Wales gives his Daughters to the Looms; England,
>   nursing Mothers . . ."

Again,

> "And all the Arts of Life they chang'd into the Arts of
>   Death in Albion
>   The hour-glass contemn'd because its simple workman-
>   ship
>   Was like the workmanship of the plowman & the water
>   wheel

That raises water into cisterns, broken & burn'd with fire
Because its workmanship was like the workmanship of the
    shepherd;
And in their stead, intricate wheels invented, wheel
    without wheel
To perplex youth in their outgoings & to bind to labours
    in Albion
Of day & night the myriads of eternity: that they may
    grind
And polish brass & Iron hour after hour, laborious task,
Kept ignorant of its use: that they might spend the days
    of wisdom
In sorrowful drudgery to obtain a scanty pittance of
    bread . . ."

These words might well have been uttered by one of those later
critics of an industrialized Britain, a Ruskin or a William
Morris, deploring the destruction of handicrafts, the monoto-
nous and soul-destroying labours of the artisan, though in their
context they have a symbolic meaning of a larger kind. The
"Furnaces of Los" are not those of Sheffield and Birmingham.
The "wheels" represent systems of materialistic thought; it
would be too minutely particular to say they forecast the
Stockton and Darlington railway (which was running before
Blake died). Yet there is no reason to deny Blake, who was so
intuitive, an intuition of what was going on in the world of his
later years, even if he had no direct contact with it. To pursue
the matter no further, one may feel that the Industrial Revolution is conveyed (in a quite modern fashion) by the choice and
vibration of words and imagery.

Throughout, one thing changes into another as in a dream.
London from Kensington Gardens to the "Isle of Leutha's
Dogs", from the Surrey hills to "the Jew's-harp house & the
Green Man", a city of the "Minute particulars" on which
Blake insisted, co-exists with, merges into, the tumultuous
world of spirits. The names of those concerned in the brawl at
Felpham, the trial at Chichester, are listed like a catalogue of
barbaric minor deities: autobiography and myth conjoin. The
offensive soldier, Scholfield, becomes one of the "Giants of
Albion" (the primitive men earlier imagined by Spenser) who

"smell the blood of the English" and accumulate in "A World in which Man is by his Nature the Enemy of Man". "Scofeld & Kox are let loose upon my Saxons." Puzzling over the fabulous "Kox", one realizes with some surprise that this is the Private Cock who stood by while Scholfield was ejected from Blake's garden. The difficulties of interpretation can be gauged by the celebrated line "Go thou to Skofield: ask him if he is Bath or if he is Canterbury." Is this, as Mr. Max Plowman has said, "a heartfelt prayer to the man of war beseeching him to let us know whether his war is spiritual, like Canterbury, or the war of swords and spears (typified by Roman Bath)"? Or is Skofield, as Mr. Joseph Wicksteed argues, "The life of Man" faced with the alternative between "the pursuit of happiness" (Bath—construed as a symbol of bodily healing) and "lofty religious duty (Canterbury)"? The question is complicated after a few lines more by what seems a purely individual defiance hurled by Blake at the offending dragoon, "Tell him I will dash him into shivers where & at what time I please."

It is possible that Blake himself would have rejected none of these alternatives, and allowed for fluid meanings or layer upon layer, changing with the perspective in which they were viewed. "Inspiration" here reached the farthest point from the classic lucidity and perfect union of form and meaning which Blake so bitterly assailed. The art of Homer and Virgil in telling a story in the words that best conveyed it to an audience was not that which he had chosen. He had no audience: his aim was expression. The physical action which Homer and Virgil delighted in was to him a barbarous pleasure in warfare, witness to the benighted condition of a warlike State. "It is," he said, in his remarks on Homer and Virgil, in 1820, "the Classics & not Goths nor Monks that desolate Europe with wars." It was a more wholesome as well as a more difficult task to give shape to the conflict of good and evil in the mind.

Containing, as it did, every element of the romantic evolution, the *Jerusalem* remains distinct as a religious testament, an extraordinary compound of tradition, legend, borrowed doctrines, memories, personal experiences, bound together by an indomitable optimism—which is ultimately its only explanation.

6

THE HOUSE OF THE INTERPRETER

THE "tremendous" quality in the romantic struggle does not disguise the fact that it achieved no sweeping general change, that many of the traits noted as typical in the eighteenth century were still to be encountered in the Regency period of Blake's old age. The rough humours of Hogarth, though not his improving intention, flavoured the drawings of the contemporary of Blake whom he regarded with antipathy, Thomas Rowlandson. The world of fashion had not discarded its mocking grace, its sneering refinement, and in the days of the Prince Regent, the *beau*—like George Bryan Brummell—could still combine the grand manner of Lord Chesterfield with the affectations of Vanbrugh's Lord Foppington. Reynolds had died in 1792 but the search for the principles of taste, the unassailable criterion, in the Mediterranean lands, went on. It reached a climax when Thomas Bruce, seventh Earl of Elgin, visited Athens and engineered the removal to England of the Parthenon frieze and other sculptures from the Acropolis between 1803 and 1812. Fuseli, dragged to see them by the enthusiasm of his pupil, Benjamin Robert Haydon, was forced to acknowledge a beauty with which he might not have been expected to be in sympathy. The figures which Blake would have criticized as "the daughters of memory" (as opposed to the "daughters of inspiration") were on view in the new buildings of the British Museum not very long after he had pronounced that "Grecian is Mathematic Form: Gothic is living form". The revival of Gothic architecture had begun; in 1816 Edward Blore was building Abbotsford for Sir Walter Scott; but (diverted by Gothic as he was) John Nash achieved the last triumphs of classic planning in London between 1811 and 1820. Romantic poetry was in exile. Byron, satanically defiant, had retired to Italy, his attention divided between *Don Juan* and the

Countess Guiccioli (Blake's "revelation", *The Ghost of Abel*, in 1822, was dedicated to "Lord Byron in the Wilderness"). In the same year Shelley, in whom all the love of liberty of an older generation had still flamed, was drowned at Spezzia.

Blake in his sixties was a poor, elderly man in an unsympathetic age. Economically speaking, he lived even more than in the pre-Felpham days "by miracle". As an engraver he belonged to an outmoded school; this was an age when reproductive engraving had greatly "improved", when a new race of craftsmen produced astonishing feats of minute shading in steel plates, rendering the tone and suggesting in their delicacy of black-and-white the colour of a topographical drawing, even the atmospheric effect of a vignette by Turner. There was much work of this kind to be done but it did not come Blake's way nor was it of a kind to suit him. His writing was not calculated to earn money; much of it not getting beyond the manuscript stage, though the manuscripts or the visions they recorded absorbed him. There is pathos in the remark of Mrs. Blake in her old age: "I see so little of Mr. Blake now. He is always in Paradise". Butts was a faithful patron still, yet there were limits to the number of paintings and drawings one man could buy or the amount of support he could give. Only an occasional small sum came in from his printed books. He had never had any social ambitions and to see him in relation to the prodigal pleasure-loving society of the Regency needs some mental effort. By chance he appears on one occasion at the dinner table of Lady Caroline Lamb in 1820. To another of the guests, Lady Charlotte Bury, it was an "ill-assorted' party of artists, litterati and fine folk, and Blake (though she was interested in him) a pathetic waif from a lower social stratum. "I should fear," the lady observed, "that he is one of those whose feelings are far superior to their station in life." She does not seem to have known he was a poet and assumed he was a species of amateur painter though she had never seen anything he had done. He evidently lacked "that worldly wisdom and that grace of manner which make a man sure of eminence in his profession and succeed in society". The revolutionary, the man of startling paradox, the writer of splendid lyrics, the designer whom even Academicians respected, these were aspects of Blake hidden from her, yet somehow the quiet old fellow claimed her attention rather than the famous and fashionable Sir Thomas Lawrence, who was also one of the guests.

The kindly and not unintelligent account of Lady Charlotte Bury indicates the depth of obscurity in which he now lived. There were presumably at least two rooms on the first floor of No. 3 Fountain Court, Strand, which after leaving South Molton Street the couple rented from Mrs. Blake's brother-in-law; one being a rather dark "show-room", though attention fixes on that bed-sitting, studio room which has been variously described. It seemed to Crabb Robinson smaller and more squalid than to such younger visitors as Samuel Palmer or George Richmond. The barrister sat on the edge of the bed, not trusting the one chair, looked with a somewhat bleak eye at the "mean yard" outside. On the other hand the river comes into Richmond's description, the room expands—a fireplace in the far right-hand corner, the bed on the left hand, a long engraver's table under the window (A "delightful working corner" said Palmer loyally). A pile of books on the floor, portfolios of his drawings, completed the spartan equipment of the interior. But there was no squalor, insisted Palmer, all was neat, clean, and orderly. The feeling of what the French call "bienséance" was reflected from the personalities of the tenants. Even Robinson observed the cleanliness of Blake's linen, the whiteness of his hands. Adversity and age had not broken his spirit nor dimmed his faculties, but had given him a saintlike fortitude. The fiery energy, the outbursts of spleen, could not now be guessed at: his look was one of gentle benevolence. As sketched by George Richmond, in a broad-brimmed hat, and wearing the tail-coat and "tights" of the period, he has the amiable aspect of the Mr. Pickwick whom Charles Dickens was to describe in the following decade.

"The house of the interpreter", so a few fervent disciples described the lodgings in Fountain Court. It was here that the two great works of his last years, the illustrations to the Book of Job and the water-colours to Dante's Divine Comedy, were carried out.

"The interpreter." He gained the name, out of Bunyan's *Pilgrim's Progress*, as one who for a group of young men suddenly illumined and interpreted the existence in which they enthusiastically but gropingly struggled. They found him at the height of his creative powers. They revered equally his personality and his work and in these last years, neglect was tempered by their attention. Emerson has said that if a great man were to bury himself in a cabin in the heart of a forest, sooner or later there would be a beaten track to his door. Through the human forest of London, the young admirers found their way to the great unknown.

John Linnell claims notice first as an individual character, and for the help and encouragement he gave to Blake. Linnell was a middle-class Londoner, born in the neighbourhood of Hart Street, Bloomsbury, in 1792. His father, after a number of ups and downs, had built up a prospering business as frame-maker and gilder, dealing incidentally in pictures and prints. John, the second son, had little or no schooling, but began to draw as a child, and when he was twelve or thirteen was employed by his father in making copies of George Morland's popular farmyard pictures. William Fleetwood Varley found him one day, making notes of a Girtin water-colour at Christie's salerooms, and suggested that the boy should go and see John Varley, his elder brother, well-known as water-colourist and art master. John Varley was a natural teacher, interested in anyone who showed the slightest aptitude for painting. He welcomed the young Linnell and made him free of the studio, where Linnell met William Henry Hunt, later so highly praised by Ruskin for his minutely stippled water-colours of birds' nests, peaches and plums; and William Mulready, Varley's brother-in-law, a young Irishman and a promising Royal Academy student. In 1805 Linnell himself began work in the Academy Schools.

It was a transitional period in academic art, in which the early Victorian school of "genre" or anecdotal painting was evolving, though Fuseli was still the Keeper of the Academy, and Linnell worked under him. In spite of his example—or of Reynolds' precepts—many students took most readily to imitating the realism and humours of Dutch and Flemish art. In this vein, David Wilkie scored his first success with the *Village Politicians* of 1806, while Mulready in 1815 was to be made Associate of the Academy on the strength of a picture called *The Idle Boys*. It says something for Linnell's independence of mind, and perhaps also for Fuseli's teaching, that he did not share the fashionable and youthful aversion for Michelangelo and the Florentine school.

He fits, more generally speaking, into the pattern of liberalism and nonconformity. William Godwin still had his circle, presided over the family group which was so remarkable and confused an illustration of the gospel of freedom. Linnell gave drawing lessons to Mary Godwin and to Charles Clairmont, son of Godwin's second wife. Whatever lessons or warning he derived from the suicide of Fanny Imlay, Mary Wollstonecraft's daughter, the attachment of Shelley to Fanny's half-sister, the suicide of Shelley's first wife, the affair of Claire Clairmont with Byron, he arrived, at all events, if not at advocacy of sex freedom, at some kind of radicalism that reflected Godwin's revolutionary thought. He had also that desire for a remodelled and purified religion so marked in the middle-class. The third of the Varley brothers, Cornelius, persuaded him to go to the Baptist Church in Keppel Street, Bloomsbury, where the Rev. John Martin preached. The pastor's "simple, earnest and logical" sermons converted him to Baptism in 1812.

In the Baptist congregation he formed various ties. There Linnell came into contact with Thomas Palmer, a Baptist "coal merchant and bookseller" who had a shop in Swallow Street. Linnell was to marry his daughter, Mary, and later to become the brother-in-law of the genius among the Blake disciples, Samuel Palmer. He met also Charles Heathcote Tatham, architect, whose daughter Julia married George Richmond (another of the group); whose son Frederick Tatham, in misguided zeal, was to burn Blake's manuscripts after his death.

An intelligent, able and determined young man, Linnell, by the time he was twenty-five, had made headway in his profession and his cleverness was not merely superficial. A visit to Wales did not lure him into the obvious picturesque that Varley had extracted from its mountainous scenery; rather, it recalled the old masters and the need for as careful and searching drawing in landscape as in figure study. In the portraits (by which he had managed to accumulate £500) there was a firmness that spoke of his devotion to Albrecht Dürer. A refusal to compromise is shown by his insistence on a civil marriage in which no element of "priesthood" remained. In 1817 he and Mary Palmer went to Scotland where the simple declaration before a magistrate in Edinburgh legally united them.

It was soon after his marriage that Linnell came to know Blake and the friendship which lasted until the latter's death is indeed a pleasant episode. Linnell's shrewdness divined the great powers of the older man. He recognized also, and admired, a tenacity in matters of principle equal to his own. His help was given in the least obtrusive and most encouraging fashion possible. He bought the original drawings of the "visionary heads" that resulted from the evening sittings with Varley and copies of the set of water-colours illustrative of the Book of Job that Blake had designed for Thomas Butts; and finally, in 1823, commissioned the engravings from them at £5 a plate. It was understood that Blake was to receive £100 more from whatever profits the work produced, but, no profits resulting, Linnell paid an extra £50. In 1825 he gave Blake that book of a hundred sheets of fine Dutch paper on which he commissioned him to make a series of water colours from Dante, with a view to their later being engraved.

Without Linnell, it is not likely that Blake would have undertaken or been able to carry through triumphantly, these two great series, the crown of his achievement. The tension, the drama of the *Job*, the magnificence of gesture like that of the universally famous illustration in which "the morning Stars sang together & all the Sons of God shouted for joy" are beyond criticism. The meaning, which Mr. Joseph Wicksteed has so admirably interpreted, subtly referring the whole appearance of external action and conflict back to Job's own inward spiritual conflict is not, it is true, a factor in its aesthetic impressiveness (though it is clearly desirable to know what Blake intended). The symbolism, indicating good or bad by the advance of the left or the right foot, may be considered irrelevant to the effect of a work of art. The influence of Michelangelo makes for some uneasy comparisons, and seems to have been, as in the figure of the Deity, a barrier preventing Blake's wholly original expression. But in the Dante series, no such disturbing reminiscence is left, no double meanings need distract the attention, the rhythm and unity of form and colour have become complete and seemingly effortless.

MIDSUMMER NIGHT'S DREAM, by Fuseli

OBERON, TITANIA AND PUCK, by Blake

A PINDARIC ODE.   97

' Hark, how each giant-oak, and defert-cave,
' Sigh to the torrent's awful voice beneath!
' O'er thee, oh King! their hundred arms
        ' they wave,
' Revenge on thee in hoarfer murmurs breathe;
' Vocal no more, fince Cambria's fatal day,
' To high-born Hoel's harp, or foft Llewel-
        ' lyn's lay.

                 I. 3.
' Cold is Cadwallo's tongue,
' That hufh'd the ftormy main:
' Brave Urien fleeps upon his craggy-bed:
' Mountains, ye mourn in vain
' Modred, whofe magic fong
' Made huge Plinlimmon bow his cloud-top'd
        ' head.

        G 4   ' On

"... NOW EACH GIANT OAK,"
Illustration to "THE BARD" by Blake

The engravings for Job were made on that long work table under the window in Fountain Court, Strand; there also were the drawings for Dante conceived, and the artist's visitors were intensely aware of the exalted atmosphere of creative affort.

Linnell, in his thirties, cannot be described as a follower. He had his own appointed way which he pursued with great industry and success. His portraits were bringing him wealth: in landscape he had a feeling for nature which Blake did not share. He seems to have combined a personal respect and affection with a pleasure in exerting an ability to *manage*: if he had known Blake earlier and had been simply his agent, it is possible that he would have handled his affairs as successfully as his own. A busy man, dividing his time between Collins' Farm, North End, Hampstead (where his wife and the children that came in steady succession enjoyed a bracing air) and his studio at Cirencester Place, Fitzroy Square, he was however the best of friends. They went to exhibitions together, dined at Cirencester Place, and on Sundays Blake would brave the atmosphere of the northern London heights to which he had a curious allergy, and submit himself gratefully to the affectionate fuss that Mrs. Linnell made of him.

Younger men approached Fountain Court with more of awe and if not quite so intimate were nearer in adoration. This was the attitude of Samuel Palmer, whom Linnell introduced to Blake in 1824, when Palmer was not quite twenty. Palmer, too, was one of the nonconformist middle-class. His maternal grandfather, William Giles, was a well-to-do banker, a Baptist, who had "written books" and was known in the family as The Author. His father, Samuel Palmer the elder, had also turned Baptist and was a bookseller. The younger Samuel Palmer, one of two brothers, was born in Walworth in 1805 and at an early age had shown signs of a romantic and emotional sensibility at variance with his comfortable South London setting.

He was, in the words of his son, "abnormally sensitive". Words, events, things seen had an intense effect. A couplet quoted by his nurse:

> "Fond man! the vision of a moment made!
> Dream of a dream and shadow of a shade!"

filled him with a never-forgotten emotion. The death of his
mother in 1817 "pierced him like a sharp sword". That sense
of the romantic past which had grown ever more acute since
the days of Chatterton and of Blake's youth instilled into him,
as he has recorded, "a passionate love (the expression is not too
strong) for the traditions and monuments of the Church; its
cloistered abbeys, cathedrals and minsters which I was always
imagining and trying to draw". "Sedentary and precociously
grave", he was given lessons at home by his father, in Greek
and Latin, introduced to "a wide range of English literature", and spent only a few months at Merchant Taylors'
School in 1817. Without system, he began to draw and paint:
had lessons from one of the many obscure landscape painters
and art masters of the period, William Wate, became wild with
excitement at the sight of Turner's *The Orange Merchantman* in
the Academy of 1819. He tried out the conventional recipes of
the popular water-colourists with "a boyish uncertainty":
scored some youthful successes at the exhibitions, and was in
danger of being spoilt as an artist, when John Linnell came "as
a good angel from Heaven to pluck me from the pit of modern
art". The painter of thirty, who recognized some merit in one
of Palmer's exhibited sepia drawings, took the youth in hand.
He introduced him to Varley and Mulready, still more usefully
directed him to study Dürer and Michelangelo. With Linnell
he went to the house of the German merchant, Charles Aders,
to see such a collection of early German and Flemish painting
as was then rare. He talked of Blake and his drawings. Palmer
became aware that painting was a greater and more exacting
calling than he had dreamed of. It was in a mood of predisposed reverence that in 1824 he paid, in Linnell's company, his
first visit to Blake at Fountain Court.

Blake (then sixty-seven) was in bed, having scalded his foot,
but sitting up and at work on one of the Dante drawings.
"Like one of the Antique patriarchs or a dying Michelangelo." Palmer was overwhelmed to find that in spite of the
difference in their ages he treated him with the utmost courtesy
and consideration. The humble room, in which genius dwelt,
seemed a spiritual island in the middle of an ocean, a "place of
primitive grandeur whether in the persons of Mr. and Mrs.
Blake, or in the things hanging on the walls. . . ."

There was sympathy on both sides. Palmer's admission that he, like his host, began a drawing "in fear and trembling" was approved. In the early experience of both there was a love of Gothic. "Everything connected with Gothic art and churches and their builders was a *passion* with him," recalled Palmer in later life: but even more than his art or his thoughts upon art it seems to have been Blake the man who made a profound impression and had an inspiring effect. He radiated goodness, the serenity of a spirit that no adversity or hardship could shake or depress. It was indeed in this serenity of his old age that Blake seemed to have disengaged himself at last from the romanticism with which he had had so many contacts —the romanticism which in the 1820's had in others become sullen, fretful, disappointed, egomaniac, uncertain, despairing. The reaction following the Napoleonic wars fostered the germ of romantic unrest that like a physical ailment entered into those who were not conscious whence it came. De Quincey, in a passage of the *Confessions*, has described how the events of the time could become a dark and despairing background even in a schoolboy's mind. Samuel Palmer, unlike De Quincey in having no view of or attitude to his time in general —save for a shrinking dislike of London, "this most false, corrupt and genteelly stupid town", was no less its product—a romantic of the new generation, liable to fevers of feeling, full of doubt and yearning. It was thus the comforting thing in Blake not only that he was good but that he was strong, a rock of strength, who caused doubts to disappear, whose affirmations replaced darkness by hope, who, in his own sense of proportion, transformed the whole aspect of life as if by magic and shone a dazzling light on the path ahead. "A man without a mask, his aim single, his path straightforward and his wants few; so he was free, noble and happy."

In the formation of a group of young men round Blake both Linnell and Palmer had a part. Edward Calvert was brought into it through the Palmer connection. A stalwart fellow in his twenties, "redolent of the sea and in white trousers", he had then recently left the navy and decided to turn artist. His early boyhood had been spent in Devon and Cornwall. He was born at Appledore in 1799, educated at the Bodmin grammar school, had become a midshipman at the age of fifteen, serving in

H.M.S. *Albion* at the bombardment of Algiers, when he was
slightly wounded. During the *Albion's* subsequent cruises in the
Mediterranean, he began to draw, and on reaching the age of
twenty-one left the service and took up painting with a local
artist, A. B. Johns of Plymouth. He was married before he
came to London in 1824, arriving with his young wife, an
introduction to Fuseli, and some shares his mother had given
him to provide working capital. The stockbroker he dealt
with was John Giles, Samuel Palmer's cousin—young, garru-
lous, with whimsical turns of speech and a veneration for his
cousin's idol, the "divine Blake". Through Giles and through
their meetings at the Academy and in its Schools, Palmer and
Calvert became friends and Calvert too was taken to see Blake
and came under his spell.

He bought a copy of the *Songs of Innocence and Experience* at
Fountain Court. He invited Blake to visit him at 17 Russell
Street, Brixton, where he settled, and his house became a
meeting-place of the disciples. Palmer would drop in for two
or three minutes, and sometimes stay "a week or a fortnight at
a time". There is no account of Calvert's first meeting with
Blake and few particulars of the latter's visit to Brixton, though
they seem to have discussed and experimented with modes of
etching. When a vessel containing etching-ground burst and
caused an alarming blaze, Blake expressed anxiety only lest
Mrs. Calvert should be disturbed.

Linnell's friendship with the architect Tatham brought
Tatham's sons, Arthur and Frederick, into the group round
Blake, and Frederick became as close to him as any. When
Blake, shortly before his death, was finishing his last work—
the Ancient of Days striking the first Circle of the Earth—he
said "There, I have done all I can! It is the best I have ever
finished. I hope Mr. Tatham will like it . . ." Then there was
George Richmond, son of the miniature painter, Thomas
Richmond, who met Palmer and Calvert at the Academy where
he was a student, who was introduced to Blake at the Tathams'
house, and, wonderful experience for a boy of sixteen,
walked home with him. Francis Oliver Finch was another
painter devotee in his early twenties when he first met Blake:
a pupil of Varley who became an accomplished water-colourist.

Here was the main nucleus of what might have been a

"school", if there had been any question of working with, and
carrying out the conceptions of, the master: though there was
not, and a "School of Blake", in view of his unique individu-
ality, was clearly impossible. It is true, and a fact of some
interest, that the young men now clustering round him were all
painters and would-be painters. Though they scribbled down
impressions and sentiments, there were no poets among them
or, in the intellectual sense, men of ideas. They were, all of
them, it must be admitted, far below Blake in mental power and
range, though aware of his greatness as a kind of sacred
mystery. They recoiled from the volcanic and destructive
element in his thought—as far as they were aware of it. Palmer,
half understanding Blake's advocacy of excess, took it to mean
that if a picture was to be brilliant, it could not be too brilliant,
a line to be sharp it could not be too sharp: which was all right
as far as it went but was far from completely interpreting the
purport of the *Marriage of Heaven and Hell*. Yet the witty,
subversive, violent Blake was largely hidden from them by the
gentleness of his manners: that tracts of his mind were mysterious increased veneration. Though they did not speak of
religion, their veneration was in spirit religious: and the main
result of their being privileged to see his drawings and to talk
with him was not to foster a particular style but to produce an
idealism and earnestness which subdued, at least for the time
being, what was commonplace in their make-up and brought
what gifts they had to the highest point and greatest intensity.

The nature of their idealism varied according to the individual character and a number of influences on each. At no
time did Palmer forswear that study of nature which Linnell
had drilled into him, for which Blake had so often expressed his
contempt (though Palmer attempted to show that in conversation, the "interpreter" was more moderate in his views than his
writings would suggest). But this simple devotion was accompanied by some thwarted need for the affirmation of faith by
ritual and colour, a reaction to Catholicism and mediaevalism
against the severities of the nonconformist belief in which he had
been brought up. Calvert's idealism on the other hand was
classical. H.M.S. *Albion* had skirted the coasts of the Aegean,
had visited the Isles of Greece. The memory of his midshipman
days was not merely that of rough service in the fleet that had

been Nelson's, but of Mediterranean sunshine, of tantalizing glimpses of Homeric lands of mountains and groves where Pan might be imagined to rule and nymphs and satyrs dance. These sunny visions remained at the back of his mind and perhaps did not obtrude themselves in conversation with Blake who had so frequently expressed his contempt for pagan myth, who abhorred the "classic" in any form.

There was, however, one minor product of Blake's old age, which made a deep impression on his disciples, to some extent reconciled differences of taste and theory, and, as it were, established the key in which their beautiful early productions were conceived. This was the series of original wood-cuts which he contributed in 1820 to Dr. Thornton's edition of Virgil's Pastorals. Technically they were as delightful to look at as the vignettes of Bewick, and Blake showed an admirable feeling for the simplifications suited to the medium; but quite wonderful was the expression concentrated within a small space, the way in which they conveyed not so much the spirit of Augustan verse as of some archaic existence, superbly primitive rather than classical, a simple life to which the sun, moon and stars played a passionate accompaniment. This was the romantic vision that left its trace on the mind of Palmer, Calvert, Richmond and even Linnell and aroused in them the same mood though not the imitation of style.

Two to three years the contact with genius lasted. For Blake, productive years made happy by friendship and relief from care; for his disciples a period of their lives never to be forgotten. Tatham, at Blake's deathbed in 1827, observed the nobility of his parting, his last affectionate words to his wife— "Kate, you have been a good wife : I will draw your portrait"; the hosannahs and songs of gladness with which he happily greeted, not, to him, death, but his entry into the spiritual life. "In truth he died like a saint", said George Richmond. He, Calvert and the Tathams helped to make the funeral arrangements and followed the coffin to Bunhill Fields—the sensitive Palmer who was in Kent could not bring himself to attend. Catherine Blake was taken care of and housed at Cirencester Place by Linnell. The extraordinary man had gone, yet there had begun, under his influence, an extraordinary episode in the history of art which has still to be described.

7

THE ANCIENTS OF SHOREHAM

I T was William Blake who keyed up the group of young men
to an exalted pitch by the singular influence of his personality; but the great adventure of their youth, the formation
of a kind of artist community, detaching itself from the world
and for a time living a rural idyll, was their own idea, an
experience in which, while they felt themselves under his
beneficent influence, they obeyed a natural and instinctive
prompting.

One can understand it better by considering the stage that
romantic feeling had reached in Europe generally. The hope
of a splendid new social and political order had, for the time
being at least, been quenched: there remained a mood of disappointment and disillusion which the reaction after the Napoleonic struggles increased. On the one hand there was the
recklessness and despair which tinges with a morbid significance
the period round about 1830 as the climax of Romanticism—
the moral sickness, gloomily analysed by Alfred de Musset in
his *Confessions d'un Enfant du Siècle* (1835). The end of several
artists, whatever the element of accident in it, gives the impression that life had become of little account to them—to the
brilliant Géricault who died, seeming to have abandoned all
hope, in 1825, aged thirty-three, to Byron, fever-stricken in
Greek campaigning in 1823, and, it may be, to Shelley drowned
in a storm off Leghorn in 1822. While not exactly to be compared with them, Samuel Palmer betrays more than one sign
of the "maladie morale", the inquietude of what de Musset
called the "ardent, pale and nervous generation".

Another facet of the romantic mood was the desire for escape,
the road of escape leading to some form of almost monastic
seclusion. The Lake School was one of its products, communion
with nature was a cure for the romantic sense of hurt; but the

monastic seclusion of the past also suggested its own kind of withdrawal in which the return to an historically earlier purity of idealism had its place. Thus the band of German painters called "Nazarenes" ensconced themselves in a monastic retreat in Rome early in the new century. The frugal life they lived reflected their respect for the old monkish painter whose art was unworldly. The religion of the Middle Ages was scarcely to be separated from their art. The German Protestant painter Overbeck, a leader of the "Nazarenes", turned Catholic: "Art-Catholic" was a somewhat disapproving description of the movement. The elements of the problem existed in Britain; the conversion of Augustus Welby Pugin to Catholicism followed from the family devotion to Gothic architecture. Samuel Palmer, with, in his own words, "a passionate love—the expression is not too strong—for the traditions and monuments of the Church", was just such a disciple as the Nazarenes would have welcomed. Though his religious feelings remained indeterminate, he was a stray from the Baptist fold with the yearning his relatives sensed and disapproved towards what was to become known as "High Church".

If there is a "Nazarene" element in the group of Blake's followers there is, also, something of the school of Barbizon, which can be defined, though its history covers many years, as "the School of 1830". The French painters who composed it felt the same need for withdrawal. Nature was their church; without the complex nostalgias of the Germans or English they found in a small village the equivalent of monastic retreat, in the forest of Fontainebleau, the gravity and melancholy that answered to their state of mind. Nature, likewise, in a passionate and romantic sense of the word, was an ideal of the so-called "Ancients" of Shoreham.

Shoreham, a village in the apple and hop growing country of Kent, was only twenty miles from London, but at this time seemed utterly remote from it and from any kind of modern life. Set in a little valley through which the river Darent flowed, sheltered by chalk ridges, richly wooded, it had, save for the carrier's and the market waggons, hardly any communication with the outside world. It was all old; the church, the haunted Grange, the trees, the costume of the villagers—the shepherds still wearing the archaic smock. It seemed in its tranquillity and to the eyes of young men agitated by the confusion of ideas, the disturbance of town living, to possess the secret of some profound wisdom, to belong to a timeless golden age.

This "valley of vision" was the discovery of Samuel Palmer. In that brief period during which he knew Blake, he went there at intervals, first to recover from some ailment and afterwards out of a growing fondness which decided him to live there altogether. He inherited a sum from his grandfather providing him with a small income. His father gave up his bookselling business and joined him early in 1827. For seven years, "sometimes by ourselves, sometimes visited by friends of congenial taste, literature and art and ancient music whiled away the hours, and a small independence made me heedless, for the time, of further gain; the beautiful was loved for itself. . . ."

The friends were Edward Calvert, George Richmond, Francis Oliver Finch, Frederick Tatham and those minor and, to us, dimmer figures, Henry Walter and Welby Sherman. John Giles, the stockbroker, though not a painter, was also of the company. John Linnell was an occasional and not altogether sympathetic visitor. Blake himself, some months before his death in August, 1827, made a single visit to Shoreham.

A curious interest attaches to this solitary excursion of one with so little liking for the country, for nature. Still, it was only twenty miles; and one can imagine him good-naturedly yielding to the enthusiastic pleading of Palmer. He stayed long enough to go on a ghost-hunting expedition to the Grange with his young friends: when a mysterious tapping that excited them proved to be no more than a snail crawling up the window. Yet it was neither Blake's visit, nor his greater works, but the series of small wood-cut illustrations that he had designed seven years earlier for Dr. Thornton's edition of Virgil's Pastorals that played a main part in creating the spirit of Shoreham. The stream, the shepherd, the moon, as seen in these tiny masterpieces were almost prophetic of Shoreham as his followers saw it, or a medium through which they perceived, in Kent, the "Golden Age".

The Golden Age—it was the tantalizing thought of it that led them to call themselves "The Ancients". The title had all the romantic nostalgia for another and better time—without being specific about any period in particular. It was often used in conversation by John Giles, who was prone to contrast the "grandeur and superior wisdom of the Ancients" with modern faultiness. "Why, they were cutting a tunnel the other day, sir; they began at both ends and didn't meet in the middle! Why, the Ancients, sir, the Ancients would have cut it to a hair." If Giles had the engineers of Rome in mind he did not say so. It would have been consistent with his outlook in general that he should hark back to the Middle Ages. His admiration for that period brought him, to the alarm of his Baptist relatives, even nearer to Catholicism than Palmer. Yet "the Ideal of our dear Friend" in Calvert's words was really a "primaeval world", for the group as a whole was like that fabulous memory of an entirely happy state that haunted the poetry of Blake.

Blake died in 1827: the "Shoreham period" lasted until 1833, a time of fervour, of which there are various glowing accounts by the "Ancients" themselves, or their biographers. Alone of Blake's later friends, John Linnell stood somewhat apart. He was older, a busy and a married man. He had his portraits to paint and seldom went out of town: and he was not entirely in sympathy with the young enthusiasts even though he had his own influence upon them, distinct from and not entirely consistent with that of Blake. It was he who had so strongly counselled Palmer to study nature: and he had his own puritanical conception of a simple and patriarchal life. In Bayswater, where he had moved from Hampstead, he set his growing family to work, to dig, to grind corn, to help with bread making and the brewing of the household beer (to which he gave special attention). There was this feeling for patriarchal life in his landscapes: in a sketch made at Shoreham of a shepherd boy in his smock, with a long staff, and playing on his pipe, he shows himself mildly appreciative of that rustic idyll which enraptured the younger men.

Yet he felt with a certain pique that he was excluded from their circle, even though contempt on his part for make-believe and immature enthusiasms made the exclusion an act of his own. "I am out of the pale, I fear, too far to taste the salt of Art with such society," he wrote in 1839, "but I ought to remember that I was not one of the monthly-meeting *élite*— when at the platonic feast of reason and flow of soul only real Greeks from Hackney and Lisson Grove were admitted."

"Real Greeks from Hackey and Lisson Grove . . ." a sneer at "The Ancients", at the excited meetings in the house of the Calverts.

It is evident that from Linnell's point of view the countryside was something to be used, for health or profit, but he had as much distaste for living in it as Blake himself though on different grounds. In London one mixed and exchanged ideas with those who were powerful or helpful to a struggling professional man, who would in due course make him "known". It was reasonable to produce for their inspection and pleasure a landscape painted in such a place as Shoreham: but to cut oneself off from society, to bury oneself there, was plainly another matter. He expressed himself grateful to Palmer, for a short stay at Shoreham as a result of which he felt physically better. "I have found so much benefit from my short visit to your valley and the very agreeable way we spent the time that I shall be under the necessity of seeing you again very soon at Shoreham. I dream of being there every night almost, and when I wake it is some time before I recollect that I am at Bayswater." (1826). But he evidently gave a candid warning to old Mr. Palmer of what he thought would happen to his son. "Mr. Linnell foretells that your voluntary secession from artists will end in the withering of art in your mind." Samuel Palmer was startled and evidently shocked by what, if not quite an act of treachery, was certainly a cold denial of all he believed in. There was, Linnell admitted, and pointed out, money to be made from Shoreham. "Mr. Linnell tells me that, by making studies of the Shoreham scenery, I could get a thousand a year directly. Though I am making studies for Mr. Linnell, I will, God help me, never be a naturalist by profession"—meaning by "naturalist" one who turned out pretty landscapes, as his son remarks, "warranted to sell".

One can well imagine the romantic horror with which Palmer would view the suggestion that he should commercialize the valley of vision. This indeed was far from that unworldly enthusiasm which Blake had imparted—underlined the difference between him and Linnell, even though the latter had so generously helped the great artist. Yet all sympathy cannot be withheld from Linnell. In his worldliness there was a strain of puritanism not without its purity. He liked that which was

clear and definite, in money matters as well as in the determinate outlines of a Blake drawing. It was a candid con-
struction of living, freed from muddle and obscurity; it had the
beauty of order, of exact and lucid system. His view was social
just as the typically romantic view was anti-social—he delighted
in the society for which he worked and was at pains to study its
requirements, to identify himself with it. The prudent manage-
ment of its rewards was an ethical responsibility of success.

But all this was far removed from the creation of a separate
community, an innocent unworldly world: an enterprise
requiring both genius and will-power. Linnell looked for
neither in the younger men. On the other hand, among these,
there was no feeling of "voluntary secession from artists" but
rather of a union giving strength. In the high spirits of youth
they would meet in King William Street and set off for Kent,
along the route of Chaucer's Canterbury Pilgrims, sometimes
on foot. A twenty-mile walk in those days seemed less formidable than now: a bowl of apples and "a huge Kettle of green
tea" gave them refreshment enough when they arrived. They
would go on talking all through the night.

George Richmond was eighteen when he first walked out to
Shoreham in 1827—to stay there for as long as strict economy
would allow three guineas to last—renting a room in a
labourer's cottage for two shillings a week. He learnt to live on
10s. 6d. a week, keeping an account book, which shows spartan
minuteness in the daily expenditure on bread, cheese and
milk: a somewhat more lavish allowance for candles (as he
often worked into the small hours). These were "among the
very happiest weeks of my long life". The memory of his
meeting with Blake was still fresh and powerful in his mind and
it was at this time that he engraved a shepherd with his flock,
leaning on his staff, against a background of low hills; a
graceful and mannered adaptation of a pastoral by Blake in the
Thornton series of woodcuts that in some strange way like the
work of his companions (which he imitates) is full of fervour,
breathes devotion.

Frederick Tatham as a person appears less distinctly,
although he was one of the first to accompany Palmer to
Shoreham and perhaps of them all had been closest to Blake.
"I hope Mr. Tatham will like it," the words Blake had mur-

mured as he drew on his death-bed *The Ancient of Days Striking the first Circle of the Earth* are indicative of regard. It was Tatham who with Richmond and Calvert had arranged the funeral and followed the humble cortège to Bunhill Fields, who was later to write a short biography of the great man, with some florid exercise of language but with genuine feeling: though as an artist he seems of little note. He drew Mrs. Blake in pencil no longer like the "Britomart in Merlin's wondrous glass" who (Tatham wrote) "instantly recognized her future partner" but in the worn kindliness of age with blunt and homely peasant features. Among the Ancients, however, he is a minor figure (like Henry Walter and Welby Sherman). He stands out mainly as the well-meaning vandal who was to destroy many of Blake's manuscripts.

Francis Oliver Finch, the pupil of Varley, seems to have remained little affected by the landscape of Shoreham, though he joined in the enthusiasms of the group. A mildly romantic painter, who in 1820 had sent to the exhibition of the Society of Painters in Water Colours a subject from Ossian, "Garmallion's Tomb", he was a devotee of Claude and Poussin: and though he admired Blake and has a certain link of outlook with him in his Swedenborgianism, he belongs in his art to that other early nineteenth-century world of pleasant landscape echoes and reflections of the European masters.

In all groups of artists there are always some who seem to take part by chance and the fleeting kinship of youth which for a time hides the greatest differences. They are unnecessary, save that they give an appearance of numbers and strength. Thus, the Pre-Raphaelites and Impressionists had for a while their adherents who were with them and yet not of them, easily and quickly dispensable from their history. It was the same with the Ancients of Shoreham. A Finch, a Tatham, a Sherman, a Walter, a Richmond ... really when all is said and done it is only Palmer and Calvert of the whole confrèrie who create its style and idealism: and yet the others were a background and a buttress which they needed. Numbers made interesting those heroic walks and talks continued far into the night, provided an audience, the presence of which brought out the magic of quotations from Milton and Keats. It is notable that they had the taste of a romantic generation for the "embalmèd darkness", the mystery of moonlight, but this too could be sympathetically shared: and several participants were certainly wanted in those little dramas of mystery and horror for which the Kentish lanes, transformed by night, were an apt setting. The fantastically crawling and contorted roots and branches of old beech trees in one such lane (the scene of a murder some years before) provided the young men with the décor of Macbeth—they threw themselves with a will into the chanting of the witches round their cauldron. The glades, eerie in moonshine, suggested tableaux vivants in the spirit of the Gothic novel; one of the group, a hooded spectre materializing from the dense shadow, would seize and carry off another acting the hapless traveller, who would feel for a moment some thrill of quite genuine terror. Together, also, they were better able to appreciate the ancient and self-contained life of the villagers, who were probably less alarmed by a party waking the echoes in deserted chalkpits with song in the stilly hours than they would have been by the odd behaviour of some single enthusiast. With their own rustic poetry, the villagers referred to these strange incursionists from London as the "extollagers", a word with its undefined but vivid aroma of witchcraft, ecstasy and astrology.

Palmer—in the seventh heaven—was certainly the outstanding member of the fraternity. His delight in the place, for a time, produced in him a decision and certainty which did not normally belong to his character; rapture in itself made him a leader. The miniature painted by George Richmond in 1830 (National Portrait Gallery) reflects an air of authority as well as devotion, in contrast with the sensitive perplexity of the self-portrait two years before. It was accentuated by the beard and long hair which the painter now affected. Hair and beard, together with a long cloak falling to his heels, must have given him something of the appearance of one of the German Nazarenes who stalked through the streets of Rome in just such a garb: and the many points of resemblance are curious evidence of the consistency with which the spirit of the age impressed its stamp on the type of artist receptive to it. Palmer shows a pious strain like that of the Nazarene apostles, Cornelius and Overbeck; the same desire for a Christian artist-life purged of every source of corruption. For him, as for them, Rome was neither pagan, nor the luxurious city of the Renaissance but "holy ground, where St. Peter & St. Paul have walked before you". Writing a very long letter to George Richmond when the latter was proposing a visit to Rome, Palmer observed in true Nazarene style, that such a visit should "reimpress upon us with the force of local retrospection the spirit & genius of Christianity" with "poverty for its true riches, simplicity its logic". A few years later we find him hanging in his "little chapel" prints of "the venerable Fisher & one of his friend & fellow martyr St. T. More . . . that they may frown vice, levity & infidelity out of my house and out of my heart".

He had reached this stage of desire for an ancient purity of faith, similar enough to the desires of the German "art-Catholic"—for he assumed as they did that holiness and virtue were a chastening process of art itself and that the old religion had made its artists—he had hankered after the distant gleam of mediaeval towers and spires in his earlier youth, yet in the paintings made at Shoreham there is no obvious trace of the Germanic yearning for the Middle Ages, nor did he, as the Nazarenes did, attempt religious themes. It was in fact the "vegetable" world Blake had so despised that inspired him. To that extent he was more directly the pupil of Linnell, studying "Nature" as the latter had advised. Yet how valuable, and how different from "naturalism" was the intensity of feeling he brought to the task. In this rather than in style or subject Blake was still the power that guided his hand. The moon, crescent or full, was a symbol of all that romantic nocturnal delight Palmer and his fellow-Ancients had found among the chalk pits and the dark lanes. The great billowing cumulus, the "Bright Cloud" that appears so often in his sepia and ink drawings, especially those of 1831 to 1832, was not simply a cloud study such as Constable would have made but a symbol of his happiness : and, perhaps, even more than happiness, of the religious feeling he wished to express, the equivalent of those celestial figures in which the religious feeling of Blake had taken human shape. There was an element in it of the mysticism that Blake himself had acquired from others, the sense of hidden meanings that came from "not things by themselves but, wings, terraces or outbuildings to the great edifice of the divine human form", profound contemplation or in moments of revelation. The apple blossom in a Shoreham garden, or the lichen on the roof of a barn, intensely seen but not descriptively studied, express, almost like the paintings of Vincent van Gogh, the artist's wonder and thanksgiving. Here, indeed, is nature transformed by a temperament. A surprising (certainly by no means a necessary) result is the power and resource of design, "determinate" as Blake would have had it, curiously interesting in pattern and dramatic in contrast; in the water-colours and the mixture of colour mediums he used, oil, tempera, gouache, the golden glow which is not that of Kent but of a self-contained pictorial world, best to be compared with that of the minor German masters, Altdorfer or Elsheimer.

To Edward Calvert, Shoreham "looked as if the Devil had not found it out". "How kindly I have been again welcomed!" he wrote to his wife who was then at Brixton in 1827, "And really what a Paradise this little village is! I do look forward in the summer to our coming down for a fortnight. Lodging is cheap. Mr. Palmer could not, though he wishes it, accommodate us all with beds as he does me at present." The influence of Blake, of Palmer, and of the valley of vision for a time had a magical effect on him, touched his work briefly, that is, with creative magic.

Calvert had a dream of his own, not only different from that of Blake and other followers of Blake, but implying an opposite view from theirs. They were, in a sense, "little Englanders", whose art had little to do with, even rejected, the classic myths, symbols and forms of which the Mediterranean was the ancient fount. There was some irony in the fact that Blake had contributed illustrations to Virgil, for Virgil was among the objects of his most John Bullish attacks. The commission to illustrate the Pastorals was one he accepted in the way of business though it must be admitted that the editor, Dr. Thornton, considered them most unsuitable. That Calvert, like Palmer, was influenced by their style and mood, is evident from such a wood engraving as *The Sheep of His Pasture*, which freely adapts an illustration by Blake to the First Eclogue; while the celebrated print *The Cyder Feast* with its rapt dancers exaggerates and somewhat stylizes the emphatic gestures and movements of Blake's figures. Yet Calvert was a lover of Virgil; he had been in the Mediterranean, at the back of his mind was

THE SHEPHERD, by George Richmond

SHEPHERDS UNDER THE FULL MOON,
by Samuel Palmer

THE CYDER FEAST, by Edward Calvert

some dimly glowing conception of a sensuous beauty untouched by the chill of northern myth, the explosive force of the Bible or the restraints of a puritanical background.

For a while his leaning towards an alternative ancient world, ultimately Greek though it had still existed for the Latins, was obscured by the atmosphere of Christian piety in which the Ancients worked: but there remained an intention "to represent a few momentary passages of a Golden Age": an impatience with Christian precept that evidently alarmed his mother. "It seems to me," she wrote, in a letter that was both affectionate and dampening, "whether on poetry, philosophy, or religion, all that you read tends to a dangerous disquiet, instead of that calm acceptance of the wonders of wisdom that you discover in the revelations of God."

The presence of divergent feelings and influences gives a unique charm to the small products of the youthful Calvert's art. They have that "determinate" outline which was Blake's legacy to the "Ancients", the fervour which somehow transferred itself from their mode of life to paper, a gem-like quality which may have come from the study of ancient gems, a reminiscence of "primitives" of northern rather than southern Europe. But what one notices also is a sensuous appreciation of the human figure that none of the others displays. Blake's figures are sexless in spite of their triumphant nudity, just as those thundering passages in which he praises passion seem rather a blow struck for personal freedom than an actual feeling for amorous delight. Palmer's figures are no more than incidental shadows in his landscape compositions. It is only when we turn to Calvert that the softness and warmth of flesh impart to the restlessly moving outlines something of physical life. The "Bride" of his exquisite copper-engraving is voluptuous in rounded and swelling form. The small wood-engraving *The Chamber Idyll*, in technical quality as beautiful a print as artist has ever produced, is erotic and unabashed, so full, simply and approvingly, of erotic pleasure without a touch of prudery, that during the prolonged tyranny of the Victorian age Calvert thought it necessary to keep it in a portfolio out of sight.

Perhaps of all, his water-colour *The Primitive City* is his most remarkable achievement, once again with its seductive feminine figure that is in piquant contrast with the simplified and "primitive" trees. This little painting with its deep stained-glass blue is like an illumination of the Middle Ages, or it may be truer to say, like a fragment of background in a work by some northern master delighting in the opportunity it gave of introducing the various detail of quaintly irregular buildings, yet having also seen and striven to emulate the figure as painted by other artists who had shed the awkwardness and restraints of the mediaeval outlook. It is the hybrid nature of this delicate hybrid that constitutes its endless fascination.

There were in Shoreham and the Shoreham period of its devotees the makings of a "School", though this is a term that can scarcely be applied. The great schools of Europe had drawn their strength and solidity from a craft steadily and expertly practised: the exercise of which, for one reason or another, was required by their world. Important though feeling was in any work of art they had not depended on feeling alone—yet this was the inevitable condition of the Ancients: it was the mental tension and exaltation derived from Blake that gave them a temporary union and power, though if once the tension were withdrawn they had no resource on which to fall back. Their passionate expression was short-lived, and this perhaps is a measure of their distance from greatness. The genius of Blake could maintain itself through a lifetime of adversity and combat: but now the roaring torrent of nine-teenth-century change was poised, ready to burst over the world in which his followers lived, sweeping them away from those moorings and bulwarks they had tried to erect against it, breaking into the valley of vision, attacking the mind itself. It is necessary to follow them further, without confining attention to their prodigious youth, not only to understand the nature of the new age but also to estimate how far the spirit and influence of Blake were capable of surviving.

8

THE ROMANTIC AFTERMATH

THE Victorian Age, intervening between us and the last
defiant phase of Romanticism in the early years of the
nineteenth century, is so decided in character that it
creates the impression of a clean break with the past and seems
to relegate Blake and those sympathetic with him to a distant
and lost realm of ideas : so that we have to remind ourselves of
subtleties in transition and the process of decay that in the new
age accompanied its extraordinary growth.

In several ways the reaction against the "classic" and
rational eighteenth century in which Blake had played so
individual a part, went on. Awakened religious feeling, dividing
itself between a leaning towards the old faith and various types
of nonconformity, High Church and Low, became ever stronger.
The sense of identification with the Gothic past produced the
long series of churches and other buildings in the Gothic style.
A decaying romanticism is to be found in the paintings of
historical themes which transported the middle-class patron to
scenes of unaccustomed splendour. On the other hand the
science Blake despised and the industry of which he knew
nothing made for a material and realistic outlook. It is a
strange medley of decadent forms and ideas and new and
hopeful conceptions that accompanies the century's extraordinary growth.

Among the pupils or followers of Fuseli, who died in 1825,
the lingering romantic strain is to be found in its most morbid
aspect. They are strange creatures indeed, whom one imagines
despairing and demented in the darkness of the 1840's : in
contrast with the average painter of the time who had by now
no other ambition than to entertain the middle class with
pictorial anecdotes. In this decade, marked principally by the
banality of art and by the uneasy compound of industrial wealth

and misery and swarming population, one encounters such a
tragic figure as Benjamin Robert Haydon, and the less distinct
but equally tragic figures of Theodor von Holst and Richard
Dadd. It was in 1846 that Haydon committed suicide after a
life in which all the romantic egotism was exaggerated. By
comparison with this wild and agonized man, with his ambitions to paint colossal "ideal subjects", his feeling of persecution
and the behaviour that invited it, causing him to be "looked at
like a monster, abused like a plague and avoided like a maniac",
Blake appears the most normal of beings. It is an irony of
Haydon's career that with his romantic mentality he should
have possessed an admirable Hogarthian talent for depicting
scenes of popular life, a talent which his own aspirations
condemned, and that he should be known to posterity by two
such pieces, the *Mock Election* and *Chairing the Member* (in the
Tate Gallery) rather than by his huge *Macbeth* or *The Burning
of Rome by Nero*.

The mysterious Theodor von Holst, born in 1810, of Livo-
nian origin, was a pupil of Fuseli at the Royal Academy, and so
closely one of his followers that some of his works seem to have
been attributed to Fuseli. The title of one of his paintings
Satan and the Virgin Mary dancing on the Edge of the World sufficiently indicates the strange and wild quality of his imagination.
The pathological element is to be gleaned from a passage in
William Bell Scott's memoirs, in which he describes his meeting as a young man with various artists in the London of the
1840's—vivid is his account of this person of deranged imagination and the persecution mania which would suddenly cause
him, for no apparent reason and in the middle of a conversation,
to make off in panic and leap down a whole flight of stairs.

Von Holst died in 1844. With him, even more a figure of
strangeness and terror, it seems natural to place Richard Dadd,
who was born in 1817 and came to the Royal Academy Schools
not long after Fuseli died. Here again was an imagination
trembling on the verge of insanity, irrevocably merged with it,
after a crisis which led to his murdering his father and a life-
long confinement (he lived until 1887) in Bethlehem Hospital
and Broadmoor. One of the strangest of English nineteenth-
century paintings is the unfortunate Dadd's *The Fairy Feller's
Masterstroke*—a kind of Midsummer Night's Dream such as

Fuseli might have conceived, with full-bosomed and enigmatic elves which might be Fuseli's own, yet with something of a Victorian appearance. There is a prodigious and perhaps an insane industry in the minuteness of detail, the blades of grass and stones among which the gruesome little people stand and the "fairy feller" swings his hammer, like the work of a demented Pre-Raphaelite. There is something horrifying in the detailed realism and the fancy to which it gives an authentic and unpleasant life. Again, by comparison, the fancy of a Blake is that of sanity.

There was no "school of Fuseli", though there were these exaggerations of the mood which led him to declare he aimed rather to build "a pyramid than a cottage", the grandiose ambition that becomes paranoiac in Haydon, the delight in the macabre that becomes the disquieting fairyland of Dadd. The work of the Ancients of Shoreham never displayed this dramatic violence but the later history of Blake's admirers and followers has its own drama. Either they turned by degrees into typical and successful Victorians or else drifted into an ineffective and submissive relationship with their time, lost in gentle and confused dreaming or speculation and pathetically divested of that creative power that Blake had awakened and for a brief while sustained in them. Of the first evolution, John Linnell and George Richmond are examples; of the second, Palmer and Calvert.

In the life of John Linnell one follows the making of a Victorian—that gradual change in the individual, as revealing of the character of the age as the advent of railways and the tremendous expansion of industry, converting the lively and not unattractive young man of the Regency into the hardened and dominant paterfamilias of the mid-century.

The delicacy and kindness of his behaviour towards Blake is beyond question, nor did he fail in loyalty after Blake's death. He was good to Mrs. Blake, installing her in the house in Cirencester Place which he used mainly as a studio and where previously he would have been glad for both her and her husband to have lived. Here she stayed for the best part of a year, and meanwhile Linnell bestirred himself on her behalf. Little exception could be taken to the plain and yet modest account of his assistance in his effort to dispose of a number of Blake's

works to Lord Egremont. "Mr. Linnell was intimately
acquainted with the author, and was his employer in the above
work when he had nothing to do. Mr. Linnell's means were not
adequate to pay Mr. Blake according to his merit, or such a
work should have placed him in moderate independence . . .
Mr. Linnell begs permission also to mention that he has in his
possession about one hundred original designs by Mr. Blake on
a larger scale, forming a complete illustration to the whole of
Dante.

"Many are in an unfinished state, but the greater number
are, and are more powerfully coloured and finished than he
usually did. They were done for Mr. Linnell in return for
moneys advanced to Mr. Blake when he had no other resources." (Mrs. Blake had sent them to Linnell as his property,
seeing that he had paid for them).

"The sum, however, was inconsiderable compared to the
value of the drawings and Mr. Linnell's object being only to
relieve the necessities of his friend as far as he was able, he is
now willing to part with the drawings for the benefit of the
widow, and if he can obtain a price something more adequate
he will engage to hand over the difference to Mrs. Blake."

Lord Egremont did not buy the Dante series, though he paid
eighty guineas for one large water colour: but if the Dante
drawings can now be admired by the public in the Tate Gallery,
Linnell must be thanked for conserving them and making this
ultimately possible. He would, indeed, have been the ideal
executor, a man of method as well as reverence, who would
have allowed no fragment of Blake's efforts to be overlooked,
wasted or uselessly dispersed. It is unfortunate that the executor (if so definite a word is appropriate) was not Linnell
but Frederick Tatham, into whose possession the bulk of
Blake's manuscripts and designs passed on the death of Catherine Blake in 1831. That this was a bequest, investing Tatham
with full discretion, is implied in Gilchrist's Life of Blake,
though Linnell in his copy wrote at this point his emphatic
"No". He refused to give up the Dante drawings on Tatham's
demand, which proved the value of the businesslike written
agreement he had made and can only have the warmest
approval.

The singular and lamentable episode of the destruction of

Blake's manuscripts by Tatham, one of his most valued friends, is a commentary on two things—the fact that he had revealed himself to his followers in only one aspect, and that therefore they imperfectly understood him; and secondly on the growing Puritanism of the nonconformity that had always characterized the circles in which Blake moved. Blake's thought, daring, revolutionary, anti-Puritan, the thought of a man who had known and sympathized with Godwin and Paine, was beyond his followers. They could not appreciate the sequence of ideas and events that had moulded an earlier generation any more than those conditioned to the second World War of the twentieth century could understand the rebellious scepticism of the 1920's. And, good simple creatures as they were, it must be confessed that they were conventional enough to be shocked by some extravagance of Blake's, too limited in intellect and too humourless to respond to his paradoxes. Even Linnell, whose intelligence, if narrow, was not exactly conventional, was eventually critical of Blake's opinions and expression in words, as may be gathered from the paper of 1855 found among his "literary remains". "A saint amongst the infidels, a heretic with the orthodox"—this is an admirable and hardly disapproving estimate of the master. "But," he adds, "with all the admiration (possible) for Blake, it must be confessed that he said many things tending to the corruption of Christian morals, even when unprovoked by controversy, and when opposed by the superstitious, the crafty, or the proud, he outraged all common-sense and rationality by the opinions he advanced, occasionally even indulging in the support of the most lax interpretation of the precepts of the Scriptures." So far was the mid-Victorian mood from the romantic defiance of a half-century earlier. Frederick Tatham was not content merely to note these presumable failings and flaws in the great man he had known. He had become an "Irvingite", a follower, that is, of the Scottish preacher, Edward Irving (1792–1834) and in due course was a member of that "Catholic and Apostolic" Church which was founded on Irving's teaching. It was one of the many nonconformist efforts to expand and make a contemporary creed of the basic truths of the Christian religion. In its insistence on the oneness of all with Christ in the attributes of humanity, the importance it attached to prophetic utterance, its anticipation of revelation to come, it seems, to a lay mind, to have its points of likeness with the Swedenborgianism Blake had once professed and even with beliefs from which he never departed. Yet for the groping and intensely serious mind, the more devoted to severe and literal precept because of the need to extricate itself from confusion and bewilderment, it was impossible to overlook or condone the witty diabolism of Blake's utterances. It was necessary, for the sake of Blake himself, that this side of him should be kept from view. Religious zeal and personal affection alike consigned precious and unpublished documents to the flames.

One might think that Linnell in his severity of principle was another example of this growing tendency to suppression; though Linnell as a man of religion is a peculiar study and in this aspect very near to Blake seeing that he found it impossible to attach himself for long to any organized body or intermediary with heaven: was too nonconformist even to recognize nonconformity. His correspondence, mainly of the year 1830, with the Quaker poet, Bernard Barton, is interesting in showing his wish to associate himself with the Quakers and the pugnacious independence that prevented him from doing so.

The letters begin with a discussion of Blake, whose illustrations of Job Linnell had sent for Barton to look at. The Quaker poet could not but wish that Blake "could have clothed his imaginative creations in a garb more attractive to ordinary mortals" while allowing "a more enduring meed of praise . . . to the excellence and sterling worth of the man": but an amiable enough attitude to art turned into doubt whether as Linnell proposed an artist should or could become a Quaker. "I see no irreconcilable hostility between the religious principles of Friends and the indulgence of a taste for painting." On the other hand, "I am quite aware that a Quaker painter would be a still greater novelty than a Quaker poet, and am almost inclined to doubt whether the former would not have a still more difficult and delicate task to perform than the latter if he hoped to be regarded by the body as orthodox and consistent." Pictures were "a species of laxity and latitudinarianism . . . barely tolerated amongst us". This, however, was not the main issue. When it came to the point, as Barton perceived, Linnell was ready to subscribe to the Quaker faith only so far as it suited him. "I fear when you say that 'the unanimity of religious sentiment must be cordial and entire not doubtful or partial' that you mean something like a submission of the judgment to human authority"—which Linnell would die rather than admit.

He did not turn Quaker; nor, at a later date, did he pin his loyalty to the Plymouth Brethren, though in the 1840's he felt a certain sympathy with them from their equality among themselves and the absence of appointed ministers or preachers. But even here organization asserted itself, there were those who sought to become leaders and priests and once again Linnell refused to accept any such authority. The slightest hint of "priestcraft" was anathema to him. After giving up the Brethren he claimed the right to worship in his own way; and in fact arrived as Blake had done at a religion of his own.

This determination to be free, this rooted dislike of all ritual, ceremony and acknowledgment of man-made rules, gives to Linnell a semblance of being in some respects an unconventional person. When George Richmond in 1831 made a runaway marriage with Julia Tatham, Frederick's sister, in defiance of the father's opposition to the match, Linnell approved. To fly to Gretna Green was preferable to enduring the pomp of a church service; and when the senior Tatham came to him with the anger and grief of outraged parental tyranny, he was met with cool and deflating opinion. "It is you," said Linnell, "who are making a great mistake. This marriage is a matter of strong congratulation for I am convinced that Mr. Richmond will one day prove a great honour to your family." In the same way, when Samuel Palmer in 1837 desired to marry Linnell's eldest daughter, Hannah, the father insisted that they should be married "according to the new Act of Parliament" at the Registrar's Office, Marylebone. It is to be remarked that he "insisted". His word was law, though he flouted custom. A consequence of his refusal to bend the knee was that others should bend the knee to him; disdaining priesthood he himself became a species of high priest; and more than that, in his sole or direct communication with divine authority, he assumed its prerogative, turning into a domestic Jehovah.

This role and his sense of power were fostered by a material

prosperity partly due to his industry and thrift and partly to
the increasing middle-class wealth that now made many new
patrons of art. The basis of Linnell's fortune was portraiture
for which he was principally known until about 1847 (in that
year he was fifty-six). His portraits included those of Sir Thomas
Peel and (1844) of Thomas Carlyle. His commissions were
endless and to the house he built for himself at Porchester
Terrace, Bayswater, he added a studio of suitable dignity—a
precursor of the great Victorian studios, fifty feet by twenty
with three top lights. Yet landscape was his main interest and
in middle-age not only was he able to devote himself to it but
his landscapes were no less popular than his portraits. The new
type of patronage from the wealthy men of the industrial world
and the scale of prices that a successful painter might now
command are shown by the commissions he received from the
Birmingham manufacturer of pen-nibs, Joseph Gillott, who
paid £1,000 for Linnell's *The Eve of the Deluge*, exhibited at the
Royal Academy in 1848.

In his early days in Bayswater there were fields all round the
house: a landscape painter need not stir more than a few
hundred yards for his study of a grassy bank with grazing
sheep, of fine old trees: but during the 1840's the tide of London
building swept over the rural surroundings, and he began to
think of moving into the country. The railways were spreading
out from the metropolis; and it was near Redhill Junction on
the London—Brighton line that he found a place suiting him,
no valley of vision but a hill commanding the district around.
Here he built a roomy villa, styleless and ugly in a Victorian
fashion, but with large windows giving (among other aspects
of nature) an excellent view of the Surrey sunset. He quietly
bought parcels of the surrounding woodland until he owned
some eighty acres. In due course, Redstone Wood became a
"colony"; satellite villas were built for Linnell's sons, James
and William. He reigned over his wife, children and grand-
children in patriarchal, in Old Testament state.

There was something in this mode of life of that self-
sufficiency for which William Morris (in Linnell's lifetime)
yearned. The grinding of corn, the making of flour, the baking
of bread, the brewing of beer, the collection of honey from his
beehives, the preparation of the pure pigments he used, all this

made up his existence as well as painting. He seemed, like
many Victorians, to gain energy from the energetic times; and
the hard physical labour he enjoyed had a beneficial effect on
an originally delicate frame. He lived to be ninety, painting
until the end (he died in 1882). He married a second time, a
year after the death of his wife, and when he was seventy-four
(1866)—at the Reigate registry office. In these later days, when
picture buying had become a vogue, his landscapes were sold
before they were finished—for anything from 1,500 to 2,000
guineas—prices at which Blake might well have wondered.

In his own domain he had absolute power, which according
to a famous aphorism, corrupts absolutely. Suddenly one is
aware of a dark side to this interesting and individual career;
aware that the independent yet sedulously cultivated religion
might become, in his grandson's word, "dreadful"; that the
delight in the "beauty of cash payments" could turn into the
miserly greed that hugged bags of gold; that the reign of this
"house-despot" had its stifling and cruel side, could be feared
and hated even by those within the family circle who were submissive to it. It was perhaps through a like pious materialism,
through a similar sense of personal power, never checked and
thus tending to a sadistic tyranny, that the father of Elizabeth
Barrett became that remarkable tyrant whom the modern
mind has no hesitation in pillorying but finds it difficult to
comprehend. It is from this unprepossessing aspect that we
view Linnell when we consider the life and work of Samuel
Palmer after the Shoreham period. His son regarded his life
as a tragedy and was, there are many indications, convinced
the Linnell family was responsible for a tragic frustration.
There can be no doubt it was an uncomfortable association,
nor that Palmer was one of the casualties of this new, harsh,
ugly, striving, confused and confusing epoch from which the
consoling and powerful idealism of Blake seemed already so far
away.

Even in the valley of vision and before the Victorian age
began there was the restlessness of coming change, of the trend
of events that was to destroy the idyllic contentment of rural
England: to alter the balance of power between agriculture and
industry: to give the Industrial Revolution and the manufac-
turers of the industrial towns a legalized triumph. The Reform

Bill of 1832 in retrospect is an inevitable measure—but to one
like Palmer seemed an abominable thing, the project of a
"profane and atrocious faction" who caused, and played upon,
agricultural distress, inciting the labourers to burn the ricks of
their employers, as part of a plan to encompass the ruin of all
that was beautiful and old. His *Address to the Electors of West
Kent* survives only in the fiery excerpts quoted disapprovingly
by the *Maidstone Gazette* as "gross invectives and foul vitupera-
tions", but from these it is evident how bitterly Palmer resented
the "march of progress" in the form of political Radicalism.
"It is strange," says A. H. Palmer in the life of his father, "that
in spite of his wide reading, in spite of the almost universal
misery of the agricultural classes—misery of which he must
have heard even in thrice-happy Shoreham—his arguments
should have leaned in the most party-spirited manner possible
to the side opposed to reform." Alas, it is all too clear that Palmer was trying to prolong the enchantment he had personally
found in his youthful years, that the reality of present and an
apprehended future threatened the romantic dream that had
placed church, village and peasantry in his conservative and
backward-looking imagination beyond the reach of change. It
was an instinctive aversion from the Victorian age to come
that caused this single polemic outburst on a matter of politics,
with which otherwise he had little concern.

Palmer's limited income put an end to his stay at Shoreham
in 1833. To be professionally self-supporting it was necessary
to live and work in London (whence the visits of his friends to
the "valley" had become less frequent). From 1833 until his
marriage in 1838 he lived alone (his father had taken to school-
mastering) looked after by his old nurse, Mary Ward, at a
small house in Grove Street, Lisson Grove, not very far from
the Linnells at Porchester Terrace and the Calverts at Park
Place, Paddington.

It is in these years that a mood of anxiety and uncertainty
begins to show itself in his letters and memoranda. With a view
to "enlarging his vision" he made painting expeditions, with
Calvert and Henry Walter, into Devonshire and North Wales.
For a whole succession of watercolourists the Welsh journey
had been an inspiring experience, yet the mountains disturbed
and impressed Palmer rather than inspired him. The pastoral

had "stretched into an epic", which daunted him. Tintern Abbey (the "highest Gothic") alone called out real enthusiasm; for it he "would give all the Welsh mountains grand as they are". He was short enough of money to call on George Richmond for the loan of three pounds to get home. "Poetic vapours have subsided, and the sad realities of life blot the field of vision: the burden of the theme is a heavy one . . . O! miserable poverty! How it wipes off the bloom from everything around me . . ." He felt "as if I alone of all mankind were fated to get no bread by the sweat of my brow".

Was it that he was being torn from his moorings, was it his new anxiety to embark on a professional career, in an efficient manner productive of material return, that caused his confidence to waver? In fretful notes he accused himself of "*Feebleness* of first conception through bodily weakness, and consequent timidity of execution". He reminded himself of the need to "aim at once at some splendid arrangement", to "let everything be colour", to "try to get something beautiful in the first design". These were excellent intentions but his splendid work at Shoreham had shown no need of such reminders. It was precisely in the beauty of first design, and, when he used colour, in its unsullied glow, that he had excelled, with both daring and decision. Yet then he had been single-minded, as Blake had been; now, attempting to look at life in a more practical fashion, its problems rose huge before him, making him waver. The weakness which was a kind of bewilderment, dispelled for a time by the example of Blake's courageous assertion, returned. If there was an evil genius in this it lies in his own self-consciousness. He had, one might almost think, begun to imagine himself into mediocrity.

On the quaking mental foundation was laid the heavy weight of the Linnell alliance. It did not, perhaps, augur well for his marriage with Hannah Linnell that the father-in-law should insist on the absence of that ceremony both would have preferred. With retrospective bitterness of exclamation, the aged Palmer entered in his note-book, "S.P. was married at the Courthouse, Marylebone; he, a churchman!" The will of the father-in-law pursued them on their honeymoon—without stirring from Bayswater he was able to direct their activities in Rome. He had planned—and even at the outset of Queen

Victoria's reign this seems very Victorian—a whole series of edifying and improving tasks for his daughter in particular, against which she had no thought of rebellion. She spent every day in making the copies of Raphael's Stanze and the frescoes in the Sistine Chapel her father had instructed her to make. "My dear daughter Hannah," he writes in September 1838, "I am very glad to find you are struggling with the real difficulties of the Art; as I have no doubt but with Mr. Palmer's assistance you will accomplish enough to produce some beautiful works; and, what is of more consequence, increase your capability of receiving those inspiring impressions of beauty and sublimity that nature was intended to produce." This, being translated, meant a regime of constant hard labour (added to the Palmers' poverty) during a stay in Italy which extended into two years.

"A wilderness of wonders", was Palmer's description of Rome, and his choice of the word "wilderness" suggests the difficulty he found in adapting himself to or deriving any benefit from the capital of art, although the letters he wrote to his friends, Giles, Calvert, the Richmonds, are full of the proper enthusiasm with which a tourist should write. His main impressions were of blue skies, a light more brilliant than that of his own country, of glittering palaces; but of what use were these impressions to one who had found his true pleasure in the twilights and moonlights of Kent? It is from this journey that one may date not only the loss of romantic intensity in his paintings and drawings but of a vain effort to catch the brightness of the Mediterranean atmosphere, to give a richness of colour that unfortunately became garish in its warmth. He did not simply copy masters, he looked at the place with a vision insidiously readjusted to the imitation of reality, an external and objective reality with which (as much of a "little Englander" in spirit as Blake) he had nothing to do. The epic of European architecture and painting, the landscape he could know only in tourist fashion, overwhelmed the lyricism of Shoreham. It would perhaps have been better if, like his revered master, he had never left English ground.

It is evident, as Blake became a figure of memory, that Palmer turned to Linnell for advice and encouragement, some of which was unexceptionable, and if Linnell did not kindle the spirit in the same way, this is the faculty only of the very exceptional being. Linnell spoke indeed somewhat deprecatingly of his own efforts and successes, "pleasing those most who know but little of Art but who are kind enough to employ me. I endeavour to learn contentment, notwithstanding a deep sense of professional insufficiency . . ." He spoke warmly of a "spiritual Art". "Anyone like Mr. Richmond, leaving the Vanity Fair of Art and entering the wicket-gate to go to the New Jerusalem, is such a reproach to those who stay behind, from whichever cause, that I could despise myself for not following him if I did not feel that my family is an excuse which I have no right to evade." Yet he did not advise Palmer to think only of profit. "You, I feel, are in the right road to distinction and need not care about present and immediate return so much . . ." In fact (1839) he was decidedly averse to Palmer's desperate, money-making plan of "little oil pictures and drawings painted in a day at once from Nature". Said Linnell, "Don't think at present of doing anything of the pot-boiling description." Better to teach for money, and take pains with some outstanding work "for reputation". Even so his native shrewdness presents this course as a matter of policy and not idealism alone. "One successful picture in the Exhibition will raise the value of all you have by you 100 per cent."

A man of thirty-four, Palmer came back from the glow of Italy to the darkness and depression of London in the 1840's with little comfort. He was keenly aware of his deficiencies professionally, especially in oil-painting which he had never mastered. Neither he nor his wife could sell their pictures. "Mr. Ruskin and others," we read in 1842, "were shown our drawings," but Ruskin, a young man who had just taken his B.A. degree and had not yet given the world the first volume of *Modern Painters*, was presumably not impressed, seeing that there is no further mention of the budding critic and patron. Palmer made a small living as one of the many tutors in water-colour painting who gave instruction in families regarding it as a polite amateur accomplishment. His uncertainty as to his aims is further illustrated by some notes of 1843 in which he attempts to reconcile opposites. "Try to make my things first Poetic; second Effective." "Poetic" were the subjects he loved— "British; Romantic; Classic; Ideal". "Effective" means the

effect of Nature, the realism of the new age; "studying phenomena in the country". Here was the difficulty which it needed
a powerful character to resolve, the problem of rejecting or
accepting the present or the past. If Blake had been at his
elbow, how quickly that fine intelligence would have affirmed
the desire for what was romantic or poetic, have pointed out the
essential conflict between the Poetic and the Effective, have
destroyed, with telling phrase, the study of "phenomena" as
that of the "vegetative universe". The study of phenomena, on
the other hand, if defended firmly, would have relegated
poetry and romance to the past, would have declared it a
falsity in this age of scientific, industrial and social advance or
complication. This was the decade in which the liberal, or
radical, sentiment Palmer so feared and hated made men look
at things as they were, at life as it was; the decade in which the
French painter, Gustave Courbet, declared himself a "realist",
painting with sullen weight the rocks of his countryside, the
straining muscles of peasant and artisan. Yet France was far
away. If the theories and work of a Courbet were unpalatable
to fellow-countrymen, artists and others, how much more so
would they have been to a conservative Englishman. It is
likely that Courbet's pictures would have offended Palmer by
the uncompromising and even brutal fashion in which they
spurned the idyll. Palmer's own note hints at a compromise
that refused to face, or was not aware of, the issues profoundly
involved.

Through the mid-Victorian years Palmer struggled not only
with these questions of art but with a poverty from which he
could not extricate himself and the responsibility of a family.
They moved in 1848 from Marylebone to 1a Victoria Road,
Kensington, a detached cottage, and after three years there to
Douro Place, not far away. A. H. Palmer, the son, who was
keenly aware of the shortcomings of Victorian architecture,
speaks of their dwelling there with contempt as "a hideous little
semi-detached house with a prim little garden at the back and
front, and an ample opportunity of profiting by the next-door
neighbours' musical proclivities". The sculptor, John Bell,
whose coldly sweet statuary was prominent in the Great Exhibition, lived at one end in some prosperity, but at the other was a
high wall and squalor. The vast studio of Linnell, impressive in

THE WHIRLWIND OF LOVERS (from Dante), by Blake

DANTE'S DREAM, by D. G. Rossetti

End of "THE SONG OF JERUSALEM," by Blake

its effect on dealers and clients, was not for Palmer. He had none. The little "drawing-room" facing south, equipped with shabby scantiness, kitchen chairs, a student's easel, and untidy home-made portfolios, served the purpose. The gay tinkle of the barrel-organ—squalor made audible—drifted in derisively from the street as he toiled with dissatisfaction at the "continuous movement of works for sale".

Blake would not have been downcast by such material conditions, had indeed patiently endured them most of his life. To do Palmer justice he struggled manfully, and, as he put it in one of his quaintly humorous phrases, like a "Christian bulldog" : but far worse than poverty and squalor was that state of indecision as to what he really wanted to achieve which made him hanker so often after "a new plan", a "New Style". Why, he asked himself, did he wish for a New Style? His own answers are not very convincing: "to save time" ; "to govern all by broad powerful chiaroscuro" ; "to ABOLISH all NIGGLE" but these matters seem incidental to some greater issue he had not touched on. He absorbed himself in questions of craftsmanship—the craft of oil painting, the craft of etching, yet in a tentative amateur vein rather than as a master in middle-age. The confident young man of Shoreham had, as it were, become another person. When he, Calvert and Giles foregathered of an evening, it was a pleasure mixed with sadness to turn over the drawings, dusty now in their tattered portfolios, that brought back for a moment his early inspiration : and the unwearying delight with which Giles pored over them seemed to be devoted to some dead and forgotten genius.

This period of Palmer's life came to an end in 1861. It was in that year his eldest son, More Palmer, died at the age of nineteen. He was called More after the saintly Sir Thomas whom Samuel Palmer so venerated. All his father's affection was concentrated on him. He showed talent, though it was a matter of some parental regret that this was for music rather than painting. Yet poor More fell ill and died while on holiday at a farmhouse near Abinger in Surrey. In agony of mind, Samuel Palmer was taken to Linnell's house at Redhill. He was too sensitive to endure the last rites. Linnell whose opposition to ceremony applied equally to a funeral as to a wedding, did not attend. More's mother mourned at Abinger alone.

The family moved after this trial to a villa near Redhill— Furze Hill House, rather because it happened to be vacant than out of deliberate preference. It was even more hideously Victorian in A. H. Palmer's eyes than Douro Place, a genteel "Gothic villa" of the 1860's "pretentious outside and inconvenient within". The "railway town" nearby was "as ugly as you could find", though if you chose to overlook it there were lovely views of the surrounding country. It was also Linnell country; the Palmers were now within the zone, physical and spiritual, of the patriarchal colony, and this must have been an added misery to those Samuel Palmer already had to bear.

There was more than one cause of conflict. It was a standing grievance of Linnell in his ultimate nonconformity that his daughter should belong to the Church of England, and be married to a man not only of this adherence but suspect of leanings to Rome. Warfare, consequently, took the form of an attempt to wean Palmer's wife from her allegiance and of a campaign of sneers and ridicule at his "Puseyite" or "Jesuitical" tendencies. To this Linnell applied himself in a cruel and cutting fashion, the habit of mind that had grown with power, the prickliness that had in the past antagonized many fellow-artists and caused him to be cold-shouldered by the Royal Academy. An early letter (1839) already shows his type of what A. H. Palmer called "mental pugilism" in the letter written after dispute to "Dear Palmer, You say you are related to the Fox family. I thought so. It is a pity you were not named Fox Palmer instead of Samuel. It wd. be so characteristic of your doubles & turns in argument. Why," said Linnell with ferocious joviality, "you are like Mrs. Quickly—a man knows not where to have you—here in the last letter received only yesterday you pretend to be innocent of all provoking language & take great praise to yourself for not roaring like a Lion. Whoever heard a Fox do so? No, he gains his point by secret sly means."

It was also a reason for contempt in this hardened successful man that Palmer was a failure. It is true that even the latter's unworldliness was unable to resist the late-Victorian picture-buying wave, though others might have profited by it more. In spite of himself he sold pictures enough in his later years to live comfortably. Yet what was he in the eyes of his relations but an insignificant member of the Water-Colour Society? An ineffective eccentric, this was how he appeared in the eyes of the Linnell family group which whatever the differences and hatreds it contained within itself could combine against the stranger. If we go by the notes on his character supplied by Linnell's son, John, to his father's biographer, they granted him humour, but otherwise deemed his sentiment "puerile", his mind "too fanciful and wild"; decided that he lived "in atmosphere of sentimental imagination and feeling not always in touch with truth or *real fact*". Almost, he acquiesced in the view they took of him, choosing to appear, as he remarked in wistful musing on the young man he had been, "only a poor good-natured fellow fond of a harmless jest".

He did not retaliate actively against Linnell; in the years of hostile neighbourliness it is strange to think of them together, two little bearded men in their heavy Victorian artists' suits with double-breasted waistcoats and in that corner of Surrey from which by some untoward enchantment of the time all things seemed turned to ugliness, all sense of art to be lost. The one, dry, acrid, masterful, the other mild and enclosing his inoffensiveness and his sense of failure in a show of humour. It was a sign of submission that Samuel Palmer, in spite of the manifest gulf existing between him and his father-in-law, should in painting have grown like him. Highly finished, sometimes unpleasantly or discordantly warm in key of colour, realistic and yet somehow lacking in the conviction or spirit of reality, their landscapes are often very similar. Even in art the stronger personality dominated the other, though neither rose above a middle level of their period or anywhere near the sphere of greatness.

Both continued to paint until nearly the end of their days, Linnell outliving Palmer by a year. Holman Hunt visited Linnell in the year before his death, described the old man lifting a Bible in his trembling hand as he asked Hunt "if he had made sure of his eternal salvation". Far indeed had Linnell and Palmer travelled from the time when they knew William Blake, into an entirely different age which had engraved its stamp on both, yet those early days had seen them at their best.

The pattern of success and failure is repeated in the careers of George Richmond and Edward Calvert. It is a sensitive and attractive face that looks out at us from the miniature self portrait inscribed "George Richmond, painted by himself for our marriage" in 1830. He was twenty-one, the beautiful Julia Tatham somewhat younger. Their departure in January, 1831, (properly enough) in separate post-chaises that careered through the snow to Gretna Green, was quite in the spirit of the romantic decade. He struck an observer of the time as "Byronic in appearance", she as "a dainty little fairy" : but neither was unpractical. They settled down at once to making a career. The Virgilian pastoral in the manner of Blake, the attempt to paint cosmic events, such as "The Creation of Light", in the spirit of the Job engravings, the Dante water-colours, gave way to the painting of portraits at a few guineas each and a fortunate introduction started Richmond off on a highly successful course. They were invited to dine with Sir Robert Inglis, friend of Wilberforce and guardian of the nine orphan children of the wealthy banker, Henry Thornton. Through the kindly planning of this household the young painter made a portrait of Wilberforce himself. He caught the aged advocate of the abolition of slavery in a typical pose, pensively comparing, as was his habit, the time kept by the two watches he carried. Wilberforce died in the same year, the portrait was engraved and became widely known; its painter was sought after.

Samuel Palmer, writing from Shoreham in 1834, observes, "As you are now become a great man, I will address you on a sheet of my best writing-paper . . ." Richmond was twenty-eight with a practice that brought him in some £1,000 a year when in 1837 he set off for Rome with his wife and a small son, staying for two years in circumstances that contrast strongly with those of the Palmers. Instead of penury and laborious copying, they enjoyed the acquaintance of Joseph Severn, the painter friend of Keats and one of the lights of Roman society. They made useful contact with distinguished tourists; with Henry Wordsworth Acland, later the famous Regius Professor of Medicine at Oxford, the young William Ewart Gladstone, then Conservative M.P. for Newark. It was at Rome in 1840 that Richmond met John Ruskin, fresh from Oxford, where he had won the Newdigate Prize in the previous year, embarked on his first European travels, and also to become a later friend.

Richmond's was a long, industrious and full life—in which there was nothing to regret for he had in his art done all that was natural to him or that he was capable of doing. Those early essays in Blake's style were simply essays, they could be given up without pain or struggling afterthought. The Victorian Age welcomed him with open arms, he became completely identified with it. He lived to be eighty-seven, until 1896, uneventfully in a sense, unless one chooses to call each of his sitters an event; in which case his career becomes a brilliant and bustling panorama of politics and the Church, of letters and science. He drew or painted Manning, Newman and Keble, Faraday and Darwin, Harriet Martineau, Charlotte Brontë, Mrs. Gaskell, Elizabeth Fry, Samuel Rogers, Thomas Moore, Hallam, Macaulay, Thackeray, Gladstone, Lord Salisbury, the Prince of Wales. His knack of keeping a likeness while contriving, if not to flatter, at all events to bring out the best in his sitter, was generally recognized and approved.

Of the marriage ten children lived to grow up. He ruled his house with the strictness which had become general with the revival of Puritanism, with something of Linnell's patriarchal authority. His sons rose when he entered the room, remained standing until he left. None of them had a latchkey, this he did not permit, and he expected from them obedience without question. One member of the family who spoke jestingly of Abraham he rebuked with the solemn words, "I do not consider it right to speak with levity of the Friend of God."

No longer Byronic; hard and matter-of-fact, his photograph in middle-age invites speculation on the way in which a career like his or the period in which he lived or both together could gradually mould and change the features. The youthful mouth upturned, in 1830, in readiness to smile, now with the passage of years droops grimly; the face is set in rigid and determined lines. His wife, the "dainty little fairy", is changed too; matron of the 1860's, the foot resting on a stool, invisible beneath immense and unbeautiful folds of black satin, she too has a formidable seriousness. The nature of nineteenth-century photography may well have exaggerated this serious air but the feeling remains that what was joyful and spontaneous did not enter into their lives, that they were enclosed in earnestness, respectability and dress like prisoners who were no longer conscious of their imprisonment.

Again the influence of Blake, though Richmond always remembered him with veneration, faded quickly away. This also happened with Edward Calvert, though he, of gentler or more poetic temperament, like Palmer, did not turn to money-making but became wrapped up in his own dream-world.

It is sad to consider Calvert's later drawings and paintings in comparison with those few small and exquisite works of his youth. They are totally changed; not in aiming at some merely commercial or unworthy end, but in a falsity which, strangely enough, seems not at all incompatible with an entire sincerity of character and intention. He was under no necessity, like his friends, of bestirring himself to sell his work and therefore of giving attention to what would sell. His moderate private income sufficed. Nor was he driven and goaded by ambition to seek for fame. Landseer, it is related, borrowed his studio for an equestrian portrait: but, being interested only in painting the horse, proposed that Calvert should contribute the portrait of its rider. This Calvert declined to do, causing his wife to exclaim in affectionate vexation, "Oh, Edward, you will never do anything to make you famous!"

In the new, crowded, sooty, fog-drenched London, spreading and sprawling, with its contrasts of wealth and abject misery, its festering slums and soulless gentility, he walked amiably, seeing not, mentally basking in the sun of an ideal golden land, where Pan played on his pipes and nymphs danced among the rocks and fragrant shrubs. "He is always in Paradise," Mrs. Blake had said of her husband; of Calvert in his later years it might be said he was always in Arcady. The midshipman's glimpse of the Mediterranean, the classics which remained his study, had taken hold of his mind, supplanting anything he might have gained directly from Blake, or in a secondary form through Palmer's briefly ecstatic vision. His heart was in ancient Greece rather than Shoreham. He dreamed, while living at Paddington, of building in his garden a studio like a Greek temple. George Richmond's son retained a vivid memory of the altar "erected to the honour of the great god Pan" (at about the time of the Great Exhibition when Calvert was living at Hampton Court); and of receiving "from the mouth of the ancient sage (Calvert however was only in his fifties) many a picturesque vision in words of the relationship of the ancient gods with the modern world!" When Calvert chose to go abroad it was to Greece (in 1844). His travel notes dwell fondly on the beautiful names, each seeming to evoke and animate a landscape merely by its music. "Wednesday, 15th May—Rise at five. At seven leave Athens on the route to Cephissia. Pass through the village of Amarysia, *hod.*, Macrousi, the country residence of Plato, and a place honoured by the Artemisian Goddess and adding her appellations. (She was the Amarysian Artemis.) Well might it so have been. I had never seen grounds more apparently congenial to her joys than in the slopes and hills of this neighbourhood. Thickets of evergreen oak, lentiscus and pine . . . Afterwards visited the Cave of the Nymphs watered by the Cephissus" . . . Reality in the form of a party of Greek soldiers with the blood-stained corpses of three bandits slung over their horses was a distressing intrusion into the idyllic day-dream, into which he quickly relapsed with the soothing murmur of Mnemosyne and Lethe on his tongue, the thought in his mind of the Castalian spring, the Oracle of Delphi, the fountain and the votive niche. Attachment to Greece entailed that study of the human form of which the ancient artist had such mastery. In this respect Calvert was not unaware of a need for science. In the 1840's he worked sedulously in the Life Academy, St. Martin's Lane, alongside that devoted student of the nude, William Etty. He took up anatomy at St. Bartholomew's Hospital and the School of Anatomy in Gerrard Street. On these excursions into the medical world he came to know Sir James Leighton, who had been physician to the Tsar of Russia, and his grandson, the young Frederic Leighton whose drawing both Etty and Calvert admired, who was to be the famous exemplar of the "classicism" Calvert already pursued.

Colour too had its science. It was on his way back from Greece that Calvert, pausing at Venice, was deeply impressed by the magnificent technique of the Venetian masters. This Venetian richness of colouring appealed to him also in the painting of Etty: Etty who so well copied the *Concert* of Giorgione, "one of the most grateful melodies with which painting presents us". One of the results of reading Plato was Calvert's constantly renewed search for first principles. Many were the tables and plans he drew up, designed to reveal the true basis of art, among them a system of musical colour that transferred the four musical modes of the Greeks—Aeolian, Dorian, Lydian, Phrygian—into visual terms, and sought to establish in detailed tabulation the equivalence of the painter's and the composer's melody.

His remarks on the beauty of Greek myth and legend, on the art of the Venetian masters, on the correspondences between music and painting, are those of a sensitive, a poetic and ingenious mind : it is when the works they produced are examined that doubts arise. Long-lived, like the other principal followers of Blake—he was eighty-four when he died in 1883,—he seems a minor member of that group of baffled searchers after the secret of beauty whose art is so typical and yet incongruous an accompaniment of the later Victorian time. It is in a similar yearning for a classic ideal of form, complicated and confused by an admiration for Venetian colour, that the art of G. F. Watts loses itself in unreality. The follower of Blake, the partner of Samuel Palmer in the Shoreham days is replaced by the contemporary of Watts and Leighton.

His painting indeed had become the opposite of everything that Blake had stood for. Gone completely was the "determinate" outline; instead was the melting softness he had admired in the Venetians, yet could not rescue from an indecisive dimness. The too large problems of technique brought out the amateur rather than the master. For the intense Christian vigour he substituted a literary paganism, a delusive shadow of pastoral and mythic existence among the mountains and olive groves of ancient Greece. That malign and subtle element in the period into which he had come, which while creating on the one hand a robust ugliness, on the other deprived the artist's idealism of its strength, imparted to them an unbearable and saccharine sweetness.

Yet in his retired existence in Darley Road, Hackney, his final place of residence, Calvert, in old age handsome and benevolent-looking with a mane of silky white hair, a square-cut beard, appears the best-intentioned, the most sincere and incorruptible of men in his steadfast pursuit of beauty. Of his early friends John Giles remained (until his death in 1880) h intimate. While that amiable character was uncritical and approving of Calvert's Grecian idylls, yet "he was never tired", Calvert's son records, "of musing over my father's early engravings—the *Ploughman*, the *Cyder Feast*, the *Return Home*, and of all others, the little *Chamber Idyll*, the simplicity of which so transported him". One might apply to Calvert the words he used in tribute to Francis O. Finch: "Living in times adverse to poetic tendencies in pictorial representation (he) pursued his way and his work undiscouraged by neglect, undiverted by example." He said of himself that he had lived "for art's sake"; but the artist in him had not outlasted his youth, the pursuit of the "Beautiful in Life" had become an empty dream.

9

THE INTERPRETER RE-INTERPRETED

ONE might say that Blake after his death was forgotten —in so far as he had ever been known; yet he lived in the memory of those artists who had come into contact with him, however far in their own work they might have shed his influence: he had been a light in their lives, for them no less brilliant as it receded in the distance of time. It was not really long before he again took vivid shape in description. The Scottish poet and journalist, Alan Cunningham, who had worked for Cromek and had some slight acquaintance with Blake, included him no more than two years after his death in his series of "Lives of the Most Eminent British Painters", providing—with information supplied by Linnell and Varley— a highly coloured account of the séances at which Blake drew his mystic apparitions; and paying tribute to his lyric gifts while deploring his "extravagances". Cunningham had been in his youth a stonemason as well as poet, was for many years clerical assistant in the busy studio of the sculptor, Sir Francis Chantrey, and on this account might claim to write with understanding of artists. "I know Blake's character, for I knew the man," he wrote to Linnell. "I shall make a *judicious* use of my materials and be merciful where sympathy is needed." Mercy as regards Blake's poetry is represented by a concluding comment on the unpublished volumes of verse—"If they are as wild and mystical as the poetry of his *Urizen* they are as well in manuscript—if they are as natural and touching as many of his *Songs of Innocence* a judicious selection might be safely published."

Cunningham was not unadmiring, but it is evident that like other contemporary observers he was interested in a strangeness or oddity of character in which he did not find any method or intelligible motive. Blake, to him, was an interesting departure from the general run of humanity, but in no sense one with whom others might feel a close affinity. It was, however, no more than twenty years after, that those again appeared who could feel with Blake, were able to relish his "extravagance" and discern in his career a consistent attitude to life and art, which had some present meaning. In the formation of the Pre-Raphaelite movement, Blake was a concealed yet an important factor; through the two Rossetti brothers, Dante Gabriel and William Michael, he was not only reinstated in a position of honour but became a means of resolving or a factor in the attempt to resolve the place and purpose of the artist in the Victorian age.

The pre-Raphaelite did not escape the characteristic Victorian difficulty of reconciling imagination and reality, past and present. It is a remarkable thing that the movement thrived on the contradictions that had sorely puzzled Samuel Palmer. It was half-romantic, half realist; romantic in its love of the Gothic past, of an alternative world to that with which it was confronted; realist in its doctrine of "Truth to Nature". The contradictions were also those of contradictory personalities within the movement. Its realism, in which it was very contemporary, was that of Holman Hunt and John Everett Millais, its romanticism was that of Rossetti. The former established a link with Linnell. "Truth to Nature" was entirely in accordance with his ideas, nor can he have been displeased by a youthful rebellion against the Royal Academicians who, he felt, had so often slighted or ignored him. "About his generous recognition of our school when it was new, and had enemies innumerable and savage among the elder of the profession," said Holman Hunt, "I can never speak with too much admiration . . . And his seeking us out on one varnishing morning and giving us a cordial invitation to come and spend a Sunday with him at Redhill was a proof that independent judgment in a generous mind would champion us." The "us" of Holman Hunt's memory is not likely to have included Rossetti. Certainly he, who never exhibited at the Royal Academy, would not have been present on Varnishing Day. Probably Hunt and Millais, at some time in the early 1850's, went out to Redhill Junction and thence to dine, Homerically, in "a large hall with the door open to the breezy hills" on fare, simple but accompanied by choice wine from Linnell's cellar (choice, in the sense that he, who always insisted on "the best", had selected the cask at the docks and himself convoyed it home to his cellar). Sympathy is evident between Linnell and Holman Hunt. The strain of Puritanism, of unbending principle, was strong in both. It was far different with Dante Gabriel Rossetti.

As a poet he was better able than his fellow-members of the Pre-Raphaelite Brotherhood to understand the poetic element that since the later eighteenth century had come into letters and sought to be infused into the visual arts. Instinct gave to his preferences historical perspective, each stage of the great romantic development found in him its advocate. Chatterton, for example, was one of his admirations, inevitably so, in the whole cast and temper of his mind, his self-identification with a lost Gothic world of colour and marvel. The sharpness with which, in his later years, Rossetti reproved Hall Caine's conventional comment that Chatterton was a charlatan and a fraud, was the sharpness of one who felt himself part of a scheme of things to which Chatterton necessarily belonged. The attempt to tear down "Rowley" was, in a way, if not intentionally, levelled at Rossetti's own imaginative life; in it Blake had an equally vital and consecutive part.

It was before the Pre-Raphaelite Brotherhood was formally launched, in 1847, that the young man discovered Blake. In the haphazard fashion from which many great works have suffered, the famous MS Volume of Blake's designs and writings in prose and verse, now known as the "Rossetti MS.", had fallen into the hands of Samuel Palmer's brother William. It was supposed that Mrs. Blake had given the volume to him, though why she should have done so is not clear. William Palmer, it would seem (like Blake's brother, John) was the reprehensible member of the family, "weak", "inept", and "foolish", in the view of his nephew, A. H. Palmer. It is possible that from the holocaust decreed by Frederick Tatham he contrived to make off with this surreptitious trophy. In the Shoreham period Samuel Palmer had hopes that his brother would become an artist: but eventually (about the time that Samuel married) a place was found for William as attendant in the Antique Galleries of the British Museum. Perhaps because it had no obvious market value, he had hung on to the Blake volume; but in 1847 he was willing to part with it to a strangely enthusiastic youth called Rossetti for as little as 10s. 6d. (which Gabriel borrowed for the purpose from his brother, William Michael). It remained a treasured family possession until after the death of Dante Gabriel Rossetti in 1882 it was sold for £110 5s. od.

What he gained from it can hardly be overestimated. In so many ways Rossetti was like Blake. He had the double gift of writing poetry and of giving visual shape to his poetic ideas. He had the same affinity with the craftsman of the Middle Ages, the same comprehensive intellect which could range far and wide, absorbing and turning to his own use whatever seemed of value: the same deep-rooted belief in the world constructed from the imagination; the same lack of conventional respect for authority. Any such analysis of resemblances will not obscure the fact that in total their personalities were quite distinct; but in the early days of the Pre-Raphaelite Brotherhood, as far as Rossetti was able to direct it, Blake's attitude appears. Rossetti's humour instantly responded to the humour of Blake's epigrams which gave him his habit of writing "limericks": but their militant intention also was not lost on him. The diatribes against Sir Joshua Reynolds and the Royal Academy delighted Rossetti, he contrived other variants of his own on the President's name, like that contained in Blake's lines

"These verses were written by a very Envious Man
    Who, whatever likeness he may have to Michelangelo
    Never can have any to Sir Jehoshuan."

These attacks (which probably made Holman Hunt and John Millais somewhat uncomfortable) did duty against the Academy of 1808. The wider background was the same. There was the same contempt for a materialist view of painting, the same implicit revolt against the later European masters, the same implied respect for the pure and spiritual quality of a "primitive" Christian art. Fortified by the possession of the precious volume, Dante Gabriel Rossetti was able to give to the movement he helped to start an impetus of which his colleagues never quite learned the secret. If Blake may be said to have been the first main spearhead of revolt against the classic

Renaissance, his efforts were thus renewed and carried further by Pre-Raphaelitism. Rossetti's water-colours were conceived in the same spirit as those of Blake, however different the result; the linear design for which he showed so great an aptitude was derived ultimately from the *Songs of Innocence*: while the Blake-like duality of his expression, in poetry and painting, contributed to that exaltation of feeling which Pre-Raphaelitism never lost. In any direct fashion it would be less easy to trace Blake's influence on William Morris than on Rossetti, yet here again we are confronted with persistent resemblances: the poet-designer, the "illuminator" of books in mediaeval fashion, (the Kelmscott Press is in essence Blake's own plan of publication) and, not least, the rebel. The aspiration towards the brother-hood of man which is a virile impulse in Blake's work and thought is strong also in Morris though he conceived his programme in less spiritual terms and with the realism that industry and the machine made necessary. The mind of Blake becomes more intelligible when related not only to the new thought-currents of his own time but also to those of the age that followed.

It is not surprising that the famous *Life of William Blake* by Alexander Gilchrist should have, to no small extent, turned into a Pre-Raphaelite interpretation of the great man, though the preparation of the biography was in the main the work of Gilchrist and his wife, Anne. Gilchrist, in 1860, was a young man, by William Michael Rossetti's account "animated, clear-headed, and bent upon producing good work—he was then regarded, in my own circle, as the best-equipped and ablest of the various art-critics on the periodical press": the wife "entering with zest into all his ideas, and capable not only of serving, but of furthering their development". He had already produced a Life of William Etty, a conscientious but not remarkable book, which, it must be admitted, added no sparkle to the humdrum details of that painter's career: but in 1860 he was in touch with the Rossettis. "A man (one Gilchrist who lives next door to Carlyle and is as near him in other respects as he can manage)", Dante Gabriel told his friend, William Allingham, "wrote to me the other day, saying he was writing a life of Blake and wanted to see my manuscript by that genius." He expressed, in his humorous way, readiness to give "a shove to the concern". The manuscript was lent, together with that "precious and almost undiscoverable *brochure*", Varley's treatise on *Zodiacal Physiognomy*, with the engraved heads by Blake.

Gilchrist died in 1861, though in the short intervening time he was intimate with Rossetti and no doubt derived from the intimacy that vitalization of ideas it was Rossetti's magic to impart: and he, after Gilchrist's death, helped Mrs. Gilchrist by acting as "selector, editor and elucidator of the poems and prose-writings". In characteristic fashion he made it a communal enterprise. While Gilchrist lived, Rossetti proposed that the wife of his young friend Edward (Burne) Jones would be very likely to succeed as "a satisfactory copyist for the Blakes" —"besides, Jones would be there to give help without trouble to himself." He took Swinburne, as enthusiastic as he about Blake's poetry, to confer with Gilchrist at the "Cheshire Cheese", and in 1861, sympathizing with Mrs. Gilchrist in the loss of her husband, repeated his offer of help in completing the Blake—"I know enough of his (Gilchrist's) plans to be able perhaps to recognize where anything remains to be done." In the following year, the death of Rossetti's wife, (the wife whom he had "influenced magnetically" as Blake had influenced *his* wife) creating, as he said, a "bond of misery" with Mrs. Gilchrist, led him to desire all the more a task that would absorb him.

It was fortunate that the book was thus finally moulded by collaborators with understanding. Dante Gabriel Rossetti was somewhat free in his corrections of Blake's grammar and on other points; on the other hand, as a poet, he could appreciate the mysterious power of passages in which he did not profess to find a literal meaning. Both he and William Michael were able to see that "the pervading idea of the 'Daughters of Albion' is one which was continually seething in Blake's mind, and flustering Propriety if she had either troubled herself to read the oracles, or succeeded in understanding them". In the 1860's, for the detached observer at least, "the unnatural and terrible result in which, in modern society, ascetic doctrines in theology and morals have involved the relation of the sexes" was painfully evident. In "uprearing the banner of heresy and nonconformity" Blake had made a truly prophetic criticism of the Victorian morality to come. The reality of Victorian censorship dictated Mrs. Gilchrist's attitude to the passages on this matter William Michael Rossetti wished to insert. "I was afraid to adopt entirely that most vigorous and admirable little bit apropos of the 'Daughters of Albion'. But it was no use to put in what I was perfectly certain Macmillan (who reads all the Proofs) would take out again."

Swinburne, too, was dying to make some vigorous remarks on the subject but the same caution applied. "It might perhaps be well to mention to Mr. Swinburne . . . that it would be perfectly useless to attempt to handle this side of Blake's writings—that Mr. Macmillan is far more inexorable against any shade of heterodoxy in morals than in religion—and that in fact, 'poor flustered propriety' would have to be most tenderly and indulgently dealt with." That the mystic, if made comprehensible, should be distressingly and indelicately plain-spoken, was an embarrassing discovery. The amount of explosive and revolutionary matter in the work of the "gentle visionary" had to be handled with care, though it was no longer possible to overlook its existence.

Yet how many greater difficulties and possible misrepresentations would have arisen with other collaborators. That Mrs. Gilchrist was beset by factions, in dealing with which the Rossettis were intimate and sensible counsellors, is clear enough. There was Tatham still, with MSS of his own, "forcible and striking work in their peculiar way". In confiding her doubts of him to William Michael Rossetti, Mrs. Gilchrist gives an interesting little sketch of his later career as well as lifting the curtain slightly on those small frictions and disputes of the world beneath Blake's level.

Abandoning sculpture, Tatham had taken to crayon portraits, by which he made a sufficient income "until the evil days (for this class of artist) began". He had then ("ineffectually I fear") taken to oil painting. Apart from this it was "an ugly circumstance" that while Miss Blake, the artist's sister, was reduced to penury, "such absolute want that I have heard a rumour she died by her own hand," Tatham had been selling the engraved books "for thirty years", and "at good prices".

Then there was the question whether Linnell's behaviour had been so wholly admirable as it seemed. Mrs. Blake, it appeared, as far as the Gilchrists could gather, had disliked Linnell, had said a considerable sum was still due on those Dante drawings which he was supposed to have paid for; that Tatham's claim for this sum had resulted in their never having spoken afterwards. The Gilchrists had come to the conclusion that Linnell was blameless. They could not acquit Tatham of blame in the matter of the destroyed manuscripts. He said that he was instigated to it by influential members of his Irvingite sect who believed that Blake was inspired by Satan. Irving's friend and the Gilchrists' neighbour, Thomas Carlyle, was certain that Irving himself had nothing to do with all this.

Linnell offered his help in the completion of the book yet he frankly said "that he might put in or take out what he did not agree with". If she had sent him the proofs, Mrs. Gilchrist concluded, glad she had not done so, "he would have struck out as false every fact he had not communicated himself".

What a relief in these circumstances to have helpers so unprejudiced and broadminded as the Rossettis; who could regard the *Everlasting Gospel* in its daring splendour of thought as "one of the finest things Blake ever wrote". Patient scholarship has since given a much fuller and more satisfactory explanation of Blake's symbolism than the Gilchrist Life attempted, yet many still will feel, with Rossetti, that as a poet Blake is not to be confined to literal meaning or his work to be made simply a honeycomb of allusion. "The truth is that as regards such a poem as *My Spectre* I do not understand it a bit better than anybody else, only I know better than some may know that it has claims as poetry apart from the question of understanding it . . ."

"What an admirable man Rossetti must be!" wrote Samuel Palmer to Mrs. Gilchrist. He felt the abundance of sympathy in the biographers and their aid; memory, painful and delightful, flooded once more into his mind. He himself contributed his glowing description of the "man without a mask", though even on Palmer the piety of the age laid its stern hand. "I think," he advised, "the whole page at the top of which I have made a cross in red chalk would at once exclude the work from every drawing-room table in England . . . I should let no passage appear in which the word Bible, or those of the peasons of the Blessed Trinity, or the Messiah were irreverently connected . . . I should simply put x x x s; and in case of omitting a page or chapter simply say 'The —th Chapter is omitted'." The essential timidity and even the lack of understanding with which the painter–disciple approached the man of ideas comes out. He suggested that Blake had not always meant what he said, or that he was to be excused for having written "in anger and rhetorically". Difficult indeed was it in the 1860's entirely to appreciate one who had known the revolutionary fervour of 1790. Yet the final result pleased Palmer beyond measure— "I could not wait for the paper-knife but fell upon it, reading all in between—now I have cut the first volume and read wildly everywhere:—and now again I begin at the beginning, and meanwhile write to tell you how it has delighted me; raising, however, a strange ferment of distressing and delicious thought."

The "respectable"—"who keep gigs and 'by sweet reserve and modesty grow fat' will be enraged by it—an excellent symptom . . ." The spade work was done by the Gilchrists but one cannot overlook the element of Pre-Raphaelite piety that in many respects gave the biography life. It was left to Dante Gabriel Rossetti to indicate in his additions that Blake did not stand entirely alone but that there was such a thing as "British poetic art". Rossetti's references to "succeeding British artists who have shown unmistakeably something of his influence on their works" were incomplete and sketchy but at least he made the attempt to place such a painter as von Holst ("in some sort the Edgar Poe of painting") in relation with the greater man; and Rossetti himself might have been added as a spiritual kinsman though with something of tragedy and warping in his later life from which Blake was happily free.

x x x x x

Even more than "fourfold", the story of William Blake is that of all the souls with whom he had had contact, which he had assembled in the complex system of his mental life, deriving from some, and to others giving, sustenance. It is this composite existence, in which religion, poetry and painting are intermingled, that makes him infinite in variety and requires that he should constantly be studied afresh. In one way the man is simpler than the words "mystic" or "visionary" would suggest.   A little man, with much of the eighteenth-century John Bull about him, pugnacious, stubborn, prejudiced, insular with the insularity of one who never left his native island, one who would give a good account of himself in a fight and would never be beaten, more of a "Christian bull-dog" than Samuel Palmer imagined himself to be.   He could bear poverty cheerfully, though he did not attach to it the mystical virtue which those who were better off may have imagined, and was quite clear about the preferable advantages of some measure of appreciation and material reward.   His life was an open book and what was called his madness was often more an index to the foolishness of those he met with than anything else.

Yet in intellectual and spiritual terms he is almost to be described as an age, an epoch, rather than an individual : and no error could be greater than to treat him as an isolated freak of genius, without relation to anything that had happened before or would happen later.   To say that he was part of a "movement" may sound academic, but in the great transformation of the eighteenth century, in the struggle towards a new life of the imagination and spirit, there was no intellectual warrior more active and completely armed : none shared more fully in the rediscovery of lost beauties and wonders in art and poetry, the search for the essential spring of inspiration, the exultant hopes of freedom and brotherhood.   If all this was "romantic" he was a romantic of the purest kind—the word ceases to be applicable only in that disordered phase of early nineteenth-century "Romanticism" when a despair (to which he never succumbed) seized on so many artists, with a desire to seek refuge in "Nature" (of which he was so consistently contemptuous).   Some part of Blake is Ossian, is Chatterton, is the Gothic Revival, is Tom Paine's revolutionary fervour and Mary Wollstonecraft's desire for emancipation : is Swedenborg's vision of celestial spheres and Wesley's buoyant optimism, is all that is best in Dante Gabriel Rossetti; through them one can not only better understand him but also trace a whole phase of imaginative life.

BIBLIOGRAPHICAL NOTE

Among biographical and critical works bearing on the theme of this book are the following; Bailey Saunders *James Macpherson*; E. H. W. Meyerstein *Thomas Chatterton*; Sigve Toksvig *Emmanuel Swedenborg, Scientist and Mystic*; W. G. Constable *John Flaxman*; Mrs. Bray *Thomas Stothard*; J. Knowles *Henry Fuseli*; Edmond Jaloux *Johann Heinrich Füssli*; Alfred Story *James Holmes and John Varley*; Morchard Bishop *Blake's Hayley*; M. Linford *Mary Wollstonecraft*; C. Kegan Paul *William Godwin, his Friends and Contemporaries*; Alfred Story *John Linnell*; A. H. Palmer *Samuel Palmer*; Geoffrey Grigson *Samuel Palmer, The Visionary Years*; *Edward Calvert* (Memoir by his son); A. M. W. Stirling *The Richmond Papers*; Laurence Binyon *The Followers of William Blake*; H. H. Gilchrist *Anne Gilchrist*; Kerrison Preston *Blake and Rossetti*. Also such general studies as Mario Praz *The Romantic Agony*; C. E. Vaughan *The Romantic Revolt*; F. C. Gill *The Romantic Movement and Methodism*. From the very large number of works concerned with Blake himself it may be only needful to refer here, with the gratitude all students of Blake must feel, to Archibald G. B. Russell's edition of the Letters (with Frederick Tatham's *Life*); Geoffrey Keynes's complete edition of the written works; the admirable *Life* by Mona Wilson and Ruthven Todd's (Everyman) edition of Gilchrist's *Life*; the two latter works containing full bibliographies. The great beauty of the colour facsimile of Blake's *Jerusalem*, produced under the auspices of the William Blake Trust and the great interest of the Commentary on *Jerusalem* by Joseph Wicksteed also need to be signalized. Valuable catalogues accompanied the Blake Exhibition of 1947, organized by the British Council (introduction by A. G. B. Russell), Blake's Tempera Paintings, 1951 (Arts Council—introduction by Geoffrey Keynes) and the Arts Council Fuseli Exhibition, 1950 (introduction by Nicolas Powell).

INDEX